She gasped, a whisper c

And then she did it again, a c
that wound him up tight.

His breath caught and held b
nothing, God, not even breathe, even if it led to his ultimate
suffocation and death—to force her along at this moment.

But…where was this going?

Slowly she pulled back, her face wet with tears and her breasts heaving with uneven panting that sounded, to his confused ears at least, like passion rather than pain. Then she raised her lids to stare at him with wet eyes that glittered with every conceivable shade of brown, from amber to deepest mahogany. And then…

Was he imagining this? Was this a dream after all? A hallucination?

And then she leaned closer…tipped up her chin, just a little…and waited.

Disbelief pinned Beau right where he sat, dazed and frozen, and he could swear he felt his skin vibrate with leashed tension that strained away from his control.

She had to know that he would swallow her whole right now.

Was that what she wanted?

Could he get this lucky? Was this a test? Did anyone really expect him to let this opportunity pass him by when he'd prayed for it for years?

He wanted to do the right thing, but he'd be damned if he knew what that was. "Jillian?"

There. He'd been honorable and raised the question, dumbass that he was. This was her chance. If she wanted this train to stop so she could hop off and run away, now was the time. *Run while you can, Jill.*

Books by Ann Christopher

Kimani Romance

Just About Sex
Tender Secrets
Road to Seduction
Campaign for Seduction
Redemption's Kiss

ANN CHRISTOPHER

is a full-time chauffeur for her two overscheduled children. She is also a wife, former lawyer, and decent cook. In between trips to various sporting practices and games, Target, and the grocery store, she likes to write the occasional romance novel featuring a devastatingly handsome alpha male. She lives in Cincinnati and spends her time with her family, which includes two spoiled rescue cats, Sadie and Savannah.

If you'd like to recommend a great book, share a recipe for homemade cake of any kind or suggest a tip for getting your children to do what you say the *first* time you say it, Ann would love to hear from you through her Web site, www.AnnChristopher.com.

Redemption's KISS

ANN CHRISTOPHER

To Richard

A million thanks to writer pals Kristina Cook, Lori Devoti, Laura Drewry, Caroline Linden, Sally MacKenzie and Eve Silver for their invaluable friendship and support, and especially to Naked Sally, for helping me with a crucial plot point.

KIMANI PRESS™

ISBN-13: 978-0-373-86161-3

REDEMPTION'S KISS

www.kimanipress.com

Printed in U.S.A.

Dear Readers,

Disgraced former governor Beau Taylor has nothing to live for and no one to care if he dies. Once, long ago, he had everything in the palm of his hand: career, prestige and, best of all, the love of Jillian, the woman he's always worshipped. But then things went horribly wrong, he made poor choices and he lost it all, including his zest for life.

These days, he drinks, parties and fills the excruciating hours with meaningless women. Every day he hates himself just a little bit more than yesterday. Every day he searches for a reason to exist and comes up empty.

And then, in a nightmarish flash, everything changes.

Suddenly, Beau has a second chance at life, one he's determined not to waste. Now, nothing will stop him from healing his damaged soul and becoming a worthwhile human being. Nothing will stop him from becoming the world's best father to his precious little girl. Nothing will stop him from becoming a deserving partner to Jillian, and reclaiming her love. Nothing.

I hope you enjoy reading Beau and Jillian's story as much as I enjoyed putting them back together!

Happy reading,

Ann Christopher

P.S. Please look for my next Kimani Romance, which will be part of the Love in the Limelight series, in October!

Chapter 1

Beau Taylor wasn't sober, but he wasn't drunk, either.

Luckily, the Miami night was young enough for him to change that.

Drinking took the edge off. Drinking was good. Drinking was necessary.

How else could he survive in the toxic waste dump of his life without some sort of buffer between him and reality?

As the disgraced former governor of Virginia, Beau was only slightly higher on the social scale than, say, venereal warts, but after a couple of drinks—preferably scotch on the rocks—he could look on the bright side. People thought he was scum. That being the case, it was easy to fulfill their low expectations.

Perfect, eh?

If he wanted a drink, he'd drink. If there were a party somewhere, he'd go. If he met a woman who was beautiful and willing, he'd screw her. Why shouldn't he? Because he'd disappoint someone who loved him? Easy solution there: no one loved him.

So he found his consolations where he could. Living in Miami, with its astonishing array of after-dark activities, helped. There were always clubs to discover and drinks and women to be savored.

Lucky him.

He was momentarily between clubs, but no worries. A quick glance outside the limousine's darkened windows showed the Intracoastal Waterway streaking by and the city stretched out before him like a glittering jewel.

Man, he enjoyed Miami.

He also enjoyed being rich, one of the benefits of the beer distributorship his late father started back in the day.

Thanks, Dad.

Having money had its pluses, and riding in style was one of them. Every car should have plush leather seats, a fully stocked bar, a discreet driver and a privacy divider. Beau enjoyed riding in limousines.

Sabrina enjoyed riding him.

And she was good at it.

Sliding his hands up the shapely thighs straddling him, Beau gripped the flexing globes of her naked ass. Ahhh…nice.

Sabrina kicked it up a notch. Flashing a wicked grin, her long black curls wild and falling in her face, she pumped her hips nice and hard, taking him deeper into her body.

Worked for him.

Laughing now, she rubbed her jiggling breasts against his tailored shirt. It was all good. Nothing like a quickie in the car to loosen him up.

Then Sabrina slowed things down. Moaning loud enough to be heard on the other side of the divider, she levered herself up until only the sensitive head of his penis remained inside her.

Yeeeaaaah. That worked, too.

Her back arched and one of her walnut-tipped nipples skimmed his lips. Was that an invitation? Looked like. He sucked it, hard, into his mouth. She rewarded him with a high-pitched cry and impaled herself again, up down, up down, faster, harder, and the fun continued.

Except…the fun wasn't that much fun. Never really had been fun.

Beau let that nipple pop free, rested his head against the seat and wished again that he were drunk. Things were easier then. He didn't have to work so hard to feel alive or, depending on his mood, to sink into oblivion.

Oblivion was his own version of heaven, the blessed place where he hated himself just a shade less than he normally did. Oblivion—not another party—was his ultimate destination tonight. Too bad he couldn't seem to get there.

Staring up at Sabrina through half-closed eyes, seeing the

straining column of her neck and the faint smile on her lips, he wondered why he always did this to himself. Always picked women with sparkling amber eyes, straight brows and fine cheekbones. Always wished he were just a little drunker or could pretend just a little more that these women were someone else.

It had never worked. Not once.

Maybe he should try harder.

Holding Sabrina's hips tighter, he pumped in a blind fury of movement, screwing her mercilessly until sweat ran down his temples and Sabrina began her chanting routine. *Yes...yes...yes.* Whatever. He just wanted to be done—with this, and with her.

Waiting only long enough to hear the surprised yelp that was his signal that she'd climaxed, he came, too. For five perfect seconds, relief—and it was only relief, not pleasure—surged through him. But then it was over, and nothing had changed.

Did that make sense? Was that fair? When he thrust so much of his emptiness into another body, why did it still fill him to overflowing?

Why, God?

That emptiness always stayed, no matter what, or who, he did.

Jesus. He made himself sick.

He eased the limp Sabrina off his lap and onto the seat beside him, wishing he could shower or, better yet, spray himself with a bleach-filled pressure washer.

Like that, or anything, would ever make him clean.

Every sexual encounter these days—and there were plenty—ended this same way: with relief and disgust. Relief because his body had cooled a little, but disgust because he still hated himself and what he'd become, and knew he'd do it all again tomorrow anyway.

Disposing of the condom, he adjusted his boxer briefs, zipped up, rebuttoned his shirt and smoothed his hair. Great. Good as new. Oh, and don't forget the seat belt. He buckled up. Now he was ready for more partying.

If the self-hatred didn't kill him first.

For now, he needed to get the everlasting bitterness off the back of his tongue, so he reached for his snifter of cognac and drank deep. He waited for his brain to fog, but…nothing. Shit. He drank again, draining the glass.

Sabrina, meanwhile, adjusted her negligible black dress, reached for her glittery little purse and found her lipstick. A few minutes of primping followed. "Where are we going now?"

Beau heard the slight slur in her words and hated her for it. Why was she drunk and he wasn't? Where was the fairness in that? Reaching for more brandy, he shrugged.

"I forget. We'll let it be a surprise when we get there."

No arguments from Sabrina, who closed her compact with a snap. "How do I look?"

He would have preferred not to see her again just now—if ever—but he did the polite thing and glanced over. By the dim interior lights he surveyed the skimpy-skanky black dress, the cleavage, the bare legs, the screw-me heels, the makeup and the hair. It was funny how she looked equally naked whether she was dressed or not. How did she manage that?

Sabrina waited for his answer and, focusing on her total package, he tried to frame one. The bottom line on this lovely lady was that she was vacant, shallow and soulless enough to be his ideal companion for tonight's debauchery.

Knowing she'd never hear the sarcasm in his voice, he raised his snifter in a toast and flashed a smile that felt as natural as shoving glass shards through his cheeks. "You look perfect—"

The sudden painful glare of headlights directly into the car was their first warning.

Then came the earsplitting screech of tires and a violent lurch strong enough to knock the drink from Beau's hand.

His seat belt tightened across his hips and his body jerked.

Shit.

Sabrina screamed.

With a surge of full-blown panic crushing his throat, Beau whipped his head around to see Death barreling at them in a brilliant yellow glow bright enough to power two suns.

Truck, his brain registered. *Semi.*

The driver tried to veer the limo out of the way again, but that truck kept coming.

The impact took forever to come, giving random thoughts the time to flash through Beau's mind.

He was about to die.

Good.

Allegra would grow up without a father.

Tragic, but ultimately better for her.

The semi rammed into the side of the limousine with the earth-shattering force of a bomb and their screams rose up in a chorus of terror and agony.

As Beau's world spun out of control and then went black, one face filled his mind's eye. One beautiful image ushered him through the excruciating pain and fear and into the next life, if there was a next life for the sorry likes of him, which there probably wasn't.

He saw the bright amber eyes, heard the joyous laughter and felt the love.

Jillian. God, I loved you. You never knew how much.

She smiled at him and he rejoiced at what was now and had always been the most beautiful sight in his life.

And then he died.

Chapter 2

Six months later

"Someone's leased the Foster place." Blanche Rousseau, vibrating with excitement over today's gossip, hurried into the kitchen with a brown bag of groceries in each arm.

"Really?"

Jillian Warner paused in her relentless kneading of bread dough and eased the curtains aside. Peering out the window over the sink, she surveyed the Foster place, perched atop the tree-dotted hill at the end of their street.

She half expected to see a moving van speed by, buuuut… no.

Nothing about the massive and weathered white house looked any different in today's midmorning light. The wide veranda still begged for a fresh coat of paint, and so did the columns. The bushes, as usual, were overgrown monstrosities that would soon reach out to grab unsuspecting children who wandered too close, and the windows were still vacant and eerie.

She was about to return to her dough when a distant flash of movement caught her eye. A big black dog—a standard poodle, maybe—rounded the Foster place, barking with excitement. Oh, and was that the tail end of some sort of SUV in the driveway?

Maybe, but who really cared?

Jillian let the curtain drop and attacked her dough again. They didn't have time for gossip when there was bread to be made and meals to be cooked for ten hungry guests.

Blanche, meanwhile, set the bags on the wooden counter and surveyed Jillian's progress with pursed bubblegum-pink lips.

Oh, Lord. What now? Jillian tried to concentrate on her task, but there was no ignoring Blanche—not the blue-beaded chain of her cat's-eye glasses, her white-blond teased beehive circa 1962 or her plump frame squeezed into electric-blue stretch pants and a matching jacket—especially when she got in a mood.

Finally Jillian looked up, exasperated. *"What?"*

"You need to ease up on that dough, honey," Blanche drawled, her lilting Louisiana tones thick with disapproval. "You trying to make shoe leather or dinner rolls?"

"This may surprise you, Blanche, but I've made a decent batch of rolls once or twice in my life."

"That does surprise me," Blanche muttered, now eyeing Jillian's work with raised brows. Clicking her tongue, she moved along the counter.

Jillian glared after her, irritated.

Sometime soon she'd have to break the sad news to Blanche—that she was not, in fact, Queen of the Universe here at the historic Twin Oaks Bed & Breakfast outside Atlanta—but for now she'd let this latest insubordination pass.

Though she hadn't been listed on the contract for sale Jillian signed three years ago when she moved here from Virginia, Blanche had come with the B & B, just like the dormer windows, railed porch with rockers and twelve bedrooms.

Jillian was new to running the B & B and Blanche was…well, old. Since Jillian needed Blanche's experience and expertise, Jillian spent a lot of time swallowing her retorts.

Jillian floured the counter and reached for the rolling pin. "So who bought the house?"

"No one over at the grocery knows." Blanche rummaged in one bag and produced several dozen eggs and a couple pounds of butter. "Must be someone with a lot of money, though, 'cause that place needs some W-O-R-K. Maybe it's a nice man for you. Now that you're dating and all."

Jillian rolled her eyes. She'd wondered how long it'd take Blanche to raise this topic and was surprised it had required—what?—fifty whole seconds.

"I am not dating," she said, now using a floured glass to cut dough rounds and place them on the baking sheet. "I had one dinner with a man—"

"And coffee with him last week. Coffee plus dinner equals dating."

"I don't date," Jillian said flatly. "I meet the occasional nice man and have dinner."

"Very occasional." Blanche's backside poked in all its considerable glory from the depths of the refrigerator, where she was now arranging food. "Since this is the first man I've seen you have dinner with in three years."

Affronted because there was no need for such an unvarnished recitation of the sorry state of Jillian's love life this early in the day, she put the glass down and frowned at Blanche.

"You just focus on baking that chicken for lunch, okay?"

"No sex." Blanche emerged from the fridge and pulled a tragic face on Jillian's behalf. "No fried chicken. All work, no fun. No wonder you're so uptight all the time. You haven't got much to live for, far as I can tell."

Jillian laughed, but it was as hollow as most of her laughter these days. Something inside her had broken and, three years later, she still hadn't found a way to fix it. Maybe it was time to face the fact that the old Jillian, the happy one, was damaged beyond repair.

The funny thing was, she didn't really care. Here at the B & B, which she'd bought with her divorce settlement because she didn't want to return to practicing law and she needed something to do now that she was no longer the first lady of Virginia, she'd built something more lasting than happiness: peace, personal satisfaction and self-sufficiency. Even better, she'd found a mother's pleasure in seeing her child discover the world.

Wasn't that good enough?

She knew how to meet a payroll and balance the books, manage several employees, feed up to thirty people in the dining room, unclog a toilet, install storm doors and bandage scraped knees. Best of all, Allegra was happy and healthy.

Those were the important things. As long as they were on track, it didn't matter that Jillian felt dead inside—when she felt anything at all.

A clatter in the hall jarred Jillian out of her thoughts and she looked around in time to see Barbara Jean, Blanche's granddaughter, appear in the doorway.

Twenty-one and heading back to Vanderbilt in the fall, Barbara Jean spent most of her time marching to the beat of her own drum. Witness the orange and red hair, the multiple piercings and the iPod, which was always strapped to her arm. On the other hand, Barbara Jean was a straight-A student, levelheaded and responsible. She was, therefore, Allegra's well-paid and much-appreciated nanny.

Barbara Jean threw her arms wide in a flourish and bowed. "Make way for Princess Allegra!"

Jillian and Blanche, who went through this drill on a daily basis, snapped to attention and bowed as two-year-old Allegra sidled into the room, teetering on purple plastic prostitute-in-training slides with pink ostrich feathers across the open toes. Today's ensemble also included a pink leotard and tutu combination, a sparkling rhinestone crown and a blue magic wand with pink streamers.

"All hail Princess Allegra," the adults intoned.

Allegra blessed them with a serene nod. "You may rise."

Jillian crooked her finger at the girl, who came over. "Come here, Princess Allegra. Mommy's got something for you."

"What?"

"This."

Sweeping her daughter up, Jillian kissed her fat little honey-with-cream-colored cheeks and swung her in a circle. Allegra screamed with laughter, revealing one Shirley Temple dimple on the left side of her mouth and tiny white teeth. After a few seconds of this silliness, Jillian set the girl back on her wobbly legs and ruffled her sandy curls.

"Don't forget you've got a swimming lesson soon. Barbara Jean will take you."

"Nooo-ooo." Allegra backed away as though she expected to be dragged off in chains and tortured in a dungeon. "I don't want to go swimming. I want a tea party."

"Yeah, well, there's plenty of time for a tea party after you swim."

Allegra prepared for a rant by opening her mouth so wide you'd think it had a hinge, but a new distraction arrived before she could get started: someone knocked on the kitchen door.

They all looked around to see a man standing on the other side of the screen with a bouquet of red roses slung over one arm.

Jillian's pulse quickened and a hot flush crept over her cheeks. She hastily washed her hands while Blanche shot her a smirk and then sauntered to the door and swung it open.

"Adam Marshall," Blanche cried, laying the charm on so thick she'd need a putty knife in a minute. "You come right on in here and have some coffee and a muffin. How's our favorite accountant?"

"I'm pretty good now that I know there's a muffin in my future." He came inside while everyone said hello and Blanche fixed his snack. His gaze went straight to Jillian and held. "How are you, Jillian?"

"I'm good."

Adam had been the B & B's accountant for two years and had been making eyes at Jillian for a year and eleven months. There was an intimidation factor involved, Jillian supposed, because she'd been the first lady of Virginia and was the sister of the sitting president. That, combined with Adam's natural shyness, accounted for his delay in asking her out, not that Jillian was anxious, given her antidating stance.

But last week he'd finally gotten up the nerve to approach her, and they'd had coffee. Why not? She had to drink coffee, right? Why not drink it with him? Then they'd had dinner. Both had gone reasonably well. Now here he was again.

On paper he was everything a single mother like her should want: single, straight, with a nice job, a sense of humor and no lurking baby mamas. Plus, he was easy on the eyes. Dark skinned with a mustache and skull trim, he had warm brown eyes and the kind of dimpled boyish grin that probably weakened knees wherever he went.

It wasn't his fault that Jillian's knees were impervious.

So, yeah, she wasn't dating, wasn't smitten and wouldn't be falling into this guy's bed—or anyone else's, come to think of it—anytime soon. And that was just fine with her because she had a drawer full of BOBs (Battery Operated Boyfriends) upstairs.

But…he was a decent guy and she had to pass the time somehow. Why not do it with him on occasion?

Allegra tottered over on her plastic heels and stared up at Adam.

"I like your flowers."

Adam looked down at the girl. "Thank you."

Allegra's curls quivered with her bouncing excitement. "Are they for me?"

Adam, bless his heart, didn't miss a beat. Smiling, he pulled one perfect red bud out of the huge arrangement and held it out to Allegra.

"For you, your majesty."

Allegra beamed up at him. "Thank you. You may kiss my hand."

They all laughed. Adam took her tiny hand with its chipped pink nail polish and kissed it with the appropriate solemnity. Allegra tittered.

And Adam went up another notch or two in Jillian's estimation.

"Okay, princess." Barbara Jean took Allegra's hand and steered her toward the hall. "Time for swimming."

"Nooo-ooo." Allegra's wails echoed down the hall as they disappeared from sight.

Blanche presented Adam with coffee and a pumpkin muffin the size of a small melon. "I'll just leave you two to chat." She patted Adam's arm. "Enjoy your muffin."

"Thanks, Blanche." Adam watched her go and then gave the roses to Jillian. "For you."

"Thank you." It had been so long since a man had made a romantic gesture that she couldn't repress her grin. "They're beautiful."

"They're a bribe. I'm hoping you'll go out to dinner with me again."

Jillian faltered and stalled by placing the flowers on the counter. "Adam—"

"You already told me," he said good-naturedly. "You don't date."

"Oh, good. You were listening."

"Think about another dinner, though. That's all I'm asking."

She hesitated.

Thinking about it probably wouldn't kill her. Besides. His face was so pleasant and hopeful that she just couldn't say no. She was in the prime of her life, for goodness' sake. Life wasn't over just yet. As long as she was honest about not wanting a relationship, dinner with him was no big deal, right?

"Okay," she said.

"Good." Adam grinned and then apparently decided to press his luck. "Can I kiss you? I've been kicking myself for not asking the other night."

Kiss? *What?*

But Adam, for once in his life, seemed to be in an impulsive mood and didn't wait. Leaning in and catching her before her alarm could really take hold, he brushed his mouth across hers.

Nothing happened at first, but then there was a spark of something in her belly, a long-forgotten feeling of something she couldn't quite identify.

Excitement? Longing? Need?

Pulling back, Adam smiled as though he'd been granted eternal life. A similar reaction eluded her and she had to force herself to smile back. *Man.* This kissing thing threw her for a serious loop. She hadn't kissed anyone romantically in three years, and hadn't kissed a man other than her ex-husband in fifteen. How was she supposed to feel? She didn't have a clue.

"I've got to get back to work." Sounding a little husky now, Adam grabbed his muffin and gulped some coffee. "I just wanted to bring the flowers and get my kiss."

"I'll walk you out," she said, trying to get her mind right.

This was all too weird. She'd been asexual for so long, and now *this.*

It came as a huge shock that she could still affect a man, still inspire him to think about her, leave work for her and bring her flowers. She hadn't realized that such tiny miracles were possible after all this time.

They walked outside, down the cobbled path to Adam's car. The May day was beautiful, bright and clear but not yet humid, not that she could enjoy it with him staring at her with those unnerving, puppy-dog eyes.

Feeling fidgety and awkward, she glanced over at the Foster place. There were definite signs of activity now; a moving van occupied most of the long drive and in front of it sat a dark Range Rover. Uniformed movers swarmed in and out of the front door and up and down the driveway—

Without warning, Adam cupped her cheek and kissed her again, his mouth firmer and more confident this time. After one stiff second, Jillian responded with her lips but the rest of her body remained aloof, well out of Adam's reach. And then she had enough.

She pulled away, flustered. "What was that?"

"That was, 'I hope I'll see you soon.' I'll call you, okay?"

"Okay."

Watching him drive off, she touched her tingling lips and then caught herself. Don't be silly, Jill. It was time to get cracking. Those rolls still weren't in the oven and lunchtime would be here soon—

A low bark from her left startled her.

Turning, she saw the new neighbor's dog trot out from behind a forsythia bush at the edge of her property, his pink tongue lolling in a friendly doggy smile.

"Hello, cutie." She held her hand out for inspection. "Hel-looo."

The dog ambled over. He was big and black with short curly hair, pointy ears, long legs and huge paws. Probably less than a year old, he wriggled with excitement and had a red collar with a numbered tag.

He snuffled her hand, apparently decided she was okay, and then nudged her. She accepted this obvious invitation to scratch his ears, and the dog all but passed out with pleasure.

Oh, man. Her heart turned over, hard.

This wasn't a standard poodle. This guy was a Bouvier des

Flandres, the type of dog she'd had as a child. His long hair had been shaved, probably because it was so hot here in Georgia during the summer, but he looked exactly like Ishmael, and the sudden sweet nostalgia from her childhood was almost unbearable.

Just like that, she remembered the joys of pet ownership, especially during that terrible year when Mama died, leaving her and her older brother, John, alone with their grieving and distant father.

It all came back to her: the nightly warmth of Ishmael's heavy body stretched out across her feet at the end of her bed; Ishmael sprawled between her and John on the floor in front of the TV; a soap-covered Ishmael resisting his bath in the plastic pool next to their estate's enormous inground pool.

Good times, good times.

Boy, did she miss that dog. He'd died of old age when she was in high school. Come to think of it, she missed Ramona, too, the chatty Siamese she'd named after her favorite Beverly Cleary character. That silly cat. When Ramona wasn't ignoring her and John or terrorizing Ishmael, which was most of the time, she was underfoot, meowing about the general unfairness of life and demanding to have her chin scratched.

Wow. She hadn't thought about Ramona in ages. The ache of nostalgia grew. Allegra occasionally made noises about wanting a pet; maybe it was time to think about getting one.

In the meantime, this dog needed to get home before he ran out into the street, and there was no time like the present to meet the new neighbor. Those rolls could wait another minute or two.

Oh, but wait. New neighbors had to be greeted with food. It was a rule.

"Come on," she told the dog.

He followed her inside the kitchen, where she quickly washed her hands, lined a basket with a large cloth napkin and filled it with leftover pumpkin muffins from breakfast.

"Now we're ready."

The dog agreed with another bark.

What a sweetie. Scratching his head again, she led the way.

They walked up the lane to his owner's driveway, where

serious progress was now being made. Someone had lowered the ramp on the moving van, and there were various blankets and dollies lying around, but no signs of human life. A discreet glance inside the van as she passed revealed several nice pieces, including a black leather sofa and an enormous entertainment center. A man's furniture. Definitely a man's.

They climbed the shallow steps and crossed the huge veranda, which crunched beneath Jillian's feet. Hopefully, the new guy had a rake and a broom because there were dead leaves everywhere. This baby needed a lot of cleanup. It was a beautiful house, though, with clean lines, exquisite woodwork and beveled glass framing the open front door.

She knocked and waited.

No answer.

She tried again, this time using the heavy brass knocker.

Still nothing.

The dog looked up at her, and she could swear he raised his furry eyebrows in a *What now?* gesture.

Well, the door *was* open.

Stepping inside, she gasped at what had been a remarkable house and, with a little love, would be again. Several rooms spun off the foyer, the centerpiece of which was a wide staircase with a carved handrail, and every room that she could see was bathed in light from full-length windows. Ornate woodwork framed every doorway, and there was an enormous marble fireplace in what was unmistakably the living room.

No signs of life, though, and—

Oh, wait. Were those voices upstairs?

Turning back in the direction of the staircase—maybe she'd wandered a little farther inside than she should have—she opened her mouth to call out a hello, but a movement out of the corner of her eye stopped her.

A man's hand on the brass handle of a cane came into view, followed by one long khaki-trousered leg and a foot encased in an expensive loafer.

"Hello," Jillian called. "Your dog wandered down the street to say hi and I was just bringing—"

The rest of the man came into view and Jillian's words stopped dead.

Oh, God. No. God, no.

Above the khaki pants was a lean, broad-shouldered torso in a white dress shirt. Above that was the face of the man who had destroyed her marriage, her heart and her happiness—the man she hadn't spoken to directly for three years and who made regular appearances in her dreams to this day.

She staggered back a step, putting a hand on the wall for support.

Beau. It couldn't be.

But no other man in the world had those amazing hazel eyes. No other man in the world had that beautiful honey-brown skin, those slashing cheekbones or that lush mouth. No other man in the world had those silky-sexy waves of soft sable hair or that potent brand of masculinity that reduced her to a vibrating mass of overheated flesh every damn time, aeons since she'd first laid eyes on him at the orientation at Columbia Law.

"Is it you?"

Stupid question, yeah, but she had to ask, just to be sure; her untrustworthy eyes needed confirmation that it really was him. That despite all the time and distance, both physical and emotional, that she'd put between them, this man was back in her life and would be living down the street.

After an endless wait, one corner of his mouth curled.

His face. Oh, God, his beautiful, ruined face.

He had a jagged, puckered scar that cut across his cheek, went past the edge of his mouth and ended at his chin. Yet he was still breathtaking, damn him, and that was unquestionably still Beau's wry smile. Worse, those were Beau's piercing eyes staring at her with such unwavering focus, and Beau's delicious scent of fresh cotton and sporty deodorant she smelled.

"Yes," he said, and the world spun out from under her.

Chapter 3

Apparently she looked as shell-shocked as she felt. Leaning on his cane and favoring his left leg, Beau took a halting step forward and put his hand on her arm, his eyes wide with concern.

"Are you okay?"

No. "Yes."

Pull it together, Jill. You can do this.

She stepped out of his reach and away from the wall with only her pride to keep her going. This man would not get to her; she could stand on her own two feet.

He dropped his hand and stared at her until her burning face made her wish that she were in the molten crater of a volcano or the heart of hell itself—anywhere but here, with him.

Bitter tears of humiliation burned her eyes, but she blinked them back, ruthless in her determination never to shed another tear over this man. She ran through her lifetime allotment of tears for him years ago.

"It's good to see you," he told her in that deep, black-magic voice.

"I can't say the same."

A faint smile flickered across his face. "I know you can't."

She was lying, though. She had to lie. Because even now, even after all the things he'd done to her and all the ways he'd damaged her, there was a tiny corner in the dark recesses of her soul that was glad to see him.

How sick did that make her? Pretty damn sick.

Even scarred and limping, he stole her breath. Always had, always would. Even a near-fatal car accident couldn't reduce this man's effect on her and she hated him for it.

She hated herself even more.

"Is that something in the basket for me? I didn't eat breakfast."

What? *Basket?*

He pointed and she belatedly remembered the muffins. Now that her bewilderment was turning into anger, she tightened her grip on the handle and jerked the basket to one side, well out of his reach.

"They were for my new neighbor."

"That would be me."

"Not on your life."

"Ah." He let his head hang with exaggerated disappointment.

"What're you doing here, Beau?"

"I'm moving into my new house."

Having already seen the van outside, this was not breaking news. The confirmation was still a serious jolt, though, along the lines of an anvil dropped on her head.

"Did it ever cross your mind that maybe you should have given me some warning that you'd decided to relocate from Miami?"

"It did, but it's hard to give you warning when you don't return my phone calls."

Oh. She fidgeted with nerves and guilt. So that's what those voice-mail messages had been about. She'd deleted them all, the way she'd deleted him from her life.

It was all part of her policy to never speak to him again, if she could help it. A little harsh, true, but she'd managed remarkably well. In the three years since the divorce, she'd only seen and talked to him once, in the hospital after his accident, and that didn't really count because he'd been unconscious at the time.

What else could she do? Why would she talk to this man if she could avoid it? So he could hurt her again? Uh—no, thanks.

Direct communication wasn't necessary, anyway. He'd lived in Miami, she'd lived here, Barbara Jean had shuttled Allegra back and forth between them and e-mail had worked perfectly well to discuss parenting issues. Now here he was, bringing in stormy seas to rock the boat and ruining things the way he always ruined everything.

She jammed her fists on her hips. "Why didn't you e-mail me?"

"E-mail doesn't work for everything." That bright gaze held hers, but revealed none of his secrets. She was sure there were secrets; there always were with Beau. "I've decided to take a more proactive approach with several things in my life from now on."

"Such as what?"

He paused and stared, drawing out the tension and letting the panic grow in her chest. In no particular hurry to answer, he made his slow way to the only piece of furniture in the room, a console by the far wall, and leaned against it.

"For one thing, I want to be much more involved in Allegra's life. Seeing her for a couple of weekends a month isn't enough."

More time with Allegra? Over Jillian's cold, dead body. It was hard enough to part with Allegra for those weekend visits—how would she deal with her precious daughter being gone more often?

"I beg your pardon, but you haven't filed any paperwork to change—"

One hand came up, stopping her bluster in its tracks. "We don't need to involve the court with this, Jillian. We're both reasonable human beings and we can work together to find a system for me to see Allegra during the week. How hard could it be with me living right down the street?"

"Why would I want to work with you on anything?"

"Because." Unmistakable sadness darkened his eyes until they were almost brown. "Even though I was a lousy husband, I'm a good father. Since you're a good mother, you know how important it is for a young girl to have her father actively involved in her life."

Shut down on this issue—he *was* a good father and Allegra *did* miss him between visits—Jillian hitched up her chin and changed the subject.

"What about your job? You can't just up and quit—"

"I did up and quit. That's one of the benefits of having a little money."

A little money. Hah. Good one. He had a big enough stake in his family's beer distribution empire to support him and several small countries for decades to come.

"Anyway, my heart wasn't in the big-firm, corporate-lawyer life."

Jillian laughed sourly. "Well, I can certainly understand that since your heart has never stayed in one place for very long."

His jaw tightened, but he said nothing, and her anxiety increased.

"What, pray tell, is your heart into these days?"

"My heart," he said in the velvety tone that tightened her nipples and resonated deep in her belly every time she heard it, "has only ever been in one place—"

His disquieting gaze swept over her, making her shiver involuntarily.

"—but we'll get to that another time. If you're asking what I'm doing with myself these days, you can be one of the first to know. I've endowed a new charitable foundation, Phoenix Legacies. I'm running it."

Jillian couldn't tamp down her surprise or her growing sense of dread. If Beau was doing good works, she didn't need to know. Any information that interfered with her unmitigated hatred of him was a bad thing.

"Phoenix Legacies?"

"We give micro loans to worthy applicants who've taken a wrong turn with their lives and need a little help getting back on their feet."

This was too stunning for words. Beau? The former governor of Virginia and current king of Miami's fast-living, hard-partying lifestyle? A philanthropist now? *Beau?*

And she didn't want to ask—was afraid to ask—but she had to know.

"*Phoenix?* Why would you do that?"

He stared her in the face, deadly serious. "I like the idea of rising from the ashes. If I can help people put their life on the right track, then maybe my life will mean something." He paused, his jaw flexing with the effort to hold back his words, but the words won. "For a change."

So that's what this was about. Redemption for Beau. Fine. He could do all the saintly works he wanted, as long as it had nothing to do with her. Big deal; God knew he had a lot to make up for and he certainly had money to spare. She would not be impressed or interested. It would not matter to her—

"And how much of your fortune did you use to bankroll this little venture?" she demanded because her curiosity had her in a stranglehold. A million or two was nothing to him—

"Ninety-eight percent," he said, unsmiling.

Jillian's jaw dropped. He'd given it all away—everything his family had ever worked for or stood for. Gone. He still had enough to live well on, but—

Heavy male footsteps and voices distracted them just then. They looked around to see several uniformed movers descending the steps.

"Still working on the bedroom," one of them told Beau as they trooped out the front door toward the van.

"Great," he said.

"What's gotten into you?" Jillian asked the second they were alone again.

Though he stilled and didn't move by so much as a blink or a breath, Jillian felt the change come over him, the intensification of his focus on her. As though he'd wanted her to ask this exact question and they were now circling toward the heart of something important and terrifying.

"I almost died," he said simply.

This reminder did nothing for her nerves, which were already stretching and unraveling. Did he think she'd forgotten the middle-of-the-night phone call that had told her the father of her child and the only man she'd ever loved was near death in a Miami hospital?

Though she hadn't seen him in years at that point—didn't want to see him—she'd never forget the blinding horror she felt, especially when she'd heard that his companion du jour, Sabrina something, and the driver had been killed when the driver of that semi fell asleep at the wheel.

In that moment, all her rage fell away and the only thing that mattered was Beau and her need to see him again, not to let him go. So she left Allegra with Blanche and hopped on the next plane and prayed for him not to die or, if he had to die, for him not to die until she got there.

And then she'd arrived at the hospital and survived the shock of seeing the biggest, strongest, most vital man she'd ever known swollen and broken, bruised and slashed, more dead than alive, with internal injuries and a badly broken leg that was begging for amputation.

He'd coded once, the nurse told her. Probably would again, and the next time—if there was a next time—they most likely wouldn't be able to bring him back.

All through that terrible day and night, Jillian had sat with him, talked to him, prayed for him. Then the second day began and the doctor told her that Beau would live and keep his leg, and that was all she needed to hear. She left before noon, on the next plane back to Atlanta, because she'd made sure her child's father was okay, but that didn't mean she forgave him or ever wanted to see him again.

Now here he was and, God, she just couldn't breathe or think.

"I know you almost died." She spoke slowly because it was so hard to force the words past the overwhelming knot of dread in her chest and throat. "What's that got to do with you setting up a foundation, moving down the street from me and getting a dog?"

Again that relentless focus held her in its thrall, hypnotizing her with the splintered shards of bright black, green and gold visible in his eyes, even across the room.

"When I woke up in the hospital, I was sorry I wasn't dead."

This merciless honesty unnerved her. Beau dead? Even now she couldn't bear to think it. "Don't say that."

"I was." He was so matter-of-fact they might have been discussing his need for a house painter. "But then I decided that just because I'd screwed up the first half of my life didn't mean I needed to screw up the last half."

"And that means…what?"

But her body already knew the answer even if her brain

refused to accept it. It was in her lungs, which couldn't breathe, in her heart, which skittered on every other beat, and in her belly, which dropped sickeningly.

As the silence stretched, she prayed.

Please don't let him say it. Please, God, don't let anything else in this safe, new world here outside Atlanta change on her. Please...*please.*

Pushing away from the console, Beau made his painful way across the room to where she stood with her clenched fist still clutching that stupid basket of muffins. He stared down at her, doling his words out in measured amounts.

"It means that, while I was recovering in the hospital and working on strengthening my body, I also started working on strengthening my spirit and figuring out why I did the things I did." He paused, color rising high over his cheeks. "I stopped drinking. And I started counseling."

This was unbelievable. Too flustered to be coherent, she stammered the first response that came to mind.

"Y-You're not an alcoholic."

"No, but I didn't need to be drinking."

Wow. That was quite a step because Beau loved his scotch.

"I'm...proud of you."

This wasn't a pro forma attaboy; she really meant it. Knowing Beau as well as she had for all these years, she knew what a huge step this was. The change in him was profound—she felt it the way she felt the relentless beat of her pulse in her throat—and it wasn't just the physical. Whether it was from the accident or the counseling, she couldn't tell, but it petrified her.

A smile warmed his eyes and it was so achingly familiar she wanted to drown in it. "I'm trying to be a better man, Jillian."

The way he said her name hadn't changed after all these years. It was still a loving touch, a melting caress that reached places deep in her soul only he'd ever been able to access. Hearing those three syllables roll off his tongue again renewed her panic and intensified it.

Where was this going? When was he going to drop that final shoe on her? Why couldn't she breathe?

Because she couldn't look him in the face and let him see how he was ripping her to shreds all over again, she looked away. To the crown molding, to the empty hallway, to the dog, who was now drowsing on a sunny patch of the floor with his paws sticking up. If Medusa had been in the room, Jillian would have gladly looked at her swirling head of snakes and been turned to stone.

Anything to avoid Beau's gaze.

Beau waited until finally her cowardice became so humiliating that even she couldn't stand it for another second.

Be a woman, Jill. Just ask.

"What does your trying to be a better man have to do with me?"

Staring her right in the eye, he hit her with the directness that had always been both a wonderful and a terrible thing about him.

"I want my family back."

Jillian paused, the words locked tight in her throat. "You never lost Allegra."

"I want *you* back."

Chapter 4

How the hell could he do this to her?

Again?

How was it that this one man could still reach deep inside her and touch her heart? Why, after every terrible thing they'd been through together, did he still have that power over her?

Well, no more. Never again. The independence and self-confidence she'd gained since the divorce were too precious—too hard-won—to risk by letting him into her life again.

God, she was an idiot. If only she could be indifferent enough to laugh and tell him she didn't give a damn what he wanted. What a glorious day that would be when she finally managed it.

Until then, she felt sudden, choking rage, the kind that burned its way out of her body in an unstoppable eruption. Just this once—*just once, God*—she wanted to hurt him a millionth as much as he'd hurt her. If not emotionally, then physically would do just fine.

With an incoherent cry, she hurled the basket at him.

That cane didn't slow him down any. His instincts were still sharp and he deflected the attack, sending muffins flying in all directions.

"How dare you?" The movers would hear her screeching and realize she was insane, but there was time enough to be embarrassed later. "You have a near-death experience and you decide…what? That it's finally time for you to grow up and be a man? And now you show up here, where I have rebuilt my life, bit by painful bit, and move onto my street and announce you want me back? What do you expect me to do?"

"Exactly what you're doing."

The grim resignation in his voice and on his face brought her up short. How could he be so calm when she was losing it? Didn't he know he was detonating an atomic bomb right in the middle of the carefully constructed house of cards that was her life?

If only she could breathe. If only she could think. If only she'd had some warning that today wouldn't be just another quiet day at the B & B.

Maybe they needed another joint walk down memory lane.

"Let's recap, shall we?"

"Jillian—"

"You cheated on me when you were the governor. Is this ringing a bell at all?"

"Jillian—"

"We'd been having problems and I knew our marriage had been in trouble for a long time, so I forgave you. I stood by you at that podium while you gave your little press conference and apologized for the scandal and swore you'd changed. Remember that?"

"I remember."

"And then we hired Adena Brown to rehabilitate your image and save your career. And what did you do when I thought we were rebuilding our marriage? You had another affair. With her."

"I know what I did."

"So you broke my heart again. Created another scandal. Put me through another public humiliation. Made things so bad for me that I couldn't walk down the street in Richmond without being gawked at. I had to come down here after the divorce and start a new life in a new place where I could hold my head up. And I have."

"I know you have, baby."

God, she was shaking all over. He'd made her a mess, after all. Those same stupid tears seemed stuck in her eyes; they wouldn't fall and they wouldn't dry up. Worst of all, they didn't shield her from the yearning in his darkened eyes or from the telltale throb in his tight jaw that told her he was also near tears.

The sight of his raw emotion was almost worse than feeling

her own. Taking a deep breath, she willed herself to be strong and her voice not to shake.

"So, given our long and painful history together, Beau, you'll have to forgive me if I don't want any part of your little self-improvement project."

Noises startled her and for the first time in a while, she became aware that they were not the only two people in the universe. From outside in the hall came the sound of the movers returning with a mattress and trying to negotiate it up the staircase.

The poor dog hadn't managed to sleep through her shouting. He was up again, snuffling around the room and systematically eating the muffins with appreciative smacks.

All this activity went on around her and still Beau was the center of her existence. He'd always been the sun to her orbiting earth, since the day they met in law school all those years ago, no matter how she wished otherwise.

He crept closer.

Stubborn pride forced her to stand firm and keep her chin up when the smarter thing would've been to leave now, call her real estate agent and list the B & B for sale by supper. But she was still a weak fool, even now, because she held his gaze, knowing that he could play her heartstrings the way Eric Clapton played guitar.

"Do you know what I thought about when I saw that truck coming, Jill?"

"God." Pressing a hand to her chest, she tried unsuccessfully to choke back a hysterical laugh. "Are you going to use your near-death experience against me? Really, Beau?"

"I thought about you." He shrugged helplessly, as though thoughts of her at the moment of his anticipated death were inevitable and he accepted them as such. "I saw your face."

If only those words were meaningless. If only she could let them roll off her back, pity him for living in the past and move on with her life with no thoughts of him to torment her in the dark hours of the night. None of that was possible, though, and bluster was her only flimsy defense against him.

"Too bad for you." She tried to look bored. "I've moved on."

"You have in some ways," he said evenly. "But we're still in love with each other. We're not finished. We'll never be finished."

Jillian went still, too shaken even to blink. The words were such a stinging blow that he might have backhanded her across the face.

For no reason at all, she thought of Adam, her numbness when he'd kissed her earlier, and the way she'd been sleepwalking through life for years. She thought of the yawning emptiness she'd felt, and how she'd wondered if and when she'd ever feel anything deeply ever again.

And now, after ten minutes with her ex-husband, she was that same sickening knot of seething emotions—anger, pain, hurt and confusion—that she'd been when she left him.

Oh, the irony.

She gave him the kind of pitying look she knew he hated, and focused on getting out of there as soon as possible, while she was still in one piece.

"You're in denial. You should ask your therapist to work on it with you."

This seemed like a pretty good exit line and she turned to go. But Beau's face contorted with fury and he lashed out, catching her wrist.

Crying out, she wrenched away from him.

This threw him off balance, to her sinking horror.

Oh, no. She hadn't meant—

He flailed his free arm but couldn't right himself. She saw his eyes widen with dismay and all her anger evaporated in the time it took her to lunge and catch him around the waist.

Desperate not to let him fall and damage that leg any further, she locked her knees and they staggered a couple of steps together.

Then Beau shoved her away. "I can do it."

The scar puckered and reddened with his furious pride as he snarled at her. Grunting with the effort to remain upright, he wobbled again and took another five years off her life.

"Fine." Stung by his rejection and sick with worry, she watched him plant the cane with painstaking care and get both his feet under him. Panting now and looking pale—God, she hoped he wasn't still in pain—he leaned on the cane, closed his eyes and took a ragged breath. "Fall on your ass, then. See if I care."

The flash of a crooked smile was her only warning before those hazel eyes flew open and locked onto her face with a hard gleam. Then he sprang into action, caught her around the waist with a free hand that was still as powerful as it had ever been, swung her around and backed her into the wall.

"Don't."

Too late. He'd already settled against her and shifted so that her hips cradled his and there was no question about which parts of his body were still in fine working order.

Just like that, her mind emptied out and there was only the pleasure and sweet remembrance of they way they felt together, the way his hands made her body hum with energy.

Push him away, Jill. Do it.

The intent was there, but her flesh was starved and weak and he felt as unspeakably good as ever. She struggled but only wound up gripping his muscular arms, pulling him closer when she should have been yanking herself free.

This small acquiescence pushed him over an edge.

With a sound that was half groan, half growl, he dropped the cane with a clatter. Then he held her head between his hands, and forced her to look into the fractured shards of green and brown light that were his brilliant eyes.

Beau. God, Beau.

His fingers worked through her hair until they massaged her scalp and melted her like a caramel chew left in the sun. She nearly died with the rightness of being back with him like this, seeing him like this, feeling him like this.

All the old chemistry was still there, all the passion and the need. There was no pretending it wasn't, not with him this close.

"Here's the thing," he murmured. "You do care. I know you do. I remember what you told me in the hospital."

Oh, no. He couldn't have heard—

"You were out of your mind with pain and the meds," she tried. "You have no idea what—"

"Bullshit." His lips thinned with stubborn anger. "I heard what you said."

This was too much. Apparently there was no weapon he wouldn't use against her; she should have known. Distraught, she abandoned her pride and fought for survival by appealing to his conscience. She knew he had one buried deep somewhere.

"Why don't you just stab me with a knife and be done with it?" She kept her voice quiet, knowing that would affect him more than yelling. "Wouldn't that be easier than the way you keep tearing me apart every time I get my life back together?"

That did it. His face contorted with what she hoped was shame and his head dropped.

She sagged with relief.

But instead of moving away and freeing her, he rubbed his face against her cheek—his nose against her hair—and inhaled her the way a drowning man would inhale that first breath of air when he was rescued.

"I love you," he whispered in her ear. "I've always loved you, and I died loving you—"

"Don't."

"—and I wouldn't be here now if I didn't think you still loved me. I wouldn't have come if I didn't think I was ready to be the kind of husband you need. We've got to face down our demons, Jill. We've got to do it together."

No. Not that. Never that.

A renewed surge of anger and adrenalin flashed through her, giving her the burst of strength she needed. Wrenching free, she hurried a few steps away, out of his reach, and wheeled around to face him in all her terrified fury. She focused on one small part of what he'd said because that was the only thing she had the courage to confront.

"You're not my husband anymore."

"I intend to change that," he said flatly.

Chapter 5

Hurry, Jill. You can make it.

Hurry…hurry…HURRY.

But as she unceremoniously left Beau's house and sped back down the hill to the B & B, where she belonged, she didn't think she could make it at all. Overhead, the sun had begun its midmorning blaze and the air was thicker now, a humid sludge of unbreathable oxygen, all but useless to her.

Run, Jill!

No. She couldn't run. Couldn't risk Beau looking out the window and seeing what he'd reduced her to. If it killed her, and it just might, she wouldn't give him the satisfaction and ammunition of knowing how he affected her. He'd only use it against her the first chance he got.

Almost there. Hang on.

Ahead of her loomed the B & B, her beacon, the only thing saving her from collapsing in the street. For a minute it seemed like it was coming closer, but then her legs slowed down, her lungs emptied out, and her tiny safe haven from Beau remained as unreachable as a rainbow's end.

Meanwhile, her frantic heart had gone berserk and seemed determined to pump out a thousand erratic beats per minute. The staccato pounded in her tight throat and battled with her breath for supremacy. Neither won, leaving her gasping and panicked.

Passing out on the sidewalk seemed like a real possibility. With the way her luck was running today, she'd fracture her skull on the concrete as she fell, and lapse into a coma before the EMTs came.

Maybe she should sit on the curb and wait for the spell to pass. Or maybe she should drape herself around the mailbox post so the mailman would see and rescue her when he came to deliver today's batch of bills and catalogs.

No. She could do this.

One more step, Jill. You can do it. And another. Last one.

She staggered up the stairs and through the kitchen door into her refuge, where the cooler air didn't make one damn bit of difference.

No sign of Blanche, though, thank God. She could really do without any witnesses to this, her first full-blown panic attack in months.

Doubled over now, the walls spinning until only streaks of random colors and patches of sunlight passed before her eyes, she lurched into the dark pantry, slammed the door behind her and hit the cold floor right between the fifty-pound burlap sack of basmati rice and the flour bin.

Put your head between your legs, Jill. Do it.

She did it.

Breathe, Jill. Just breathe. There's no reason why you can't.

There was a reason. Beau had unleashed these demons inside her, and now they had her throat in an iron grip trapped inside a cage of paralyzing anxiety.

It was too much. This was all too much: Beau and the B & B, Allegra and single motherhood, making lunch and the guests and the payroll and facing another day after this one.

She couldn't do it.

She'd made it this far, yeah, and built a so-called new life, but she'd only been faking it, and the jig was up.

Now her horrible truth was out and the whole world would know her ugly and humiliating secret: she was a mess, unworthy of the title of mother or even woman. She couldn't fake her way through another day.

Breathe, Jill. Just breaaaathe.

The constricting pressure around her chest eased up, just a little.

It was a start. Not a good start, but a start.

Trying again, working from her belly, she sucked in another molecule or two of air and it was a miraculous triumph, the same as giving birth to a healthy child or landing a rover on Mars.

Panting and choked, she wheezed her way to a complete lungful and then another after that, and by then her training kicked in to save her.

Good thoughts, Jill, she reminded herself. Think them.

She thought about Allegra. She thought about spending a day on the beach, splashing in the waves and enjoying the sun's bright heat on her face. She thought about warm, gooey chocolate-chip cookies with pecans, and the fluffy comfort of her down-covered bed. She thought about all the emotional progress she'd made and how far she'd come.

The tension left her body by slow but sure degrees, and the crushing pressure let up until it no longer flattened her into a dark smudge on the floor. She took another tentative breath, just to be sure, and the lifesaving air didn't kick and scream its way into her lungs.

And then, just like that, it was over.

But of course it wasn't over at all because she was still a mess down to the marrow of her soul.

Exhausted, she slumped back and tried to ignore the low shelf of baking products cutting across her kidneys. The world came back to her and she became aware of the distant voices of guests in the foyer…the open and close of the front door…the heavy, rubberized footfall that announced the imminent arrival of Blanche.

Blanche. Oh, no. God help her if Blanche saw her like this.

Calling on the kind of supreme effort that Superman used to fly around the earth's circumference and reverse time, she heaved herself to her feet and tested out her wobbly knees. They trembled but held.

She was just swiping some of the wetness from her face—she wasn't sure whether it was sweat or tears and didn't really want to know—when Blanche came into the kitchen singing, or rather rapping, Public Enemy's "Fight the Power," which was just… wrong.

"Fight, fight, fight the—" Blanche chanted and, without warning, swung the pantry door open, sashayed inside and came up short when she saw Jillian.

Jillian tried to look dignified. Blanche gaped.

Apparently, Blanche couldn't get a good enough look, because she reached out and flipped the light on. Jillian wasn't prepared. Wincing, she blinked and covered her eyes. Blanche tsked and jerked Jillian's hand down.

The women faced off.

Judging from her horrified expression, Blanche knew the worst, but she asked anyway. "Have you had a panic attack?"

Jillian pulled free, flicked off the light and tried to escape before this interrogation reached full swing. "No."

Blanche didn't buy the lie, which was no surprise since the woman had the unerring instincts of a baying bloodhound on an escaped convict's trail. "You're all wild-eyed and sweaty, missy." She looked around, as though she expected to see a masked intruder. "What's going on in here?"

"Nothing." Jillian smoothed her hair and tried not to sound too defensive. "I was just…you know, checking the supplies and—"

Blanche's brows inched up toward her artificial hairline. "And—what? You were crying because there weren't enough tea bags? Don't kid a kidder, honey. What's wrong with you?"

Jillian opened her mouth to dodge and deflect, but it wasn't worth the effort. Why bother? Blanche would know soon enough anyway.

"Beau bought the Foster place."

Blanche, who knew the rough outlines of the implosion of Jillian's marriage, if not every gory detail, took this news with appropriate solemnity. With a single sharp nod, she squared her shoulders and marched to the far corner of the huge pantry, where she rummaged around behind an enormous sack of coffee beans and extracted a fifth of Patron tequila.

Whoa. The good stuff. How much was she paying Blanche, anyway? And did Blanche drink on the job? This early? She'd have to revisit these issues later, when she wasn't so overwrought and behind on the lunch preparations.

And what— *Oh, no.*

Blanche had by now produced a stack of Allegra's Dora the Explorer Dixie cups, and poured a shot for each of them.

"Blanche, I don't dr—"

Blanche shoved one of the cups at Jillian and raised the other in a toast. “Cheers. Now drink.”

Yeah. Cheers. Whatever.

Jillian drank.

The liquid courage both burned and was smooth as the finest silk going down. Jillian choked just a bit on the swallow, wondering if she'd made a terrible mistake by imbibing so soon after her panicked trauma of a few minutes ago, but then a funny thing happened. She coughed and gasped and the warmth spread through her, empowering her with enough strength to get mad.

What the hell had gotten into her?

So Beau thought he'd reappear and turn her world upside down, did he? So he thought he could just materialize and pick up where he'd left off? So he thought she'd forgive him?

Well, she had news for Beau: no freaking way.

That man had already taken enough from her. She wasn't about to give him another inch, thought or tear, not one more cry. It didn't matter where he lived. It didn't matter what he said. All of that was meaningless.

The only thing that mattered now was the life with Allegra that she'd painstakingly built here at the B & B. Everything else was sound and fury, signifying nothing—especially Beau.

Let him move down the street. It was no skin off her nose.

Catching Blanche's watchful eye, Jillian smiled and held out her cup. “Hit me again.”

“That's my girl.” Blanche beamed with approval and topped them both off. “Cheers.”

“Salut.”

They tapped cups and tossed back the tequila, which Jillian was really starting to appreciate. She was just debating whether a third hit would make the lunch prep and cleanup go any more smoothly, when there was a sharp knock at the kitchen door and her insides turned to stone.

Oh, God. That wasn't a normal knock. That was Beau's knock. She knew it.

And it was all well and good to stand there in the closet and tell herself to be brave and strong, but it was something else again to be brave when Beau was actually in the room with her.

Facing him again this soon would take another thirty years off her life. She couldn't do it.

The blind terror must have shown on her face because Blanche took charge. Hitching up her stretchy pants and reminding Jillian of Gary Cooper adjusting his holster in *High Noon* before the shoot-out, she gave her a grim nod and took charge.

"You leave him to me, honey."

Relieved as Jillian was by this offer, how humiliating was it to hide in her own damn pantry while her employee took care of her ex? Sure, she felt a little wobbly at the moment, but was she that big a coward?

Blanche had cracked open the pantry door and peered out to survey the enemy. Now she retracted her head and faced Jillian with a low whistle of feminine appreciation, looking resigned to the worst possible outcome.

"Oh, Jilly," she said. "That man's a god. You've got a big problem."

"Thanks for the news flash."

Beau knocked again, more insistently this time, and Jillian made up her mind. Hiding in the closet was for children like Allegra. She was a grown woman and needed to act like one.

Drawing on some inner reservoir that she really hoped was filled with courage rather than suicidal tendencies, Jillian gave Blanche a gentle nudge on the shoulder.

"Go on and let him in. Give me a second. I'll be fine."

Blanche didn't look at all convinced. "You sure, honey? I can tell him—"

"Now, please."

Blanche sighed and looked to heaven for strength. Either that or she was praying for Jillian's ultimate destruction to be as painless as possible. Then she marched out, a stiff soldier prepared for battle.

The second she was gone, Jillian snatched a paper towel from the roll on the shelf and dabbed her eyes and face. No need to look like she'd been teetering on the edge of a nervous breakdown. Then she fluffed her hair and grabbed the nearest thing she could find, which turned out to be a giant bag of dried cranberries, and followed Blanche out into the airy brightness of the kitchen.

Beau and Blanche stood there, shaking hands and sizing each other up, but his penetrating gaze went right to Jillian the second she appeared. Jillian focused on looking cool and unconcerned and trying not to feel the hum of electricity she always felt when they looked at each other. Maybe it was still there, but she didn't have to succumb to it. Above all, there'd be no more emotional outbursts from her today.

She set the cranberries on the counter and found her apron.

The dog, she realized, had also come down for a visit. On a leash, he'd been sitting quietly at Beau's feet, but now he walked over and settled on his haunches in front of Jillian, open adoration shining in his midnight eyes.

This guy was a beauty. Maybe she had no smiles for Beau, but she sure had an ear scratch or two for his dog, who groaned with canine ecstasy the second she touched him.

"What are you doing here, Beau?"

"We didn't really finish our talk." He leaned heavily on his cane and sweat beaded on his forehead. Was he in pain? Why had he walked all the way down here in this heat? Was he trying to kill himself and give her a heart attack in the process? And why couldn't she remember that Beau's health or lack thereof was no longer her problem? "And I was hoping I could see Allegra and tell her I've moved."

"Hmm." Jillian tied her apron. "This is Blanche."

"We've met." Blanche looked like she was working on vaporizing him with the glint from her narrowed eyes. "I was fixing to say that my mama always told me to be polite to folks, but I'll make an exception for you if you start upsetting my Jillian here—"

"Blanche—" Jillian tried, but Blanche was not to be deterred.

"—and I don't care how pretty you are. I'll snatch that cane right out of your hand and wallop you upside the head with it. And then—"

Oh, for God's sake. *"Blanche."*

"—I'll take thc broken ends and stick 'em where the sun don't shine. And that'd hurt me more'n it'd hurt you, 'cause you've got one fine ass. But I'd do it." Here Blanche paused long enough to extend a plate of pumpkin muffins and flash Beau a smile that held all the warmth of a snarl from a rabid wolf. "Help yourself, sugar. There's butter if you need it."

Grateful as she was for this massive show of support, Jillian wanted to tell Blanche to duck and run because the poor woman had no idea what she was up against. Any second now, Beau would unleash his overwhelming, devastating charm, and Blanche, who was more susceptible to a handsome man than the average woman, would be reduced to a simpering mass of blushes and giggles.

Jillian might as well pop some corn, pull up a chair and watch the show.

Only, Beau didn't fall back on his masculine appeal. He didn't even smile.

Instead—oh, wow, would he ever stop surprising her today?—he nodded in a grim show of humility and met Blanche's ferocity head-on with no excuses.

"I deserve that," he told Blanche. "Hell, if you knew all the trouble I've caused in my life, you'd go ahead and call the sheriff to escort me off the property right now."

Neither of the women had expected this and they exchanged a wide-eyed look over Beau's shoulder. Blanche recovered from her surprise quickly enough to put down the plate, fold her arms over her chest and hike up her chin as though she'd like nothing better than to take the meat mallet to him.

Beau didn't quake before this withering assessment, didn't even blink. "I'm glad Jillian has a friend like you. I hope one day I can earn your trust."

The disapproving lines around Blanche's mouth softened for a second, but then she caught herself and renewed her disdain. "Doubtful," she said.

Beau's energy seemed to dim, as though a light had gone out inside him, but he held tight to his cane and stood tall. "I understand." One corner of his mouth twisted up, crooked and humorless, and that vivid red scar puckered. "I'm not giving up, but I do understand."

Blanche shrugged. "Honey, you can do what you want. Long as you understand that I'm protecting my girl here." She looked to Jillian. "You want me to toss him out? We got lunch to fix."

Yes. Toss him out. Bolt the door. Call the sheriff.

The words were all right on the tip of Jillian's tongue, but then Beau pivoted on his good leg to submit to her verdict on his fate, and she couldn't speak to save her life.

What was this new thing about him? There was infinite patience in his expression, resignation as well as determination, and she had the terrible feeling that if she told him to come back tomorrow each day for the next fifty years, he'd come back tomorrow.

But the one thing he would not do was give up.

This put her in an untenable position, stuck squarely between her need to stay as far away from him as humanly possible, and her conflicting resolve to be brave and not let him turn her into a panic-attack-stricken mess.

Her pride won out in the end, and she shrugged in an Oscar-worthy display of indifference. Keeping her voice strong and audible was much harder.

"If you want to stand there for three minutes and watch me fix lunch for my guests, that's fine with me. I've already said everything I have to say."

A relieved grin flashed across his face, as brilliant as a streaking comet across the starry night sky. And then he sobered just as Jillian's knees were weakening to mush. "Thank you."

Oh, God, this was a mistake.

Already her pulse was flittering again in the telltale skip that told her another panic attack was in her near future, but it was too late to backtrack now. Blanche was moving toward the hall, about to leave them alone together, and there was no way Jillian could weasel out of it without looking like the full-grown, yellow-bellied coward that she was.

"Humph." Blanche pursed her lips, shot Beau a few more death sparks from her blue eyes and disappeared.

And Jillian faced Beau.

Chapter 6

Breathe, Jill. Breathe.

To give herself something to do while she waited for him to talk, she focused on the dog. "What's his name?"

"Seinfeld."

The surprise bubbled up out of her mouth in an unstoppable laugh. *Seinfeld.* That had been their favorite show a million years ago, when dinosaurs were young and they had a marriage that involved love and fun rather than the endless parade of one heartbreak after the other.

Foolish to the bitter end and beyond, she caught his eye for that one second—oh, man, he was grinning, too—and the laughter was crushed by the sweet ache of nostalgia for things that had probably never been as great as she remembered them anyway.

Turning away from Beau and his furry surrogate, she washed her hands. Forget the dog. If she was determined never to touch Beau again, she damn sure shouldn't be fawning over his stupid dog.

Seinfeld. Yeah. Right. Like that changed anything.

"What is it, Beau?" Drying her hands, she tried, with increasing frustration, to remember what meal she was supposed to be cooking. It was supper, right? This terrible day had dragged on for so long it had to be suppertime by now, didn't it? "I have work and—"

"This is a great inn." Taking baby steps, Beau turned in a loose circle to admire the kitchen and what he could see of the hall beyond. "You've worked really hard. I'm proud of you."

Jillian froze, her hand high overhead, reaching for a copper pan from the rack above the range. Chicken. They were supposed to be baking chicken.

But Beau wasn't finished reaching inside her and twisting her heart, and the unmistakable light of admiration gleaming in his eyes made everything so much worse. And that was before he spoke again.

"I don't think there's anything you can't do when you set your mind to it."

Jillian gaped at him, too undone to reply. Though this was the kind of thing he used to say all the time during their early years together, a thousand snide remarks came to mind now.

I couldn't keep you satisfied in bed, could I?

I couldn't keep you from screwing other women, could I?

I couldn't keep our family together.

Oh, yes, she wanted to hurl all that ugliness right in his face, but something stopped her. The touch of God on her shoulder, maybe, or a moment's grace. It could have been the sudden intrusion of Allegra's smile and Jillian's unwavering determination to make things work, as much as she possibly could, with her child's father.

Whatever it was, she couldn't ignore it.

So she swallowed the nastiness, which felt bitter going down and settled in her belly like a lead cannonball, and said, simply, "Thank you."

Beau turned those clear hazel eyes on her. "You're welcome."

A second was about all she could stand and then she had to look away. Beau waited, saying nothing and kicking her anxiety level even higher.

Why was he here? When would he leave? Desperate for something to do that wouldn't reveal the relentless shake of her hands, she went to the fridge and pulled out the chicken, which Blanche had put to soak in a bowl of buttermilk.

Chicken…chicken…what'd she do with it now? For the life of her, she couldn't remember. She'd have better luck trying to fillet a bowl of yak brains.

Think, Jill.

She had the pan. She had the chicken. Oh—flour. She needed flour. And then she needed to get a grip. "If that's all, Beau, I need to—"

On her way to the far cabinet to get a few more ingredients, she caught a glimpse of him out of the corner of her eye and stopped cold. Underneath the smooth golden tones of his skin, he looked pale and clammy, with a distinct green tinge.

Well, so what?

She tried not to care, but then he gritted his teeth in a discreet cringe and there was no ignoring that.

The man was in pain. Enormous pain. Terrible pain.

"Beau," she said sharply. God, was that her voice with all that anguish in it? "Sit down. You're in pain—"

"I'm fine."

Stubborn idiot. There were times when she was positive mule's blood ran through his veins.

"—and you probably need your meds."

Letting his eyes drift closed, as though he could take a quick nap standing up and then commence running a marathon—no problem—he swayed on his feet. "I don't take any meds."

He didn't take—

What?

Screw the chicken. Screw lunch. Aghast, she stalked back to stare him in the eye when she called him what he was—a maniac. She was so furious she really thought she could spit out a nail or two if she put her mind to it.

"What the hell are you doing?" Sweeping her arms wide to encompass every crazy thing he'd done this morning and those he'd been working on for years, she screeched and didn't care how many paying guests heard. "Trying to win the Martyr of the Year award?"

Those eyes flew open, blazing green now with the fervor of a zealot. "I'm no saint."

She snorted. "I think we're all clear on that, thanks. Take your meds, Beau—"

"No."

"Why not?" Jillian tried to get a grip on her overactive protective gene, but it was impossible when he was so haggard and yet so proud. She could do a lot of things; he was right about that. She could change the oil in her car, install storm windows and do a darn fine job as a single parent. The one thing she could not do and would never be able to do, not if she lived for another thousand years, was ignore his pain. "For God's sake, why not?"

"Because it reminds me!"

"Reminds you of what?"

He faltered, his expression filling with so much self-loathing and shame that she was surprised he didn't grab the nearest chef's knife and jab himself under the fingernails in punishment.

Opening his mouth, he hesitated again, and when he finally spoke it was with the helpless sincerity and vulnerability of someone unearthing a piece of his soul and exposing it to bright sunlight for the first time ever.

"All the work I have to do on myself."

Jillian stared at him.

Well, what the hell was she supposed to say to that? That he didn't have work to do? Or maybe she should emphasize the obvious—that he had so much work to do he really needed to look into overtime and weekend options.

If she was smart, she'd just wish him good luck and tell him to get started on it down the street at his own house and well away from her. Why did he have to wallow in his determined martyrdom right here in her house?

Only, he didn't look like he was wallowing or seeking pity. He looked like a man stating a simple fact without realizing that the simple fact tore her to shreds.

He had work to do on himself. Fine, Beau. *Fine*.

"Do all the work you want," she told him. "It doesn't matter one way or the other to me."

A shadow crossed his face, maybe because he knew she was lying.

"But I don't intend to watch you kill yourself." She waved a hand to the heavy oak bench against the wall under the far window. "You can sit down, or you can leave. I'd prefer that you leave, but it's your choice."

He didn't miss a beat, the bastard. "Sit with me, Jill."

She resisted for a second, hating him.

He waited.

The shallow harshness of his breath finally did her in. They'd sit. He'd gather a little strength. Then he'd leave. Brilliant. She had a plan.

"You have one minute."

Furious, she marched the few steps to the bench and sat. He followed with painstaking care, planting a foot and then the cane, a foot and then the cane.

A thousand deaths claimed her in those few seconds while she glared off in the other direction and tracked his progress with her heart in her throat, ready to spring up and catch him if he wobbled or fell.

He didn't, thank God.

Arriving at last, he sat with a poorly stifled groan and stretched out that bad leg, rubbing his thigh. Seinfeld, sensing his discomfort in the unerring way pets do, ambled over and watched, making sure he wasn't needed. When Beau was settled at last, he rested his chin on Beau's lap and looked up at him with concern in his dark brown eyes, while Jillian worked hard to hate both man and dog.

"The Celtics called," Beau said. "They want me to play forward for them. I told them I'd think about it."

This was not funny. She would not laugh at his jokes, nor would she admire his strength, determination and humility. He would not affect her; she wouldn't let him.

"Fifty seconds," she said, not looking at him. "Tick tock."

"Can I see Allegra today?"

"Of course."

"Thank you."

There was a pause during which he apparently decided to press his luck. "Can I get more time with her every week?"

No. Hell, no. A billion times no. If only she were petty enough to keep a girl from her devoted father. Life would be so much easier that way.

"Yes."

"Will you come back to me?"

What?

Jillian whipped her head around, prepared to blast him to kingdom come, but his wry half smile stopped her and dried the words right out of her mouth.

"Just thought I'd ask. While you're being so agreeable. It was worth a shot."

Okay. Game over. She'd tried to be a mature adult, but she had another seventy or eighty years of growing up to do before she'd be ready to deal with his teasing. Time for him to go. Lunging to her feet, she took a step toward the door.

"I think we're done here—"

To her utter astonishment and horror, he took her hand and, before she could protest or snatch it away, laced their fingers. Too bad her body didn't know that she'd written him off forever and that it should not, therefore, physically respond to him ever again.

Heat flashed through her, a potent and unnecessary warning that although some things had changed, other things could never change. The scorching touch of his skin still undid her and their hands still fit together like the pieces of Allegra's giant alphabet puzzle upstairs. Whether she wanted to fit with him or not didn't matter. She just did.

"I've told you." His low voice was hoarse now, overflowing with emotion. "We're not done."

The violent contraction of her heart nearly doubled her over, but she gathered her strength and tried to get free. This man would not do this to her, not in her own damn kitchen.

"No, Beau—"

Keeping her hand, he pressed it to his chest, where she felt the unrelenting pounding that matched what was going on with her own haywire pulse.

"We have a lot of work to do, Jill, but we can heal our marriage."

With rising desperation, she yanked on her hand again, ready to part with it if that was what it took to get him to stop touching her. But he let her go and she backed up a step, fueled by her fear.

"The fact that there's been a divorce means there's no marriage. You should check that out when you get a free minute. Divorce and marriage—they're mutually exclusive."

The sarcasm rolled right off him, deflected by an unholy light in his eyes that looked like determination to the millionth power.

"I don't mean to scare you and I'll try not to pressure you. But I won't give up, either. There's too much between us."

If only she could deny it. If only she could open her mouth, laugh and say, "Screw you, buddy! I felt nothing when you touched me just now! Nuuuu-thing!"

But the lie wouldn't come and her hand still tingled from his touch.

So she went on offense, which was the next best thing.

Shrugging, she did her best to look bored and indifferent. "Do what you want. It's your time to waste. But I've moved on. I'm dating someone now."

The little bit of remaining color leached away from his face, but she gave him high marks for a quick recovery and managing his shock.

"Dating? Who's the lucky guy?"

Jillian opened her mouth, ready to rub his nose in it, but that was pretty hard when she suddenly couldn't remember the guy's name or face.

"None of your business," she said instead.

Beau absorbed the blow like a man. "I'm not seeing anyone."

"Wow. That's a first. Have you called the people at Guinness?"

A flash of dark humor lit his eyes, but he said nothing.

"I have to get working on lunch, so—buh-bye."

At last—*at last, Lord, glory hallelujah*—he pressed himself to his feet, gathered his cane in one hand and Seinfeld's leash in the other, and headed for the door.

Jillian all but vaulted across the kitchen to open it for him and hold it wide.

Just as he passed through and she was beginning to breathe easier, thinking she'd survived another encounter without a second panic attack so maybe she should go buy a lotto ticket because this was her lucky day, he stopped, right in front of her, close enough that he took up her whole field of vision and threw waves of heat from his body to hers.

Looking down at her, he stared with those remarkable eyes.

Oh, God. There was more. She should've known he wouldn't go quietly.

Please, she wanted to say, *don't,* but her voice locked down when he was this near, and she was exposed and entirely at his mercy.

"I see you're still wearing the locket," he said gently.

It was the worst kind of blow, hard and punishing, and she absorbed it in every cell in her body. Her hand moved on its own and went to her throat, to the chain of white gold and, at the end of that, to the flat oval that was warm from her body.

She held it. Protected it. And didn't answer.

They stared at each other. Hitching up her chin, she tried to manage a defiant glare, but it was hard when the sudden sparkle of her tears nearly blinded her.

"I'll see you later, Jillian."

Turning away from the infinite understanding in his expression—she didn't have to see him clearly to know that it was there—she shut the door in his face.

There they were, Beau saw with knee-weakening relief. Finally.

Jillian, who had the stiff march and impassive expression of a soldier in a military drill, and Allegra, the light of his life, bouncing alongside wearing what appeared to be a ballet costume and tiara.

He stepped back from his living room window and tried to regain some chill, but it was hard with Christmas walking down the street toward him, coming early this year. He was paralyzed with hope, if not outright happiness. But he and happy had never been friends for long, so he couldn't say for sure.

The late-afternoon sun hit their heads just right and threw off flashes of gold. Their hair was exactly the same sandy color, although Allegra had long ringlets that bounced around her shoulders and Jill had one of those short bob-type dos, with curls around her ears. They held hands, his girls, and Allegra had her chubby dimpled face turned up to her mother, chattering like a squirrel.

God, he loved those two.

Moving to the door, he waited for the bell and wished he could breathe.

"Are you ready for your surprise?" Jillian asked.

"What is it? Tell me, tell me, tell me, please—"

"Ring the doorbell and find out," Jillian told her.

Allegra rang the bell, one of those twenty-second rings just to make sure anyone up in the attic or down in the basement could hear. Even though his heart was in his throat and there was no air anywhere close to his lungs, he laughed and was still laughing when he swung the door open and saw the astonished delight on his daughter's face.

They stared at each other for one breathless second during which even her curls seemed to quiver with anticipation. A smile began at one corner of her pouty mouth and spread so wide so quickly that he could almost believe he was—or could one day be—a worthwhile human being who deserved this angel's absolute adoration.

Allegra seemed to have trouble believing her eyes. Hesitating, she looked to Jillian for confirmation, as though nothing could be true until Mommy said it was true.

Jillian nodded and smiled. A less exceptional mother might have had trouble hiding her turmoil over her ex's sudden arrival, might even have scowled, but not Jill. She put her own feelings firmly on the back burner and gave her daughter unspoken permission to be delighted.

If someone had asked him three seconds ago whether he could love Jillian more, he would have said, "No, man, I'm maxed out on that already, thanks," but now he did. His heart beat with it. Expanded with it. Threatened to burst with it.

And then Allegra shrieked.

There was just enough time for him to bend and brace for the assault—he didn't trust himself enough to squat, not on this leg—before she launched at him in a flurry of sturdy limbs, childish potbelly and baby-shampoo fresh curls that had been warmed by the sun.

And then, ah, Jesus, and then she was in his arms, hugging him for all she was worth, vibrant, strong and wonderfully sweet.

Scooping her up, he straightened, staggered back against the door frame so there was no chance of toppling over and crushing the poor child to death, and held on for dear life because she—and her mother—were his life.

Don't cry, man. Do. Not. Cry.

But the hot tears wouldn't stop coming. They burned a trail up his throat, made his chin quiver, his nostrils flare and his vision blur. If he'd been in his right mind, he'd be embarrassed by this show of over-the-top emotion, but ever since the accident, everything was different and nothing was right.

And yet things were more right with him than they'd ever been.

Laughing and crying, absorbing Allegra's kisses, which were clumsy and wet, he looked at Jillian. She'd get a laugh out of seeing him reduced to this slobbering mess by a toddler, no doubt. After a quick swipe at his cheeks, their gazes connected and…

Whoa.

Jillian had the stunned look of a woman who'd just seen a lion fly or an eagle swim. So much emotion coalesced in her whiskey-brown eyes that he had to look away or risk going blind. If his thundering heart didn't give out, that was.

Fleeting thoughts raced through his mind.

To think that he'd let his pain make him self-destructive enough to nearly throw all this away. To think that he'd turned to other women when all his answers were right here. To think that Jillian had claimed it was all over between them. To think that he'd worried about what kind of greeting Allegra would give him. To think that he'd wondered if moving here was a big mistake.

Hah.

If there was one thing he had to say for himself, it was this:

When he was wrong, he was really wrong.

On this one thing, though, the big thing, he was right.

These two females were his everything. Period.

Swiping at his eyes one last time, he held Allegra high overhead. She shrieked, legs dangling and kicking.

"Stop with the kisses." He scrunched up his nose, giving her his best grossed-out face. "I don't want all those slobbery kisses. I don't even like kisses."

Allegra didn't believe him for a second. "You love my kisses!"

Beau gagged and stuck his tongue out. "Yuck."

As punishment for this insult, Allegra patted his face between her palms and planted a big one right on the tip of his nose. There might have been more, but at that moment she spied the dog and her breath caught. That one glance was enough to relegate Beau to second-class status.

"There's a dog," she whispered.

Beau settled her on his hip, ignoring the corresponding protest from his leg. Distributing the increased weight a little better, he glanced over his shoulder.

Seinfeld, who loved children and relentlessly sought them out every time he and Beau went for a walk, seemed to be in love. His delighted dark gaze was glued to Allegra and his tail-wagging exuberance threatened to levitate him until only the tips of his paws touched the ground. He crept closer, woofing a welcome.

"Daddy." Allegra could hardly speak with all her hopeful excitement. "Whose dog is that?"

"Mine."

Leaning closer, she whispered in Beau's ear as though she didn't want Seinfeld to overhear her talking about him and feel offended. "Does he like little girls?"

"He loves little girls."

"Can I pet him?"

"It's up to you."

"What's his name?"

Allegra wriggled to get down, and Beau pressed his nose to her fat little cheek one last time and breathed in as much sunshine and clean girl as his lungs could absorb before setting her free. "Seinfeld."

Jillian, meanwhile, seemed to have recovered some of her composure and was now firmly back in charge. Stepping closer, she hovered just between girl and dog, ready to intercede if needed.

"Careful, A. Make sure you let him sniff your hand first—"

But Seinfeld didn't need this kind of formality. Bypassing Allegra's outstretched fingers, he walked right up to her and licked her face. And then, when she giggled herself into hysterics, he licked the other side.

"That's hygienic," Jillian muttered.

Beau laughed. It might be disgusting, yeah, but they both knew better than to come between their daughter and her new BFF.

"Let's go in here." He grabbed Seinfeld's leash and steered him into the living room, which was a sea of boxes—some opened and some not. Allegra raced alongside, and Jillian, moving at the reluctant pace of a prisoner about to undergo a couple rounds of waterboarding, brought up the rear. Allegra plopped, cross-legged, on the floor, and Seinfeld took that as an opportunity to stretch out, belly side up, and rest his head on her lap.

"How do you like my new house, Allegra?"

"It's nice," Allegra said, now shaking Seinfeld's paw.

Beau waited for his words to sink in, which took a minute. But then Allegra's head jerked up, eyes wide with even more astonishment, and the words flew out in one hopeful gasp.

"This is your house?"

Beau grinned. "This is my house."

"Yay!"

Jumping up, she raced over to bounce in his lap and slobber a few more kisses onto his face. But then— Uh-oh.

Allegra pulled back, all shadowed expression and furrowed brows. "You can live with us—"

"No," Jillian said sharply. But then she caught herself and toned down the vehemence. "Daddy has his own house. He'll live here, but you'll get to see him all the time now. Won't that be great?"

Beau's sudden tension eased. He really had to hand it to Jillian. She'd always done a great job keeping her personal feelings out of the mix, and for that he was eternally grateful.

Whenever he had a reunion with Allegra, which was every couple of weeks or so, he half expected to start right back at square one with her:

Allegra, meet Beau. He's your father. You can call him Daddy.

When he was feeling insecure, which was most of the time, he expected Allegra to hate him on sight:

Hello, Daddy, you punk. Why did you cheat on Mommy and break up our family?

Neither scenario had ever happened, though, and he had Jillian to thank for that. Pretty much the only thing he'd gotten right in his sorry existence was to choose a woman strong and classy enough to be an outstanding mother to his child. Allegra came first with Jillian, period. Allegra's needs, Allegra's feelings and Allegra's innocence.

So, yeah, the girl didn't know he was a punk and, if it was up to Jillian, she'd never know.

Allegra frowned. "But why can't Daddy live with us? We have lots of room."

Beau held his breath, but Jillian's placid expression never wavered.

"Because Daddy bought this beautiful new house. I'll bet he even has a room for you."

That was hitting the girl where she lived. Allegra's face lit up with a glowing excitement for one brilliant second, but then she seemed to realize that she was being handled. Her pointy little chin firmed into open defiance.

"But I want Daddy to live with us."

"And I want a spotted pony," Jillian told Allegra. "Looks like we're both going to be disappointed. Now do you want to see your room, or should we leave right now?"

The females faced off in an extreme battle of wills from which only one could emerge the victor. Allegra thought it over for several tense beats, her jaw tight with stubborn defiance. Finally, she stood, looking grim.

"Where's my room, Daddy?"

Beau tried not to smile, but couldn't keep his lips from twitching. "This way."

He, Seinfeld and Allegra started for the steps and were halfway up when it occurred to him that Jillian wasn't following. He turned to discover her staring up at them from the bottom, looking forlorn and trying to hide it.

"Aren't you coming?" he asked, sounding every bit as needy as he felt.

She shrugged, keeping her expression so relentlessly upbeat that the effort must be exhausting. "I'll see it next time."

Next time. Yeah. Good. She probably wanted to give him time to reconnect with Allegra, and God knew he needed it. Outstanding. O, happy day.

Except the sun didn't seem to shine when Jillian was gone and, man, he needed that light back in his life. Even when she hated his guts and wished him a painful death and subsequent resurrection just so he could repeat the painful death cycle again, he wanted her there, in the room with him. Where he could see her smile, even if it wasn't directed at him.

But…he could be patient. She deserved that much and more from him.

Opening his mouth, he worked on pretending that her departure was no big deal and then, when that effort was a miserable failure, worked on telling her how much her cooperation with Allegra meant to him.

Aaaaaand… No. He couldn't manage that, either.

The emotion congealed in his throat, blocking everything, so he shut his mouth.

"I'll see you later, pumpkin." Jillian waved to Allegra and turned to go. "Daddy'll bring you home in a little while."

But Allegra was already gone, sprinting down the hall in a flurry of curls and pumping legs, Seinfeld at her heels. Her voice echoed down the staircase as she disappeared. "Okay, Mommy."

Beau almost made it. Almost managed the cool, unconcerned, laid-back thing. And then Jillian put her hand on the knob, and a sudden desperation rose up in him, the blind need to keep her nearby, even if it was only for another three seconds.

"Jillian."

Jillian paused, looking down at her hand or the floor, something that held her rapt attention and prevented her from looking at him. Even at this distance, he could see the thin line of her lips and the subtle pulse of a muscle in her temple.

Swallowing hard against that knot in his throat, he tried to find the words, but they remained hidden just out of his reach.

In the end, he fell back on the old standard, which was lame but the best he could manage.

"Thank you."

No reaction for the longest time and then, suddenly, she looked up and met his gaze straight on.

Jesus.

Maybe a direct lightning strike would be more of a heart-stopping jolt to his system, but he doubted it. There was so much blazing turbulence in her eyes, so much pain wrapped in anguish and surrounded by heartbreak that it nearly knocked him flat on his butt.

There was something coming next, something harsh, and he could guess what it was.

Screw you, punk.

Or maybe: I did it for Allegra, not you, so don't thank me. Punk.

Or maybe the old favorite, appropriate for almost all occasions: Drop dead.

Whatever it was, he'd earned it. So he stood tall, squared his shoulders and prepared to take it on the chin like the man he was trying to be.

Only, she didn't curse him or wish him a gruesome death followed by eternity burning in the deepest pits of hell. She didn't do much of anything except stare at him with those stormy eyes for a few more beats and then issue a warning before she slipped through the door and into the night.

"Don't make me regret it."

The dreams started up again that night.

It was Jillian's bedroom, but not. A hot breeze fluttered the sheer white curtains at the French doors, bringing in the heady scent of magnolias in bloom, and promising rain.

She stretched across her bed, nude except for the whispery touch of a pale satin sheet across her oversensitized skin, waiting...hoping. Her hungry body was beyond patience or shame, and she stroked a hand across one heavy breast, and then the other, tormenting the hard pebbles of her nipples with the sheet's sleek slide until her inner muscles clenched and throbbed for him.

Only him. Always him.

Lightning flashed once…twice…and he was there, tall and broad-shouldered, a threat and a gift, cast in shadow except for his gleaming gaze. It tracked the movement of her hand as it smoothed over the sheet, lower, between her legs.

Closing her eyes because she couldn't bear to see the satisfaction and triumph in his, she allowed herself the arch of her back and a moan, low and earthy.

Another blink of lightning, and he was closer, at the foot of the bed, pulling the sheet inch by slow inch down her body, revealing her to his hot stare.

Agonized, she stretched her arms overhead and nearly wept as the sheet trailed across her nipples…her belly…her wet sex.

"Do you want me?" he asked.

Because it was a dream, she couldn't lie.

"Yes."

"Want me to what?"

He was at the middle of the bed now, somehow, leaning over to dip his hot tongue into her belly button until she writhed and her hips lifted off the bed.

Because it was a dream, there was no embarrassment in the request.

"I want you inside me. Right now. I want it hard, and I don't want you to ever stop." At the risk of being redundant, she planted her feet, bent her knees and opened her thighs for him.

He laughed, a wicked murmur of male pleasure.

Finally, he loomed above her, naked and aroused. Magnificent. She reached for him and he settled between her legs, where he belonged, big and heavy and utterly right. With another earthy laugh, he reached between them, gripping himself.

She was ready. Past ready, because it had been too long and she could barely scrape by an existence without him.

Beau.

"Beau."

He tapped her arm, distracting her, and she twitched her arm away. *"Beau."*

"Mommy?"

Jillian bolted upright, her empty arms reaching for him, but he was gone, snatched away, and she was alone in this bed with an unsatisfied body that needed only one touch or squeeze to push her over the edge into a climax that would rip her apart.

Beau. Come back. Don't leave me alone.

Agitated and sweaty, she wanted to scream with frustration and then, when her room came into focus, along with her plain old cotton nightgown, cotton sheets and bleary-eyed daughter standing by the bed, rubbing her eyes and yawning, she wanted to scream with outrage.

God. He'd done it to her. Again.

"Mommy?"

Squeezing her head between her hands, Jillian scrunched her face and swallowed back the desperate desire and the phantom imprint of his hands on her hot skin. She remembered what she was—a single mother—and what she wasn't: a big enough fool to give that man a place in her life.

Back to the real world.

"Yes, baby?"

"I can't find Archie."

Ah, yes. Time to find Archie, the stuffed lion.

"He probably fell on the floor." Jillian stood and took Allegra's hand. The floor's chill was another layer of separation between the here and now and the dream, so she welcomed it. "Let's go find him."

Leading her daughter back to her own room via the bathroom for a cup of water, Jillian renewed her eternal pledge, the one that never quite seemed to sink in.

I'll never go back to that man. Not ever.

Chapter 7

Oh, for goodness' sake.

Not this early in the morning. Just—no. Please…no.

Not before she'd had that third cup of coffee. Not while she was running around like a headless chicken, trying to feed her guests their breakfast. Not before she'd recovered from seeing him last week and from the dream and the unsatisfied lust that still burned just beneath her skin.

Not Beau. Not again.

Balancing the bowl of fresh fruit salad—watermelon, honeydew, grapes and blueberries, very bright and healthy—in her left hand and the plate of muffins, carrot today, in her right, Jillian took a deep breath and tried to count to ten so she could calm down, but she only made it to five.

Okay, Jill. Try something else.

She squeezed her eyes closed and opened them again, refocusing and hoping that what she'd thought was Beau was merely a figment of her overwrought imagination. She could be mistaken, right? Maybe that wasn't Beau at all. Maybe there was some other really tall guy with a cane floating around. Maybe…

No. Of course not. When had her life ever been that easy?

Beau was unmistakable in his khaki suit, yellow tie, scar and cane, standing at the hostess station on the wide porch of the B & B with Seinfeld at his side.

It wasn't like he blended in with the rest of the populace anyway, what with looking like a god and all. He was taller and handsomer than all the other men there, most of whom were either beleaguered young fathers with demanding children looking for another muffin, or geriatric citizens with plaid shorts, socks and sandals.

Already all the women present were looking around with interest, trying to keep Beau in sight while pretending to read their menus or eat their eggs.

What a disgusting display.

The man and the dog waited for their table like perfect gentlemen, clearly enjoying the bright sunshine of what promised to be another beautiful day. Beau had a laptop tucked under one arm and wore a pair of sunglasses that made him look wickedly dangerous and mysterious, just in case he wasn't striking enough already.

What the hell should she do now? Other than focus on not having another panic attack, that was. The first unpleasant skitterings of her pulse had begun, and her breath was becoming shallower by the second, as though her lungs would only admit a molecule or two of oxygen at a time, nowhere near enough to sustain life.

In the kitchen on the other side of the screen door, just out of everyone's line of sight, she leaned back against the wall, closed her eyes and tried not to lose it.

Breathe, Jill, breathe. You can do it—

Wait a minute.

Her lids popped open to the red haze of her sudden anger.

What was she doing? Falling apart in the middle of the breakfast rush? Heading toward another panic attack? Because of Beau, the man who'd already stolen more of her life than she cared to admit?

Oh, hell, no.

Suck it up, girl. Put your big-girl panties on and be a woman. You can do it.

She was just squaring her shoulders and getting ready to march outside and deal with that man, the fly in her ointment and ant at her picnic, when Barbara Jean appeared at her side.

Barbara Jean gave her a bewildered glance, probably thinking that the boss was cracking up and wondering if she'd still get paid if that happened. Then she followed Jillian's line of sight and all the pieces fell into place.

Barbara Jean's breath hitched.

Jillian certainly understood the reaction. Looking at Beau was like that. As though the most powerful industrial-strength car vacuum had attached to your body to suck the thoughts out of your head and the air out of your lungs.

"He's here." Barbara Jean, who had, after all, met Beau before when she flew Allegra back and forth between the parents, spoke in an awed whisper. "Why didn't you warn me?"

"Oh, please. Get over it." Enough was enough with the whole Beau thing. Jillian found some backbone for her spine and glared at the girl as she swung the screen door open and marched out to face him. "And where's my daughter? You two are supposed to be helping down here. These guests don't refill their own coffee and get their own forks and napkins, you know."

"She's getting dressed. Purple princess today."

So much for Jillian's futile hope that Allegra would wear the cute short set she'd bought her the other day at Target. Ah, well. There was plenty of time to de-princess the child later.

Jillian stepped onto the porch. Dredging up a serene lady-of-the-manor smile that probably didn't fool anyone who wasn't legally blind, she put the food on the sideboard for all her hungry guests and met up with Beau at the hostess station.

His face brightened when she appeared, something along the magnitude of the morning sun rising on the eastern horizon. That was the thing about Beau. He'd always had a knack for making Jillian feel special. The thing she had to keep in mind was that in Beau's world, any given woman was only special until the next woman came along, a period that usually lasted less than a baseball season.

Yeah, she knew all that about him. And yet her foolish heart still went berserk.

After an arrested moment, he snatched his glasses off.

She wished he hadn't done that.

"Hi," he said.

"Good morning." She said it just like that, cool and unruffled, the same as she'd greet any other diner here at the B & B, and felt very proud of herself. "What're you doing here?"

"Eating. I hope. Since Seinfeld got all my muffins last week.

I was hoping that since you've had a little time to get used to my presence, it might—" He trailed off and waited, looking wary. "Is that okay?"

She shrugged and turned her placid smile on Seinfeld so she wouldn't have to stare into Beau's face while she lied. She'd never been a good liar.

"Why wouldn't it be?"

"Ah..." Beau said. "Because you hate me and the horse I rode in on?"

Yeah, she did.

Much as she thought she'd matured since the divorce, inside she was still a disillusioned and bitter girl with a heart of stone as far as he was concerned. No real progress had been made and now, she suspected, none would ever be made. Any thoughts she'd had of being a gracious steel magnolia above all the petty slings and arrows she could throw at him died a swift death.

Oh, yes, she hated him.

She wanted to hurt him, and then she wanted to hurt him again. No punishment was too great for him, no agony too unbearable after all he'd done and continued to do.

If she could, she'd torment him from now until the day one or the other of them died. Even then she might just have a chat with God and see if he could grant her special dispensation to torment Beau in heaven although, clearly, with this kind of thing in her heart, heaven was a questionable proposition for her.

What was that quote about hell hath no fury? Right now it felt like the yawning fires of hell were in the center of her chest, burning the remnants of her broken heart to cinders.

Only, she could never let him know what he did to her. So she turned her flat gaze on him and made it as politely puzzled as she could.

"What makes you think I care enough to bother hating you?"

It was a direct strike right between the glittering crystal of his hazel eyes, which darkened with the hurt. His whole face fell, reminding her of a punctured balloon with all the air rushing out until there was nothing left but a shriveled remnant.

Nodding as though he'd expected this sort of response, he

looked away, to a lone table at the far end of the veranda under one of the hanging ferns.

Then he looked back, his gaze shrewd.

Oh, God. He knew she was lying. Of course he knew.

"You did a pretty good impression of hating me last week."

They stared at each other, Jillian too stubborn to drop her gaze and let him see that he was right. A flush crept over her cheeks, hot and uncomfortable.

Where had this new Beau come from? When had he become this vulnerable and humble? Beau wasn't fragile. He didn't have a clingy bone in his body.

And yet it was all right there in his face—all his desperate need. She meant a lot to him and he hoped he still meant something—even hate—to her. At this point he'd be thrilled to take whatever emotion she'd toss his way.

Only, she wasn't going down that road with him—not ever again.

"I was surprised to see you," she said. "That's all."

Another nod, followed by a rough swallow that made his Adam's apple bob. He looked flattened. Defeated, even.

Good.

She felt a rush of dark triumph, but it was fleeting. The sensation of fingers closing around her throat and tight bands squeezing the air out of her chest, on the other hand, seemed to last forever.

"I'll just sit at that table in the back," he told her.

"Great. It's a buffet, so help yourself."

"Thanks."

He walked off. After settling Seinfeld under the shady canopy of the enormous oak, he came back to the porch and wove his careful way through the tables and the appreciative stares of every woman in the place, which were growing more blatant by the second.

Don't watch, Jill. You have work to do. Ignore that man. Don't care.

She did care. His limp, she noticed as she tracked his progress through her eyelashes while arranging the napkins on the sideboard and making sure there were still plenty of forks and knives, was much less pronounced today. It didn't seem to take as much effort for him to get from here to there, even though he'd walked all the way down the street again, the idiot. Why did he push himself so hard? And how was he going to balance his plate in the buffet line when he had the cane?

Not your problem, Jill.

Calling the laundry service about the sheets, which were looking a little dingy these days, was her problem. Time to go back inside.

But then one of the guests recognized him.

"Governor Taylor?"

Oh, no. Jillian cringed and tried to shrink into invisibility, and the elderly woman wasn't even talking to her.

Beau looked stricken. He faltered for one excruciating second before recovering enough to look around and discover the woman glaring, all righteous indignation and moral superiority.

"I thought that might be you," the woman said. "I can't believe you'd show your face in public."

The woman's husband—they were Mr. and Mrs. Fanelli in room 208, Jillian remembered now—appeared at his wife's elbow, looking embarrassed, and shot Beau an apologetic smile.

"Come on, Margaret." He tugged his wife's arm, trying to steer her back to their table, which was several feet away. "Let's let the man eat his breakfast in peace."

Mrs. Fanelli stood firm. "After the way he disgraced his wife? And now he's here at her bed-and-breakfast? Someone needs to school him on a thing or two."

Several people at nearby tables started to whisper. Jillian's heart sank. Even Seinfeld, sensing something in the air, raised his chin from its resting place on his paws and glanced around, ears perked.

Only Beau seemed unaffected by the brewing storm. He stood tall and kept his chin up and shoulders squared, even though a ruddy flush had begun to creep across his cheekbones.

"I'm sorry you feel that way, ma'am." That slow drawl of his, always thicker when he got upset, was now the consistency of peanut butter. "If you'll excuse me—"

Wow. Fifty points to Beau for being gracious to the old witch.

Beau kept on his trajectory to the buffet table and that would have been the end of the matter, but the woman seemed to think he deserved a little more public embarrassment and clung to his heels like a terrier.

"How could you do that to your wife?" Mrs. Fanelli asked.

"Margaret," Mr. Fanelli tried.

Okay. This was enough. Jillian didn't need perfect strangers pitying or defending her—she'd endured more than enough pity over Beau's cheating, thanks—and she really didn't need a disruption during breakfast. With her luck, one of the guests would leave here, go to one of the travel Web sites and leave a bad review about the B & B. She couldn't have that.

Hurrying over, she tacked a pleasant smile on her face. "Hello, Mrs. Fanelli. Is something wrong?"

The woman turned eyes of utmost outrage and bewilderment on Jillian, as though Beau had announced plans to rob Fort Knox and she just didn't understand how he thought he could get away with it.

"This man is here, eating at your restaurant, and I—"

Uh-uh. Wrong word choice. Jillian let her pleasant smile cool twenty or thirty degrees. "*This man* is the father of my daughter and a guest here," Jillian told her. "I assume you don't have a problem with that."

Mrs. Fanelli gaped. Only the veranda's wood-paneled floor prevented her jaw from dropping all the way to China. "You're serving him?"

Though he'd reached the buffet table at last and picked up a plate, Beau put it down now. Before Jillian could say anything—and she had a few thoughts about minding her own business that she planned to share with Mrs. Fanelli, paying customer or no—he looked to Jillian with an unspoken apology in his eyes. Then he addressed Mrs. Fanelli.

"I just meant to come and have some coffee and a muffin. Maybe a bowl of fruit. I wasn't planning on causing any scandals this morning." His gaze flickered back to Jillian. "But since I seem to be disrupting things, I think I'll go on home."

"Good idea." Mrs. Fanelli straightened the collar of her dress with grim satisfaction, her work done for now.

Something came over Jillian. Outrage at being protected like a piece of fine china on a shelf, for one, and sheer idiocy, for another. Whatever. This was her damn B & B and, since she paid the mortgage, she made the choices around here, not Mrs. Fanelli.

Putting a hand on Beau's arm, she stopped him from leaving. He froze, his brows hitching with surprise.

"Mrs. Fanelli," Jillian said. "I decide who to serve around here, thanks."

Mrs. Fanelli gasped. "But—*him?*"

She had so much disgust in her voice she may have said *it,* or *that. You serve that slime-covered, flesh-eating thing, do you, Jillian? What on God's green earth is wrong with you, girl?*

"Yes." Jillian kept her gaze narrowed and her voice iceberg cold. "*Him. He* is the father of my child. Unless he's a grand wizard of the Ku Klux Klan, he's getting a muffin. You're not a grand wizard, are you, Beau?"

Beau, who seemed to be recovering from so much shock he might have been struck by lightning, stammered and recovered fast. "Not a grand wizard, no."

"And," Jillian continued, "you do have money, right?"

Beau, who, at the time of their divorce, was worth $48 million, a generous chunk of which he paid to Jillian in the settlement, and a tiny chunk of which he still owned, even after funding his foundation, pressed his lips together and dimpled but managed not to smile.

"I think I can cover my bill, yes."

"Then it's settled." Jillian waved him back to the buffet. "Grab a plate."

Mr. Fanelli, meanwhile, took his floundering wife in hand and steered her toward the edge of the porch that led to the path to the street. "We'll just be going now. Y'all have a nice day."

Whew. Crisis averted. Jillian lapsed back into gracious hostess mode. "Where are you folks headed today?"

Mrs. Fanelli continued to glare impotently, but Mr. Fanelli seemed happy to chat. "Thought we'd check out the aquarium today. See if they have any great white sharks swimming around in a tank."

Jillian laughed. "Don't get your hopes up. See you at dinner."

They left, taking one kind of tension with them and leaving another. Now what? She didn't want to stay and couldn't make herself leave.

Beau studied her with something unsettling in his expression. It was probably the way he'd look if he discovered a naked, six-breasted woman waiting in his bed—mostly delighted, but uncertain of what to make of his unexpected good fortune.

The worst part was seeing a hopeful light in his eyes and feeling something similar in her chest. It aggravated her. Didn't she know by now that Beau and hope couldn't peacefully coexist? That Beau was a hope killer as well as a love killer? That nothing good could ever come of giving this man even an inch in her life?

"Thanks, Jill."

She scowled. "Don't thank me. And don't read anything into this. I hate to be bossed around in my own B & B and I hate to lose a paying customer. That's all."

There was subtle skepticism in his raised brows, but he had the good sense to play along. "Right."

"Well." She moved toward the kitchen door because she knew she had work to do in there, even if she couldn't remember what it was just now. "I'm just going to—"

"You probably have a million things to do, eh? Clean up from breakfast…make lunch…pay bills and make sure all the guests have their towels and pillows and brochures. The B & B keeps you hopping, doesn't it?"

Okay. Okay, so she knew what he was doing here; this little trickery wasn't going to work. By asking her about the inn, he hoped to forestall her and keep her talking; it was all part of his grand plan. It was no mystery how his mind worked. First, they'd have a conversation without killing each other. Then they'd share an unexpected smile, or maybe a laugh in an unguarded moment. This would snowball until they were back in bed together, with her hungry body firmly in charge and her brain AWOL. Or so he hoped.

Not this time, buddy. Not ever.

"It keeps me busy." This time she got two steps before his voice caught up with her.

"You love it, don't you? I can tell."

Owning and managing this inn was the most satisfying thing she'd ever done in her professional life, much better than the early years, when she'd been a corporate lawyer, and her face probably showed it. "I do love it."

"I'm glad."

Yeah, he looked it. It was hard to tell him to quit with the charming routine when his expression was bright with unmistakable pleasure at her accomplishments, almost as though someone had turned a spotlight on him when she wasn't looking.

He took advantage of her distraction by springing another question on her in an attempt to keep their little chat fest moving along. "What do you do after breakfast? Do you oversee the—"

This had to stop. They could be pleasant, but they would not be best friends forever. Period. "I'm not going to discuss my day with you, Beau."

This line in the sand did nothing to throw him off stride. "Does that mean I can't discuss my day with you?"

"Why would you want to discuss your day with me?"

"Because," he said, pulling a pained face, "it's going to be a real bitch."

This got her, as he'd surely known it would.

Glancing around at her guests, all of whom were chattering and eating like happy little pigs at the trough, she thought about the rest of her morning chores and her paperwork. Then she wondered if Barbara Jean had yet managed to strap Allegra down and get her dressed. And then she wished any of these subjects interested her half as much as Beau did.

Part of the issue was that he'd always been the strong and silent type, sharing little and shouldering everything. A severed limb was a minor injury to Beau, a catastrophic moral failing merely a challenge for growth potential. Still waters ran way deep with him. Yet now here he was, offering to open up and share.

And she was too weak to flash him the peace sign and wish him a nice day as she went about hers. "Make it quick."

Act bored, Jill. Don't look too interested.

"I'm having physical therapy and a counseling session—"

Oh, God. So he was serious about healing himself, wasn't he?

"—and I'm going to interview grant applicants."

Wow. Any one of those things would be difficult. All three together were nothing short of a full-blown nightmare day.

You can do it, Beau.

The words were right on the tip of her tongue, and how stupid was that? In the old days, the really old days, they'd supported and encouraged each other, and old habits that should have been moldering in their graves by now died hard.

They would die, though. She'd see to it.

So she swallowed the kind words and backed away from the intriguing man. Keeping her voice flat and her expression blank was much harder.

"Well," she said. "You'd better have some extra eggs for protein, then, hadn't you?"

It just about killed her to walk off.

Jillian was standing at the sideboard a little while later, refilling the coffeemaker, when Allegra finally appeared, trailed by Barbara Jean.

The girl twirled out, a Tasmanian devil of energy, her purple tutu flowing around her and creating a faint cloud of sparkles that shone in the morning light. "Mommy!"

"Where have you been, pumpkin? You know I need your help—"

The girl squealed and raced away, captivated by something over Jillian's shoulder. With a sinking heart, feeling like chopped liver that'd spoiled two days ago, Jillian pivoted in time to see another joyous reunion between father and daughter.

Allegra wove through the tables—they were mostly empty now, thank goodness—and into Beau's arms. Lifting her high overhead, he gave her a loud and wet kiss and then plunked her down on the table right in the middle of the newspaper he'd been reading. Seinfeld, looking on from his shady spot under the tree, barked and waggled.

Jillian scowled at this show of domestic bliss.

Blanche appeared at her elbow. "Don't let him rattle your cage, honey."

The automatic denial bubbled right up. "Oh, I'm fine."

"Fine?"

"Yes." Jillian caught herself gritting her teeth. *"Fahn."*

As always, when Jillian mimicked her accent, Blanche rolled her eyes but otherwise ignored her. Instead, she stared at Beau, who was now feeding Allegra muffin remnants and grinning indulgently while she talked nonstop. Jillian thought she heard something about Allegra's favorite peach-scented body wash.

"Speaking of *fine,*" Blanche muttered.

Jillian snorted. Yes, yes, yes. Beau was *fine.* They should just have a moment of universal female acknowledgment—everyone, from young women who barely made the cutoff to vote to elderly women who should be spending their time studying knitting patterns, wanted Beau—and be done with it.

Blanche's sharp gaze swung to Jillian's face and zeroed in with laser precision. "You over him, honey?"

"Yes."

The excessive vehemence was not lost on Blanche, who looked skeptical. "Just like that?"

"No—not just like that. After he cheated on me and broke my heart, we got a divorce and I took years to work through my feelings. Just like that."

Blanche said nothing, her body all but humming with doubt.

Jillian fumed, mostly at herself.

That little speech hadn't come out the way she'd meant it. She didn't sound aloof and mentally healthy. She sounded strung out and hysterical, like a nervous breakdown waiting to happen. She cleared her throat and backtracked, trying to clarify.

"What I meant was—"

Blanche dimpled with grim sympathy. "Save it, honey. I

understand perfectly." She paused long enough to let Jillian's face heat until it felt traffic-light red. "Even if you don't."

Well, that was hitting the nail right on the head. Jillian didn't understand her feelings for Beau at all, but she didn't want Blanche or anyone else pitying her. "There's nothing to under—"

Blanche took a sharp breath, her attention diverted by something behind Jillian. Judging by her sudden smile of mischievous glee, it was nothing good. Only dread kept Jillian from turning to see what it was, because, really, how much worse could her morning get, short of an outbreak of food poisoning?

"Well, lookie here," Blanche whispered in Jillian's ear, practically incandescent with delight. "If it isn't your new man, come to meet your old man." She paused. "If things keep up like this, we'll be able to cancel the satellite TV service. Your love life is so much more entertaining."

Jillian's heart nosedived down to her toes. Adam? *Adam?*

Wait—no. It couldn't—

Apparently it was. With a tiny wave, Blanche swept off, leaving Jillian to turn and stammer a greeting to Adam through lips that suddenly felt numb and oversized, like kielbasa sausages.

Smile, Jill. You can do this. Just smile, dammit.

Her mouth couldn't manage it. The best she could do was a lopsided grimace that didn't seem to slow Adam down any. Climbing up the veranda steps and coming straight to her with the unwavering trajectory of a heat-seeking missile, Adam smiled as though she planned to share the secret of a twenty-four-hour orgasm with him.

"Good morning," he said.

There was no further warning. Apparently drunk on his success from last week, he cupped her face, leaned in and kissed her, absorbing her surprised peep into his mouth.

She immediately broke the kiss, flustered into speechlessness.

Did Beau see that? He was probably watching; she had zero hope that he'd been so enthralled with, say, Allegra's recitation of her favorite lotions to miss the sight of another man kissing his ex-wife.

Don't look, Jillian. Don't— *Oh, God.*

A quick glance over Adam's shoulder at Beau's thunderstruck and murderous face was all she could take. The angry heat blazing off him felt like a dragon's fiery blast, enough to incinerate both her and her ashes, and she knew that her morning was about to get a whole hell of a lot worse.

Chapter 8

Why did you look at Beau, dummy?

With her skin feeling tight and hot now, as though it might peel off in curled strips, Jillian took a step away from Adam.

"Hi." Pausing to get her quavering voice under control, she frowned up at him and watched his postkissing glow evaporate. "I wish you wouldn't do that in public. My daughter's right over there and—"

"Oh. Sorry."

Adam followed her line of sight to where Allegra was now petting Seinfeld, clearly oblivious to her mother's romantic travails. Then he saw Beau, and his face turned thundercloud dark.

"Is that—"

Give the man ten points. "Yes."

They watched as Beau stood, tossed some money on the table and collected his cane and Seinfeld's leash. He was heading in their direction with Allegra trailing behind, his expression now implacable, when Adam recovered from his shock and turned to Jillian.

"What's he doing here?"

Okay. Now wait a minute. This man was getting on her nerves. In fact, men as a gender had, in the last several days, gotten on her last nerve. After three years of an empty bed and relative peace and quiet, now her cup was running over, and she didn't like it. At. All.

Still, she tried to be gentle because Adam was a nice man and he did seem to care about her.

"Not that it's your concern," she said, "but Beau bought the house at the end of the street to be closer to Allegra."

Adam's lips twisted into a cynical smile. "*Closer to Allegra.* Right."

"What brings you here, anyway?"

"I came to talk you into having dinner with me tonight."

"I don't—" she began, but Beau had arrived.

Looking at him just now, especially at close range, wasn't a brilliant idea, but she couldn't help it. Some little demon inside wanted to see how he, Mr. Unfaithful, liked these apples. Was he jealous? Did he appreciate the delicious irony of seeing her with another man after he'd cheated on her and torn her guts out on more than one memorable occasion? Could he swallow this taste of his own medicine?

Did it hurt, Beau?

With sudden defiance, she hitched up her chin and met his gaze with dark triumph in her heart, daring him to say one thing. Just one small thing. He had no rights as far as she was concerned, and she'd be damn sure to rub it in his face if he had the balls to complain.

Only, to her bewildered disappointment, he didn't complain.

He wasn't happy; there was no question about that. His turbulent eyes had gone a dark, muddy green, a sure sign of turmoil, and there was feverish color in his cheeks, two high arcs of red that were always a dead giveaway that he was upset about something.

But his expression was…resigned. Not defeated, though, and not despairing. He simply looked as though he knew this wasn't his day and was determined to be a man about it.

And, underneath that, she sensed his fierce determination to make sure his day came real soon. Pretty much the way she imagined Tiger Woods would behave if he lost the Masters—he'd suffered a defeat today, yeah, but tomorrow he'd be back on the course at the crack of dawn, ready to practice his swing until his palms blistered and his back seized up, prepared to do whatever it took to win. No one was going to outwork, outfocus or outstrategize Tiger—or Beau. No one wanted the prize—and the prize was Jillian—more than Beau did.

Deep inside her chest, Jillian's heart fluttered with terror.

Beau looked to Adam, which was good because Jillian couldn't breathe when he focused all that fierce attention on her. Tucking his things under his arm, he stuck out his free hand.

"Beau Taylor."

"Adam Marshall."

They shook while Jillian tried not to compare them and then, when that didn't work, tried to pretend that it didn't matter that Beau set her skin on fire and Adam didn't.

Adam was attractive, but Beau was devastating. Adam's brown skin was smooth, but Beau's was living gold, as irresistibly warm as the sun's glow. Beau's silky sable curls demanded touching and at this impossible moment she couldn't even remember if Adam had hair.

And Beau's eyes—

"You're dating Jillian?" Beau asked.

Well, hold up. *Dating* was putting too fine a point on it, for one thing, and Jillian didn't like being talked about as though she weren't there, for another, and—

"Yes," Adam said without hesitation.

"Then you're a lucky man."

Jillian stared at Beau, shocked by his graciousness.

"I know," replied Adam.

What the hell?

This was wrong. All wrong. These men shouldn't be standing around like generals staring at a map of a conquered country, divvying up the spoils. She shouldn't be standing quietly by, watching it happen. Worst of all, she should not, in the tiniest, darkest corner of her heart of hearts, be feeling so excruciatingly feminine.

Stop it, Jillian. Right now. Put an end to this disgraceful display.

"Excuse me." She kept her voice frosty, her eyes flinty. "I do not appreciate—"

Naturally, they both ignored her.

Beau wasn't quite done. "There's something you should know."

Something about Beau changed in that one-second pause. Not his expression, which remained implacable, or his voice, which was quiet and even. But both she and Adam stilled, and Jillian sensed a new...*thing* emanating from Beau, an unyielding power that she'd never felt before.

His features seemed clearer, somehow, his cheekbones sharper, as though Beau was, right now, just this moment, more of himself than he'd ever been in his life. An unstoppable force to be reckoned with.

Maybe Adam didn't know what he was dealing with here, but Jillian did, and it was thrilling. Terrifying and thrilling.

This Beau, this man standing in front of her, was the man she'd married, times a million. At the same time, he was as complete a stranger to her as an Aborigine just arrived on a flight from the Australian outback.

Jillian could only hold her breath and wait.

Adam, who apparently had a stubborn streak that bordered on foolishness, jutted his chin. "What's that, Taylor?"

Beau's gaze flickered to Jillian, and, Jesus, she felt touched, as though he were claiming every part of her. He wanted it all back, from her heart to her head, her skin, hair and every last drop of blood in her body in between.

All that naked possessiveness ran over her, and it was like Sir Edmund Hillary and Tenzing Norgay planting that flag on the summit of Everest. If Beau had anything to say about it, all of her was his, or soon would be again—from her hips and butt, nipples and thighs and sex, down to the darkest corner of her soul.

He was going to win her back or die trying, and she was facing the fight of her life if she wanted to keep him away. Which she did. Even though her skin still hummed when he entered the room, electricity still sizzled between them when their gazes met and, worst of all, she felt as though she'd reconnected with the missing other half of herself whenever she looked him in the eye.

She would not make the same mistake again. If there were going to be a fight, then she'd fight. Because she couldn't let this man destroy her again. Not again.

Beau finally spoke.

"I want my wife back, Marshall, and I don't care how many

men she has dinner with or dates or sleeps with, and I don't care if it takes the next thirty years." He paused, his jaw tight and grim, his gaze, which was still on Jillian, unwavering and unapologetic. "I want my wife back."

Beau hurried out of the elevator, through the sleek glass and chrome atrium of his office building and out the revolving door into the hot sludge that passed for Atlanta air in the springtime. A quick glance at his watch confirmed what he already knew: he was late for his first counseling session.

Dammit.

He picked up his pace—as much as he could, anyway, which wasn't much with the cane—weaving through the crowd toward the parking lot and his car.

This Phoenix Legacies business was no joke. The applicant interviews this morning had run long because there was no shortage of people wanting both a second chance and money to finance it. There'd been an organic produce farmer who'd declared bankruptcy after last year's drought and his wife's bout with cancer; he deserved a serious look. Then there'd been the woman running the after-school program in her basement, which was tough to do now that her house was in foreclosure. The bad economy had hit everyone hard, and—

"Governor Taylor?"

Beau stifled a curse and kept going. He didn't have time for any paparazzi now, and surely there had to be a limit to how many shots they could get of him to go along with their *Governor Taylor's Tragic New Life as a Cripple* stories. He was almost to his car—

"*Governor.* Can I have a minute, please?"

Shit.

He paused, not bothering to hide his irritation. Did this idiot want an official "no comment" from him? Was that it? But when he looked over his shoulder, he realized it wasn't a reporter or a photographer.

It was a young brother, as tall as Beau, but bulky enough to play for the Falcons. A quick glance told Beau almost everything he needed to know about this guy. The short dreads, tiny hoops in both ears and unidentifiable tattoo creeping up the side of his neck said he was a rebel, or at least thought he was a rebel. The thin cotton dress shirt, dark pants and unfortunate loafers, which were all clean but cheap, screamed that this guy didn't have enough money to know where he'd get his meals next week. The keen dark eyes behind the black-rimmed glasses said this guy was intelligent, if not educated.

The squared jaw was a giant F-you, even though the guy needed something from Beau. He was proud and defiant, and he hated his need, considering it a weakness, but he still needed.

This guy was mad at the world.

And Beau didn't have time for another angry black man. He was doing pretty well in that role himself at the moment. "Can I help you?"

The guy hesitated, and then stuck out his hand. "I'm Dawson Reynolds."

They shook, and the name nudged something loose in Beau's memory. "You filled out an application for Phoenix Legacies. You've just been sprung from prison, right? A sexual assault conviction? The Innocence Program did DNA testing or something and proved—"

Dawson's mouth thinned. "What I've been saying for the last three years—I didn't do it."

Interesting. That certainly explained the prison muscles and screw-the-world attitude. "Congratulations." Beau resumed walking, anxious to get to his car. "All the best to you."

Dawson kept pace, and they worked their way through the crowd. "I had an interview this morning."

"You *missed* your interview this morning." Beau veered into the parking lot and headed down the row. "We waited half an hour for you. That's why I'm late now."

"I'm sorry about that. My buddy's car had a flat, and I just got here—"

"You didn't call."

"I can't afford a cell phone, and the battery on his was dead."

Beau was ready to write the excuse off as either a lie or a tale of woe, neither of which meant anything to him, but then he saw the look on the guy's face. Dawson was embarrassed that he didn't have a car or a phone, humiliated and trying to hide it.

"What about your family? Aren't they helping you?"

The skin stretched taut over Dawson's face, tightening his features into something wild and barely controlled, like a wolf trying to pass as a puppy. "My family wrote me off before I went to prison. Now I've written them off."

"But—"

"I'll deal with my family later, when I'm ready. For now, I need a job."

Compassion or something like it sparked inside Beau, but this guy wasn't going to win him over. Everyone he'd interviewed today had a hard life, and they'd all managed to show up on time this morning.

Dawson must have sensed his ambivalence, because he pressed his case. "If I could just reschedule the interview. I have a finance degree from Duke, and I learned a lot of skills when I was locked up—"

"You want a startup loan so you can flip houses."

"Yes."

The guy seemed to hold his breath. Beau felt a moment's pity for him, but he didn't make business decisions based on pity. There were other applicants just as worthy. And they didn't have chips the size of Gibraltar on their shoulders.

"I'm sorry," Beau told him, anxious to be done with this guy, who wasn't his problem and wouldn't become his problem. "I can't help you."

Dawson's face twisted into a derisive and fearsome snarl that had no doubt kept him safe in the prison showers for the past few years. "Why doesn't that surprise me?"

"So what brings you here?" asked Dr. Desai.

This guy was an idiot, Beau thought, stretching out his leg and trying to get comfortable on this hard-ass modern sofa.

Notwithstanding the framed degrees from Stanford and Cornell on the wall, the doctor was an idiot. The doctor's receptionist out in the lobby was also an idiot and, if the man had a wife, children and a dog or cat at home, they were idiots, too.

True, Beau was mad at the world just now, but there were still a lot of idiots hanging around. Like that guy who'd had his lips wrapped around Jillian's earlier. Now *he* was an idiot, the punk.

Another man. Kissing Jillian. And it was all Beau's fault.

That pretty much made Beau the head idiot, didn't it?

"What brings me here?" Beau echoed.

Who, other than an idiot, would ask such a stupid question? Irritated, he clenched his fingers into such a tight fist that his short nails felt like razor blades against his palm. The slicing pain cleared his head, just a little, and he opened his hand and smoothed it against the black leather.

"Didn't you get my file transferred from Dr. Palmer in Miami?"

Dr. Desai opened his mouth to answer, but Beau plowed ahead. Screw it. He didn't care what foot they started on. This guy could kiss his ass for all he cared.

"And didn't you read the four million forms and questionnaires you made me fill out before you accepted me as a client?"

This time Dr. Desai got two words in edgewise. "Yes, but—"

"And you've probably seen me on the news. Doing the whole apology and resignation press conference thing. Or maybe you've seen me over on the cable comedy shows, where they've added me to the apology hall of fame. So I'm pretty sure you know why I'm here."

Dr. Desai didn't so much as blink, the crafty old SOB. Didn't frown, didn't sigh and didn't do anything reproachful, which naturally made Beau feel worse for being rude right off the bat. He simply crossed his legs and surveyed Beau with wise brown eyes that made Beau feel as though he'd been locked in the office with an owl.

The moment stretched.

Beau fidgeted, smoothing his hair and then folding his hands in his lap.

Dr. Desai tried again. "So, you're trying to…?"

"Not be such a self-destructive son of a bitch."

Wow. That got him a smile, or at least the curve of the doctor's lips and crow's-feet creases in the deep brown skin at the edges of his eyes.

"How's that going so far, Beau?"

"In terms of what? How many people hate my guts today or how many hearts I've broken or—what? You've got to give me some guidelines here."

"In terms of how you think you're doing."

Whoa. The old man went right for the jugular, didn't he? So they were going to talk turkey. No reason to sugarcoat it, then.

"Most days, I still feel like a worthless pile of shit. How's that?"

There was a pause.

"I…see," said Dr. Desai.

They stared at each other. Beau's bitterness didn't seem to disturb the man the least little bit, and neither did his sarcasm. That was a nice trick. Beau wished he could run out to the drugstore and buy a dose of the guy's equilibrium, maybe see if he could have a normal day like other people seemed to. What would life be like without the burning desire to be more than he was and the unwavering certainty that he was all he'd ever be—and that wasn't very damn much?

Dr. Desai slid his pen into the bright white hair above his ear, probably because Beau had so many outstanding issues to work on that he'd given up trying to take notes.

"You've been in therapy for several months, right? Do you still feel like as big a pile of shit as when you started out?"

That question took a little more thought. Beau gave it a second and dug deep.

He thought about a few things—a few tiny things—that he'd done that he could be proud of. He'd stopped drinking, for one thing. He'd been celibate for several months, for another. Sure, he felt as though the mojo was backing up inside, threatening to explode out of him one unfortunate day sometime soon, but he hadn't had meaningless sex since the night of the accident, and it was all meaningless unless the woman was Jillian.

It wasn't about the women, anyway. It'd never been about

the women. It was about him, and him and Jillian. And wasn't knowing the problem half the solution? He sure hoped so.

He'd attended both psychological and physical therapy religiously, and he intended to keep that up for as long as it took. And he'd always been a good father. Now that he lived down the street from Allegra, he was being a better one. With Jillian, though, he didn't know what the hell he was doing other than making it up as he went along.

Oh, and he'd done the whole giving away his fortune thing. Charitable work earned him some credit, right? Even if his soul was damaged and he hadn't found the first recipient of a grant yet? No one expected him to turn into Nelson Mandela overnight, did they?

So…on balance, there'd been some improvement. A tiny little bit.

Dr. Desai waited, apparently prepared to sit there indefinitely, if need be.

"I've made…a little progress," Beau said, hoping the admission wouldn't jinx him forever.

"So," Dr. Desai wondered, "you're—what? Only fifty percent shit now?"

That was too generous, and the new Beau was all about keeping it real. "Sixty, let's say."

"And the other forty percent?"

"A work in progress."

"Fair enough." Dr. Desai flashed something that may have been a smile but looked mostly like grim satisfaction. "Are you willing to do a little hard work with me?"

Beau felt grim, too, especially when he thought about all his areas for growth potential, but maybe he'd come to the right place after all. Maybe this guy could help him.

"I'm all about working hard, Doc."

"Good. What's standing in the way of you being where you need to be?"

That was easy. "I'm standing in my way."

"Why?"

"If I knew that, I wouldn't need you, now would I?"

"It's good to know I'm not obsolete."

Beau almost laughed. It was such a strange sensation, such a distant memory, that he wasn't quite sure what to make of it. Laughter, like happiness, was hard for him to call forth and recapture, except when he was with Allegra. But he was trying.

"What did you do before you came here, Beau? You seemed agitated."

Ah. The memory of some other man kissing Jillian. That one he had no problems with. Already his heart was thundering in his throat, his blood rushing in his ears. His face felt hot, as though there were a layer of lava between his cheeks and his flesh.

"I saw my wife kissing some other man so, yeah, you could say I was agitated. You could say I wanted to rip the man's tongue out of his head."

Dr. Desai frowned. "But you're divorced."

"Yeah." Beau tried to swallow back the bitter bile, but it just kept coming and coming in an endless supply that would probably choke and kill him sometime soon. "I'm divorced."

"I take it you still have strong feelings for your ex-wife."

This guy was funny. "Strong feelings?" Beau said. "Like when you're nearly killed and her face is the one you see when you're hovering between life and death? Like when you can't sleep without her in your bed, wrapped around you? Like when you'd agree to spend eternity in hell if only she'd smile at you one more time the way she used to? Strong feelings? Like that?"

"That about covers it," Dr. Desai said.

"Then, yeah." Beau met the man's gaze and didn't bother trying to hide his desperation and, worse than that, his bottomless fear, because what if he never got Jillian back? God knew he didn't deserve her and never had, even on a good day. "I still have strong feelings for her."

"You want her back?"

"I want her back."

Dr. Desai tipped his head back and studied the ceiling. Obviously he didn't want to stomp on Beau's dreams on the one hand, but he felt as though Beau needed a healthy dose of reality on the other. Beau could have told him not to bother. He and reality were well acquainted.

"Is it possible that you've magnified the good times and sugarcoated the bad? Sometimes people have a tendency to—"

"What? Like childbirth? You think I've forgotten all the pain?"

"Something like that."

Beau thought. He remembered the second the pain began, the moment when his glorious old life ended and the new, forever-altered one took its place. The heartbreak was still right there, in his face, in all its IMAX-worthy, Technicolor high definition. There wasn't one thing he could forget, and he'd certainly tried.

"I can assure you," Beau said coolly. "I haven't forgotten any of the pain."

Something in his face must have convinced the good doctor that Beau was sincere and free of denial. So he changed tactics.

"You know," Dr. Desai said, "the statistics on successful remarriage between the same—"

"Are terrible." Not bothering to hide his impatience, Beau checked his watch. God help him—thirty minutes left in this session. "Yeah, I know."

"Have you thought about the possibility that your ex-wife has changed, and that even if you reconciled—"

Beau glared. Did the man think he was stupid?

"Of course I've thought about it."

"And?"

"And she has changed. She's stronger. Wiser. More self-confident. She can take care of herself and she's a great mother. She's the woman I always knew she'd become."

"And?"

"And I want to be the man she deserves."

"What if you can't be?"

The distinct possibility nearly made Beau break out in hives and heave up his breakfast. But he had to acknowledge and accept it.

"Then I can't. But I have to try." He paused, and then decided to lay it all out there. "And it'd be really nice to be able to look myself in the mirror when I shave. For once."

"So you want to change. For yourself."

This was getting ridiculous. "Have you not been paying attention, Doc? I need to change for myself. Even if Jillian never takes me back, I can't go back to the way I was. I don't want that kind of life."

At last Beau seemed to have stumbled upon the right combination of words. Dr. Desai nodded, deep grooves of what looked like satisfaction bracketing his mouth.

"I think I can help you."

"Great," Beau said. "Why don't you go ahead and give your magic wand a flick. Get me straightened out before dinner."

Dr. Desai chuckled and apparently decided that, since he and Beau had reached an understanding, Beau was worth the trouble of taking notes. He untucked the pen from behind his ear and took up a yellow legal pad.

"Let's get started."

Chapter 9

Could this date have been any more painful?

Yeah, Jillian supposed. It could have. If she'd had a root canal between the appetizers and entrées. Without anesthesia.

Short of that, she and Adam had just experienced the most excruciating dinner two people could have with each other. Awkward silences. Halting conversation. Stilted jokes. It had been the perfect storm of embarrassed discomfort.

And that was just during drinks.

Adam pulled his car, a nice Toyota sedan, up to the B & B and put it in Park. Keeping up tonight's tradition of looking everywhere but directly in Adam's eyes, Jillian glanced out her window and took a quick inventory, making sure the whole place hadn't fallen apart during the couple of hours she'd been gone.

One of the hazards of ownership was her obsessive attention to detail and service, but things seemed well under control. The inn was picture-perfect, the image of a cozy hideaway far from the city's bustle. Strategic spotlights emphasized the exquisite landscaping. Several guests enjoyed the porch's quiet serenity and rocked in the chairs or swayed in the wicker swing; their quiet laughter broke the night's silence. The slight breeze ruffled the hanging ferns and hinted at the rain that was just waiting for the right moment to fall.

Man, she loved this place. It was her pride and joy, her little slice of heaven on earth.

Too bad she was on the date from hell.

Shoring up her courage, she dredged up the bright, false smile she'd been wearing all night, the one that hurt her cheeks, and glanced across the car's dim interior to Adam. It was too dark to get a good read on his expression, and maybe that was best because he'd been increasingly quiet since they left the restaurant.

"So," she said, encouraged to hear that there was only the slightest quaver in her voice. "Would you like to come in for some, ah, coffee?"

Coffee meant coffee; it wasn't code for sex and she'd be really surprised if Adam interpreted it that way at the end of such a disastrous evening. Once the words were out of her mouth, she waited to regret them, but she didn't. For some inexplicable reason, she felt this rising desperation to end the date on a high note, an outcome that seemed as likely as sticking a straw in the Pacific Ocean and drinking it dry.

Why was she so determined to make tonight work with Adam? She had no idea. Maybe it had something to do with this being her first real date in about a thousand years and the thrill of feeling like a desirable woman again. Maybe it was because of the sexy little black dress she'd shoehorned herself into and the makeup she'd let Barbara Jean shellac onto her face.

Maybe—man, she didn't even like thinking the thought.

Maybe it had something to do with proving to herself, God and everybody else that Beau's sudden reappearance hadn't disrupted her equilibrium too much, and she was still on her way to becoming the powerful and self-confident woman she thought she'd been before he showed up with his new solemnity and the same old sexy eyes.

Whatever.

The bottom line was that her fragile ego couldn't withstand another failure with another man, even if it was just an awkward date rather than a divorce.

"I've got cheesecake."

This last-minute addition made her want to slap her hand over her mouth. Was there anything more pitiful than a woman who begged and used food to entice a man? The best thing she could do for herself right now was shut up before she continued her inevitable and tragic descent from needy to pathetic.

"I can't," Adam said.

Of course he couldn't; no surprise there. Jillian was something of an expert when it came to driving men away, so why should this man be immune to that particular talent of hers?

Trying not to take it personally was a pointless exercise. How could it not be personal when your date preferred to leave at the earliest possible opportunity rather than spend a few extra minutes eating a delicious and free dessert with you?

She tried to brace for it, but it raced ahead and flattened her to pancake proportions all the same—that same old feeling of rejection and inadequacy, as familiar as Allegra's dimpled smile.

Something about her was faulty. Well…no. Maybe she was looking at it the wrong way. Why not turn it around and look at the positive? Something about her was brilliant, a van Gogh in the art of getting men to run out on her.

The fact that she wasn't wild about Adam anyway didn't matter the slightest bit. All that mattered to her ruined ego was not being an abject failure with a man. At this point in her life, any man would do.

As always, her pride took over. The most important thing was not to show how much this tiny rejection, the latest in a long line that stretched from here to eternity, hurt. So she flashed an indifferent, do-what-you-want smile as she reached for her purse on the floor.

"I understand—"

"I don't think you do."

A hard edge had crept into his voice, a husky rasp of emotion that startled her. It was there in his eyes, too—an unexpected gleam of something that made her wonder if he was more complex than his bow ties and nice but unexciting Toyota sedan had led her to believe.

"I want you," he told her.

Oh, God. He did. Jillian felt it in the sudden crackle of electricity in the air between them and saw it in his expression, which was ablaze with a new heat that prickled her skin and curled her toes.

"I've wanted you from the second you came into my office. It's taken me this long to work up the courage to tell you because you're the president's sister and you're rich and I'm not and you're incredibly beautiful and I'm your accountant."

"Oh," she said helplessly.

"I've waited this long for you and I was willing to wait some more. I didn't care about taking it slow. I was on board with all that until—"

He trailed off. What had begun as a tiny flicker of dread in her belly grew to the size of a California wildfire. She didn't want to hear this next thing, whatever it was, but she had to ask because her curiosity demanded it.

"Until…what?"

He stared at her. "Until I saw you with your ex-husband."

No. Oh, no.

She opened her mouth, and out flew one of her automatic denials. If she kept issuing them, she had to get better at it—right?

"I don't have any feelings for Beau."

The bitterness in her voice gave her away. It was so brittle and ugly that even she could hear it, and it didn't matter that she'd been trying to speak in the genteel car voice she always wished Allegra would use.

I don't have any feelings for Beau.

Right. The sentence was as convincing as a kid telling his mom he hadn't eaten all the brownies when he had a ring of chocolate around his mouth.

Adam didn't argue, but his unblinking gaze, quiet with reproach, made her long for some sort of explosive outburst. Embarrassed heat crawled up her face and prickled in her scalp until she had to look away, out her window.

Seconds passed. Several very long seconds. For reasons that eluded her, it seemed critically important to convince this man, this near stranger, that she was a whole person, as mentally healthy and at one with the universe as a Tibetan monk meditating in his temple. That Beau had no hold on her life or her emotions and never would again.

Even if her heart of hearts told her that was a damn lie.

"Beau and I have a long history, yeah. Most of it painful. We push each other's buttons sometimes, but that doesn't mean—"

"Are you trying to convince yourself?" Adam cocked his head and raised his brows with what looked like a burning desire to get to the bottom of a mystery that kept him awake nights. "Because you're not convincing me."

Stymied, she shut up.

There was no arguing with someone filled with so much absolute certainty, much as she wanted to. She'd only wind up looking like an idiot. Well…a worse idiot. And there was a tiny part of her rational mind left that whispered that Adam was right. What kind of fool would he have to be to get involved in the emotional knot she and Beau still had wrapped around each other?

Adam, she was beginning to realize, was no fool. Nice? Yeah. Strong and honorable? Definitely. The kind of man she should want and would be lucky to have in her life? You betcha. He was the elusive good man of all the legendary stories, and he was nothing like her bad-boy ex-husband.

Which naturally meant that he wanted nothing to do with her.

Ah, hell. Who was she kidding? Eventually all men rejected her. If a flying saucer full of men from a neighboring universe flew in looking for women to help repopulate their dying planet, they'd reject her, too.

God, her face was hot. It felt like it was lit with a red flame bright enough to illuminate the car's dark interior. That was what utter and complete humiliation did for you.

Get out of the vehicle, Jill. Now.

"Well," she said, reaching for the door handle, "thanks for dinner. I'm sorry I wasted your time."

Adam didn't look any too happy to finally be getting rid of her. In fact, judging from the fleeting eye contact that was all she could maintain at the moment, he seemed so sad and deflated that she actually felt a little better. Still embarrassed, but less so.

"Jillian."

With her heart thumping and one foot out the door, she waited.

To her astonishment, he cupped her cheek and stroked it with more tenderness than she deserved, all things considered. When her lips parted on a gasp, he used his thumb to gently stroke those, too.

Deep in her belly, the reawakened passion she'd felt in the last several days twisted and tightened to a sweet ache. Vibrant with agitation, she shoved aside the jumbled images in her mind.

Adam. Beau. Adam and Beau. Adam and her. Beau…

And her.

Her lungs heaved, straining for air.

Through lids that had slipped to half-mast, she saw the glint in Adam's eyes, the terrible doomed want. It excited her and she despised herself for it.

"When you get over him," Adam told her in a voice that was low and husky, "I hope you'll call me."

They stared at each other until, helpless to do otherwise, she nodded.

Satisfied, Adam ran his fingers under her hair into her nape and exerted gentle pressure that she could have resisted. She didn't. And then his lips were on hers, moving and caressing and…ah, God, it was sweet…so unbearably sweet.

The sensations rose and swirled, coalesced and deepened until a tiny gasp escaped from a needy, dark place inside her that she wished she could tamp out forever.

And in her heart, she knew the truth:

The mouth and hands on her were Adam's.

The face in her mind's eye and her body's responses belonged to Beau. Beau. Always Beau.

The bastard.

A new kind of tension shot through her body and, catching herself, she pulled back. Afraid to look into Adam's eyes, she pressed her fingers to her lips. Did Adam know how screwed-up she was? Could he taste her confusion?

Maybe not. Heaving a harsh sigh, Adam turned away, rested his elbow on his window and rubbed his own lips. Sexual frustration obviously had him tight around the neck.

He wasn't the only one.

"Good night, Adam."

"Good night."

She got out, her skin prickling with sudden anger. She wanted to slam the car door, stomp up the path to the inn and rant in an adrenaline-fueled frenzy, to rage at the unfairness of life.

But somehow she kept an iron leash on her emotions and did none of those things. Slipping into the side door that was her private entrance to the house, she made her way through the darkened vestibule and up the back stairs.

With each step, she added another item to the list of unforgivable transgressions Beau had committed against her.

That man had single-handedly ruined everything in her life that had ever been beautiful or happy. It wasn't enough that he cheated and destroyed their marriage, shattering her heart, soul and confidence in the process. It wasn't enough that the Beau she thought she'd married—the best friend, the generous lover, the protector and provider and playmate—had never existed at all, but had only been a figment of her girlish imagination. It wasn't enough that he'd turned her out in bed, awakening and teaching her until her body was a slave to the pleasure that only he could provide, so much so that even now, years after they'd last had sex, the touch of another man evoked only desires for him.

Oh, no. All that wasn't enough. Not for Beau.

He had to follow her hundreds of miles and reappear, a ghost out of the darkness, just when she'd cobbled together something resembling a life. He had to change just enough to renew her obsession with him and make her wonder if he'd changed or was capable of changing when she knew damn well that the answer to those questions was, and always would be, an emphatic *no.*

He had to make her want him again.

Always. Still. Forever.

This whole time she'd worked on getting over her emotions, being healthy and not wasting time hating him. So much for that. She did hate him. She hated everything about him—from his wounded hazel eyes to his earnest ability to play a role and pretend he was like other humans, with sorrows and regrets, strengths and weaknesses, rather than just weaknesses; to his house and his car and his dog.

The hatred was so strong that she tasted its bitterness on the back of her tongue and smelled it in her flaring nostrils. She wished he were dead. She wished he'd died in that car accident rather than come up here to torment her. She wished she could kill him now with her bare hands. Would anyone blame her? Surely everyone who knew their tortured history together would understand. She wished—

Oh, God.

Cracking open Allegra's door and poking her head inside the dim room, which was illuminated only by a pink-and-white butterfly lamp on the nightstand, she froze, stopping so suddenly her feet may have been fixed to the floor with invisible clamps.

Beau sat on the edge of the bed, leaning over a sleeping Allegra and pressing a kiss to her forehead.

He was glaringly, outrageously out of place among the girly-girl frills, a shot of high-octane testosterone amid all the sweetness. The squared shoulders encased in a simple dark T-shirt of indeterminate color, the muscled arms, the strong thighs stretched along the bed—all those things radiated pure masculinity as jarring as a peek into an NFL locker room after a playoff game.

Dumbstruck, Jillian could only stare. For one upside-down millisecond, she had a thought so disturbing she wondered if she should leave now and head for the nearest insane asylum to check herself in for evaluation.

Beau's home.

And then all her anger rushed back, bigger and blacker than ever.

The girl rustled and stirred, turning from her back to her side and settling her favorite stuffed animal, a fluffy yellow lion cub named Archie, under her chin.

Beau hesitated, clearly not wanting to wake her, and then, when Allegra didn't move again, got up, planting his cane underneath him. He tucked a picture book under his arm—*Click, Clack, Moo,* Allegra's current favorite—and crept toward the door.

That was when he saw Jillian and hesitated.

The blazing hatred she felt toward him must have been unmistakable, because his face paled; she could tell even in the relative darkness.

Even as his discreet gaze flickered over her, taking in the sexy dress, the cleavage, the bare arms and legs and the heels, she felt his new stillness and saw the subtle squaring of his shoulders. It thrilled her in an ugly way that made her heart pound and her fists clench.

Yeah, you bastard.

We're about to throw down up in here.

Because she had a couple new additions to her list, didn't she?

It wasn't enough that he'd moved down the street. It wasn't enough that now she'd have to share her precious daughter with him half the time, which was much more than she wanted, even though it was best for Allegra. It wasn't enough that she'd have to see his terrible, beautiful face every single day.

Oh, no.

Beau had to invade her peaceful sanctuary. Had to come here, to her inn. And not just to the public rooms, where she could grudgingly tolerate him. He had to come into the private rooms. Show up in Allegra's bedroom late at night, when Jillian least expected him to be there.

Hell, maybe she should check the master suite to see if he'd cleared out a drawer for his socks and put his toothbrush in the holder by the sink.

When she least expected it, there he was.

In. Her. Freaking. House.

The anger flared into a rage so powerful she could probably lift a jet one-handed with it.

"What are you doing here?" she demanded.

Chapter 10

Before Beau could answer, Barbara Jean materialized in the hall by Jillian's side. She'd probably been right next door in the private sitting room adjacent to Jillian's bedroom, watching TV, texting her friends or doing whatever the hell it was youngsters did these days.

"Hi." Something in Jillian's expression must have struck her as particularly grave, because Barbara Jean took the extraordinary step of pulling out the earbuds and giving the situation her full attention. "You're back."

"Yeah." Jillian didn't bother transferring her glare from Beau to Barbara Jean; of the two of them, Beau was the one she needed to keep her eye on. "I'm back."

Barbara Jean twisted her hands in the first show of concern Jillian had ever seen from her. "I, ah, hope you don't mind, but I called Beau—"

Beau. Brilliant. Beau was now on a first-name basis with her nanny. Beau had wormed his way into yet another female heart.

Beau was like Big Brother—omnipresent and inescapable.

"—because Allegra wanted him to tuck her in and wouldn't go to sleep without him. I tried to read her an extra story, but she—"

Barbara Jean trailed off with an uncomfortable shrug, withering before Jillian's frigid disapproval.

Though Beau was the ground zero of all Jillian's fury, she had a little to spare for the nanny, beloved though she was, who'd invited this…this…man into Jillian's private zone.

Did Barbara Jean think that was okay? Did she not have the most basic level of common sense and sensitivity? If Dracula showed up on the doorstep and gave the girl the hypnotic eye, would Barbara Jean invite him in, too?

Peeling her gaze away from Beau—she'd deal with him in a minute—Jillian turned at last to Barbara Jean, who swallowed visibly and seemed to brace herself.

"Thanks for your help tonight." The swelling tightness in Jillian's throat almost blocked her voice. She struggled to manage another sentence with relative calm. "You can go now."

"Great."

With visible relief, Barbara Jean scurried back into the sitting room, grabbed her backpack and hurried down the hall and away, sparing one worried glance over her shoulder at Beau, as though she wasn't sure she'd ever see him alive again. Then she disappeared down the steps.

Beau had by now limped his way across Allegra's room and edged past Jillian through the doorway into the hall. He kept his gaze averted and seemed determined not to make any further eye contact with her, which was the appropriate protocol when it came to angry ex-wives and rabid dogs alike.

"I'm going, too." He kept his voice to a low murmur, as though he knew the sound of it would only escalate the situation. "I'm just going to get my cell phone. I think I left it in— Yeah. There it is."

He headed into the sitting room, to where, sure enough, his phone sat on the coffee table. Jillian followed with the single-minded focus of a spring bride at the Filene's Basement sale, and when Beau turned to leave, she was right there in his face, blocking him.

He pulled up short and hesitated, still not looking at her.

"Going so soon?" she asked.

"That seems like a good idea, yeah."

Jillian paused, wondering, for one wild second, if she'd heard right. Surely those words hadn't just come out of that man's mouth. She'd better check.

"A...*good idea?*"

Beau had sense enough to keep his mouth shut.

Which only pissed her off more.

"By 'good idea,' do you mean like the good idea you had

to show up here in the private rooms of my inn while I was gone?"

"Allegra wouldn't go to sleep—" he began.

"Or like the brilliant idea you had to move to my city and my street without any advance notice or consideration for my feelings? Is that what you mean by 'good idea'?"

For the first time he looked up at her, and the shock of the connection nearly toppled her over backward. His hazel eyes now flashed a muddy brown, a color she'd seen only a few terrible times in their relationship; it never boded well. She stared at him, filled with a swelling and primal satisfaction.

Was he upset now, too?

Peachy.

Yet he remained calm, with only his eyes and the creeping red flush across his cheekbones to give him away.

"I apologize," he said to her astonishment. An alpha male to the last follicle of hair on his sleek head, he wasn't big on admitting culpability for run-of-the-mill transgressions like invading her space, so this was a first. "I should have checked with you. I just wanted to help Allegra get to sleep and I figured I'd be gone before you got back from your date. Won't happen again."

Taking advantage of her momentary speechlessness, he tried to sidestep her.

Pivoting, she blocked him a second time.

Oh, no, buddy. It's not that easy.

His head was down again, so she waited while he hesitated. Waited while he stared at the floor, his jaw flexing in back where he ground his teeth together. Waited until his gaze, hot now with the turbulence of the Caribbean during the full force of a summer hurricane, flickered back to her and held.

"What do you want, Jill?" His low voice was full of gravel. "A fight?"

Yes. A fight. That was exactly what she wanted and needed.

She scrunched her brow and widened her eyes with mock confusion.

"Isn't this where you want to be?" Marching past the coffee table, sofa and her desk in the corner, she flung open the door to her bedroom, where the nightstand lamp illuminated her enormous wrought-iron bed. Covered with a mint-green duvet and matching black-patterned pillows, it was fluffy and inviting. So much so that Beau couldn't hide the sudden flair of greedy interest in his eyes. "Don't you want to see my bedroom? That's what you came for, right?"

"Jill—"

Ignoring him, she wheeled around, yanked open the top drawer of her bureau and rummaged around inside. "Or maybe you want to see my underwear drawer. Make sure I haven't changed the kind of panties I wear since the divorce."

She withdrew a big handful of satin and lace in every color under the rainbow and stalked back from the bedroom until she was an arm's length away. Then she threw her panties at his feet.

Paralyzed or stunned—maybe a little of both—he didn't move.

"How's that? Does that satisfy your curiosity about my new life? Anything else you'd like to know? How about the number of other men I've slept with? Didn't you want to discuss that?"

This, finally, seemed to push him over some invisible line, much to her savage satisfaction. She didn't care that he'd reduced her to raving lunacy. It didn't matter that this was exactly the kind of ugly confrontation she'd always sworn she'd never engage in with him, the kind that made her look like the wrongdoer, rather than him.

All that mattered was the stricken expression on his face, as though a nuclear warhead aimed right at his chest couldn't have hurt him more than she just did.

This was what she wanted: Beau in agony.

But he was good. Really good. With a single blink, he wiped his expression clean, until it was as starkly blank as a blackboard on the first day of school. The wilder she became, the more determined he seemed to cling to his civility.

He opened his mouth and took forever to activate his husky voice. "I'm leaving."

Hysteria erupted from her body on a bitter, jeering laugh.

"Why leave now, Beau? You haven't gotten what you came for."

"Because I'm upsetting you."

His voice was nothing now. Less than a whisper from a person with laryngitis. But she didn't care about how he sounded. The only things that mattered to her in this ugly moment were the wild light in his eyes and making him unravel to the last thread of his soul.

So she taunted him with another jeer. "Upsetting me? When did you ever care about upsetting me? When you were screwing other women?"

He paused and she really had to hand it to him for keeping it so calm and cool. If she knew anything about Beau, which she did, she'd pushed him to his outer limits about five minutes ago and he now probably wanted to drive his fist through the nearest wall.

They stared at each other for several of the longest seconds of her life, with only their harsh breath to break the stony silence. Her heart, which had been alternating between skittering and pounding, pretty much stopped as she waited to see what Beau would do next.

They were teetering on the edge of a cataclysm and a single small push would send them hurtling toward something damaging, if not fatal, and she wanted it. Oh, yes, she wanted it.

Taking all the time in the world, Beau turned away, but he was no longer trying to leave. Instead, he made his careful way to the window, stared at the closed blinds and came back. There was a grim resolution in his expression, a darkness that hadn't been there before.

"I don't want to fight with you," he said. His voice was steady now, strong, determined and utterly reasonable, and she hated him for it. "But we have a lot of issues we need to address. If you want to do it with all this anger, then that's fine with me."

Oh, no. He wasn't going to make her out to be the crazy one.

"Aren't you civilized all the sudden? Who'd've thought?"

"Not at all." One corner of his mouth eased up into a terrible corruption of a smile, so dark and crooked it might have been a twisted path leading straight into the center of hell. "I'm not feeling civilized at all. But I'm trying to control the situation before it gets any worse." He hesitated and then continued as if his flood of words couldn't be sandbagged into obeying, despite all his best efforts. "Otherwise, I would have already asked if you let that man touch you tonight."

This was such a stunning reversal that it took her a long, gaping moment to recover and spit out the obligatory:

"That's none of your business."

That humorless black smile widened an inch, sending fear streaking through the depths of her belly to a place only he'd ever been able to access. "I know it's none of my business. I also know that it's my own damn fault that it's none of my business. That doesn't mean the question isn't eating my guts out."

"Poor Beau. Don't like the bed you made for yourself to lie in, do you?"

"It's killing me."

"Good."

Was it wrong to take so much fierce pleasure in someone's obvious misery? Would God punish her later? Or maybe the universe would send a wave of bad karma her way to balance the scales. That was fine. No problem. Even a fire or a plague of locusts felt like a small price to pay for the satisfaction of this moment, which had been years in the making.

What was the saying—hell hath no fury like a woman scorned?

Damn right. And she was about to unleash hell on Beau in a way she never had before. They'd never had it out. The end of their marriage, which came the day Beau admitted his second affair, had been abrupt and absolute. There'd been no closure, whatever that was. And it was possible that the lack of closure was driving her now.

Some twisted demon was in charge here, not her.

So she kept her chin up and held his gaze, determined to let him see her seething anger. Absolute power flowed through her like a superhero's electrical current, and it thrilled her.

And then, just that easy, Beau took one slow but aggressive

step toward her, breaching her space with his size and body heat, and all the power shifted.

"I am wondering, though," he drawled, "why you're so upset."

"I told you—"

He flapped his free hand. "Yeah, yeah—I know. I shouldn't be here without permission. But here's the thing. You would have given me permission if Allegra needed me. Wouldn't you?"

Paralyzed with growing dread—where was this going?—she couldn't answer.

"And I did apologize. I tried to leave. So I'm wondering whether you were upset before you ever laid eyes on me tonight."

"Of course not—"

Oh, God. Why did he keep coming closer? Why couldn't she breathe all of a sudden? She'd wanted this fight, needed this release, and he was giving her what she wanted. So why was she suddenly frozen with terror?

"And I'm also wondering why, if your personal life is going so well and what's-his-name is such a great and amazing guy, you're back home before the crickets even have a chance to start chirping for the night." He paused just long enough to let the tension build inside her. "Why's that, Jillian?"

"You've got some nerve—"

"If you're so well-adjusted and over me, then why are you so upset?"

Yeah, Jill. Tell the man why.

As if she could. As if she had any answers here.

God, she couldn't breathe. All the air was trapped in her throat, strangling her, and she placed a hand over her heart, desperate to get a grip before this turned into a full-blown panic attack—another one—and equally desperate not to let him see her gulp for air like a caught catfish.

Trapped beneath that piercing gaze, she opened her mouth and produced only silence and then more silence.

Hide, Jill. Don't let him see you like this.

"This is going nowhere." She took her time about turning and walking to the door, which she pushed wider for him. Good thing she had her own private wing in the inn. Otherwise, the guests would have gotten way more than their money's worth by now. "I'd like you to leave now."

That hard jaw of his dropped with open incredulity, and then his face twisted into a snarl. His bitter laugh was like a blast from a middle-of-the-night storm siren, jarring and shrill and a sign of terrible things to come.

"That's the story of your life, isn't it, Sweet Jill?"

Don't look at him, Jill. Keep your face turned away.

She held tight to the knob because it was the only thing keeping her upright. If only she could get a breath. One good breath. "Just leave."

"You're the only one who can control when we talk and when we don't talk, aren't you, Jill?" he taunted. "You're the one with all the rules. But here's the funny thing about your goddamn rules—they always shut me down every time I have something I need to say."

Staring at the floor, she tried not to hear him. Tried to hide behind the furious rush of blood in her ears and block him out. But it didn't work and she had more important things to do now anyway, like hide the fact that she was falling apart.

Her burning face was going to burst into flames any second. She needed to breaaaathe, and she needed God's help to get out of this mess she'd created for herself.

Opening her jaw just slightly, not enough for him to notice, she tried to drag air in through her mouth. "I don't know what you're talking about," she gasped.

"Oh, you don't?"

To her horror, he hurried over and stooped until his face was right there, right in front of her, and there was nowhere to hide that he wouldn't see her.

"Let me help you out with that. I'm talking about how it's always been all about you and what you need. Since the day we got married. It's all well and good for us to have a conversation and vent our feelings, as long as you're the only one venting. We can tell the truth as long as it's your version of the truth. We can talk about how we've let each other down and how brokenhearted we are only until it's my turn. And guess what happens then? It's time for me to leave! Conversation's over! Sharing time is done!

Too bad, Beau! Maybe next time! Well, when is my next time going to come?" He was roaring now. "Because it hasn't come yet and I've been waiting for years!"

Okay. Okay, forget the door. She let go of the knob because it was too wobbly to support her, especially with the weight of his righteous anger bearing down. Shrinking away from him and as far into the wall as she could get, she laid her palms flat and tried to stand strong.

"That's not…that's not true," she said.

But it had the ring of truth. Even through the frenetic pounding of her pulse, the shallow panting of her breath and her willful desire not to hear anything he flung at her right now, she knew: he might be right, and she couldn't bear it.

With one trembling hand, she reached for the door again. "I want you to—"

"I'm not leaving," he shouted, and slammed the door shut.

Jillian edged away and wished to heaven she hadn't opened this Pandora's box of nightmares.

The shaking began then, deep in her belly. Within seconds it had spread to her thighs, and she pressed her knees together in a futile attempt to control it, determined not to humiliate herself any further, even if she had to lean her head back and close her eyes against the swirling dizziness.

But, God, if she could only breathe—

Beau also seemed to be having problems with his lungs. After a couple of harsh rasps, he seemed calmer but not calm, reasonable but only on a thin surface layer that covered his turbulent emotions.

"Can I tell you how I feel, Jill?" he whispered. "This one time?"

"No."

A pause, and then, "Listen to me! You have to listen to me!"

With every ounce of strength she had, she raised her head from the wall, opened her eyelids and looked directly into his face for a connection that was worse than a gut punch. He was wild-eyed and desperate, Beau and yet not Beau at all, as though someone had smudged his features with an eraser, allowing glimpses of his damaged soul to emerge.

He hesitated, clearly not knowing what to make of her silence. She didn't know what to make of it, either. Taking it nice and easy, he dropped his cane, stepped closer and put his hands on the curve of her waist.

No.

She shook him off in an eruption of flailing arms, but he just kept coming and settled his hands again. This time, that gentle touch was exponentially worse. Less shocking and more comforting. And there was no way she could allow this man to comfort her.

"No."

She smacked him away for a third time, the simultaneous panic and absolute rightness of being in his arms again making her crazed.

"Please, Jill."

That quiet plea took all the fight out of her. Naturally, he knew it and wasted no time pressing his advantage—or maybe it was purely her weakness.

Reaching out again, slowly…slowly…he took both her hands in his and, oh, God, she remembered the warmth of those hands, the strength and tenderness. Worse, oh, so much worse, was the smell of him, that virile male scent of warm skin, soft cotton and the faint freshness of soap and deodorant. Earlier in the evening, she'd smelled these exact same arousing things on Adam's skin, yeah, but that was apples to oranges, a two-fingered "Chopsticks" on the piano versus a Mozart symphony.

Don't fall for this, Jill. Don't let him do this to you and—

Oh, nooo.

With a penitence that a confessional priest could only dream of, he bowed his head and rested his forehead against the backs of her hands. As if she were his queen and he were giving her all the respect she deserved. As if he worshiped her. And the vibrating tension in his body was a dead giveaway that her touch affected him in unholy ways he couldn't control.

"I love you. I always have. I always will."

Turning her hard face away, she resisted the urge to snort.

Love. From Beau? Please. She was surprised he could blaspheme the word with those lips without immediately being struck dead with a lightning bolt.

Oh, but there was more.

"I'm sorry, Jill," he whispered.

Oh. *Sorry.* Well, didn't that just cure everything?

"For what?" she wondered, and a tremor went through him at the quiet harshness of her voice. "The public humiliation? The private humiliation? The despair? Taking a woman who loved you and was confident and competent and whole—"

"All of it."

"—and turning her into a mess who doesn't trust men or her own instincts and has panic attacks? I'm just trying to understand, Beau. Which part are you sorry for? Any of that? Or are you only sorry that you lost your family and your career and had no one to care when you almost died? Help me out here. Break it down for me."

He lifted his head, much to her dismay. The situation was already fraught with way more intimacy and vulnerability than she could handle, and she didn't need to see his expression now, but no one was asking her what she wanted.

And there it was. All the unmitigated shame in those unblinking eyes, all the sorrow. It was there in the downturn of his lush lips as he tried to keep his chin from trembling, and in the strain across his cheekbones, flaring nostrils and, most terrible of all, the sheen of tears.

Seeing this kind of emotion from him was so harrowing that she forgot about her desperate struggle to breathe and her need to keep that brick wall standing tall and sturdy between them.

He pressed her hands to his heart, where she felt a pounding so violent she was surprised it didn't cause his T-shirt to ripple and bulge.

"I'm sorry for all of it, Jillian."

No.

She didn't want to hear this—

"I'm sorry I cheated on you with women I can barely remember. I'm sorry I made you cry. I'm sorry I wasn't the kind of strong husband you deserved. I'm sorry I didn't try harder.

I'm sorry I didn't get professional help sooner. I'm sorry I never showed you how much I needed you."

What a laugh. He'd almost had her there for a moment, but the whole need thing was stretching it a bit too far, even for someone as naive and trusting as she was.

Incensed again, she tried to jerk free, but he wouldn't let her go. "You've never needed anyone in your life."

Cursing, he looked up at the ceiling and took a moment to blink back his tears, not that any of it was real. It really was quite the performance. She had to hand it to him.

"This is the problem," he said, the frustration rising in his voice. "This is exactly what I'm talking about."

She raised a mocking eyebrow. "Fascinating. Do tell."

The words came in a frantic rush now, as though they'd been blocked for so long they had to run wild at last. "I needed you, Jill. I needed your optimism. Every day when I was governor, I looked forward to coming home to you. You were my consolation for a bad day at the state house or a bill that didn't pass. You were my reward for a job well done. You were my peace and my sunshine and my heart. I don't know what to do without you. I've been lost these three years. It's like I'm wandering in a forest and I can't find my way out. Nothing matters—"

Choking, he trailed off and hung his head.

And she watched him, again cursing her stupidity for landing herself in this mess. Some of these pretty words would stick with her later. Much as she wanted to block them all out, some of them would penetrate. She would wonder if he meant any of this heartfelt nonsense...she was already wondering...

Swiping at his eyes, he pressed fevered kisses to the backs of her hands, wetting them with his hot tears. When he looked up again, there was something even darker in his expression, as though the worst had yet to be said.

No. Not that.

Her lungs seized up again and she tried to break free.

"I needed you to share your pain with me, Jill—"

"Don't."

"We needed to turn to each other and help each other through—"

"I said, don't."

"And I needed you to let me in, but I couldn't reach you behind your vacant eyes. It was like my Jillian checked out and I couldn't—"

"Don't!" she shouted, and wrenched free.

They squared off now, both panting, and she sank against the wall because, Jesus, God, she couldn't breathe again, and it was all she could do to stay on her feet. Pressing a hand to her chest, she tried to keep her heart inside, where it belonged, but it seemed determined to hammer its way out of her body.

Her clutching fingers closed around her locket, which had collected her warmth, and she clung to it as the only thing keeping her from shrieking insanity. And Beau, damn him, tossed a pound of salt on all her half-healed wounds.

"When can we talk about Mary?" he asked.

Chapter 11

Jillian stilled, stunned senseless, even though she'd known this was coming. The name hung in the air for so long it became a presence of its own, an echoing reverberation that hurt both her ears and her soul. She couldn't believe he'd said it, but of course he'd said pretty much anything and everything to her tonight, so why would he stop now?

But *Mary.*

How could he do it?

"Don't you dare speak her name to me."

He plowed ahead. "We need to—"

Fueled by blind panic, she dredged up the anger that had been simmering beneath the surface, waiting just under the tight layer of her skin, and threw it in his face. She was desperate to get away from him, desperate to get to her bedroom, where she could hide in her dark closet and collapse until she'd ridden out the despair by herself.

"No." Her only goal was to divert him and escape. Well…and to hurt him a little more. That was always her underlying goal. "Don't you tell me what we need. There is no *we.* And you've had your little say, so now it's my turn. Or don't you want to know how I feel?"

He stared at her, reproachful, resigned and silent. Then he gave a sharp nod.

So it was okay if she spoke her mind, was it? Well, screw him. She didn't need his permission for a damn thing. She opened her mouth, determined to make her words as ugly and hurtful as possible.

It wasn't hard.

"I hate you Beau. I used to love you, but you killed all that two or three times over."

He kept quiet, swallowing with a hard bob of his Adam's apple.

"I hate you for breaking my heart." Continuing in a monotone, she kept going because this was a pretty long list and she wanted to finish it and get some sleep sometime tonight. "I hate you for destroying our family and forcing Allegra to grow up in a house without a father in it. I hate you for not being the man I thought you were."

Beau blinked, his gaze wavering. His chest may have heaved, but she didn't give a damn if it did. He could drown in his own tears for all she cared.

"Thanks to you, I've cried so many tears I should have collected them and had a pond dug out back. Do you understand that? I have images of you screwing other women in my head, and I can't get them out."

His face crumpled, straightened and crumpled again until he finally dropped his head and pressed his thumb and forefinger to his eyes, as though he wanted to gouge them out.

Watching him was oddly satisfying, and yet the sight didn't affect her at all. She might have been watching a movie from the other side of a Plexiglas divider; the scene before her couldn't reach her and didn't have any effect on real life as she knew it.

"Thanks to you, I've spent thousands of hours thinking about things like, hmm, 'I wonder if that woman screws better that I do? I wonder if she tastes better than I—'"

"God, Jillian, don't—"

"—do? Is it my belly? Is my belly not flat enough for you? Am I not adventurous enough for you? Is that it? Did you want to swing from the chandeliers or have a threesome, and you just didn't feel like you could indulge that side of yourself with me? What did I do wrong? What did they have that I didn't have?"

"Nothing."

"It must have been something, Beau."

"Jillian." He took a hurried step toward her, palms up, and she could feel his rising desperation, smell its salty tang on him like the sweat that shone on his brow. "I'm sorry about all that.

I'm sorry. If I could take it all back, I would. If I could die for it, I would. But I can't. And we were falling apart way before all that. That's what we need to work through—"

"No."

"—because our real problem will haunt us forever if we don't talk about it." He paused to take a deep breath and square his shoulders in a way that clearly said he may be defeated, but he wasn't quitting. No matter how much pain they had to wade through and how much she didn't want to do it. "When can we talk about—"

"No," she shrieked. *"No!"*

"—Mary?"

"This is not about…about her."

Jillian tried to keep it together, but she was failing, bit by bit, and her body could not handle this much emotion without self-destructing into a pile of ruined flesh and limbs. She couldn't breathe; her heart threatened to explode; her skin was clammy and her knees weak.

She was, in short, a disaster, and all she could think of was hurting him and escaping.

"This is about how I feel about you, Beau. I hate you. As much as I loved you before, I hate you twice as much now. Do you understand that? I have zero good feelings left for you, and you're wasting your time trying to look for any. I hate you now, I'll hate you for the rest of my life and then I'll probably be blocked at heaven's gate for hating you after I'm dead. Can I be any clearer? I. Hate. You."

Did that do it? Was that enough ugliness for one lifetime? Would he leave now so she could spend the rest of the night peacefully wallowing in her anger and despair? Had she, with that one heartfelt speech, killed Beau's determination to reconcile with her for once and for all?

They stared at each other. Actually, she stared in his direction, trying to see him through the bitter shimmer of her tears, and he watched her with an utter stillness that made her wonder if her tirade had turned him to stone.

And then, not done with her yet, he opened his mouth.

"You hate me," he said evenly. "Fair enough. But when can we talk about Mary?"

One arrested second passed.

And then she lost it.

"Get out!" The words jammed in her throat, refusing to come, but the sobs erupted freely, doubling her over with their ferocity. *"Get out!"*

Beau took one hurried step forward. Oh, thank God. She gasped in a racking breath, just trying to survive until the door closed behind him. Thank God he was leaving. Thank God, thank—

But he didn't go to the door. He reached for her, his face twisted and tormented and every bit as devastated as she felt.

"I'm sorry, Jill. I'm so sorry. But we've got to talk—"

And then his gentle, scalding hand touched her face, offering comfort that she sorely needed, and she was halfway into his arms before she remembered that she couldn't hate him forever and cry on his shoulder at the same time.

Pulling away, she wheeled around, stumbling to the doorway leading to her bedroom. So he wouldn't leave? Fine. Screw it. He could stay all he wanted to. She would leave instead.

Distraught, she slammed the door in his face and kept going to her walk-in closet. She could collapse in there. It was safe in there.

Except that his voice could still reach her and it was in her ears and in her head and her heart. And she realized that there was no safe place for her after all.

"You can't keep shutting me out like this," Beau called. "She was my daughter, too."

Ignore him, Jill. Keep going… Keep going… Keep—

Blinded by her tears, she staggered in among her clothes, purses and shoes, slamming a second door shut behind her. Then she hit the thick carpet on all fours and crawled to the farthest, darkest corner, hiding behind the row of long skirts and trying to block everything out except her desperate, heaving struggle for breath. She settled on her butt, planted her feet on the floor and put her head between her knees.

She reached for her locket with fumbling fingers that managed all the dexterity of lead pipes, and tried to focus on the comforting warmth and smoothness of the gold, its weight and its meaning, anything but Beau.

Breathe. You can do it. Ignore him. Breathe—

On the other side of the wall between them, Beau's despair came through loud and clear.

Eventually, Jillian tumbled, exhausted, into bed, where she tossed and turned like an Olympic gymnast doing her floor exercises. She fell into a troubled sleep just before dawn, and he came to her right away.

They sat on the sofa. Without a word, he swung her legs across his lap, which was a huge relief. Thank God he was touching her; thank God he'd taken the decision out of her hands.

He went to work on her feet the way he always had, gripping them in his strong hands and rubbing them, getting her used to the feel of him again.

Not that she'd ever forgotten.

"Tell me," he said.

"I can't."

"Hmm."

He ran his thumb up the sole of her right foot, from her heel to her toes, in the wonderful massage that skirted the line between delicious pain and real discomfort. She melted into the cushions, her worries slipping away despite all her efforts to hold them close and nurture them. Then he switched feet, starting the sweet torture all over again, and there went more fears and anxieties, gone like the outer layers of a baseball-sized Bermuda onion.

It was safe here and she could, just this once, be honest.

Who would know?

"Tell me," he said again.

"I need you."

"For what?"

"Everything."

His thumb zeroed in on her spot…oh, God, her spot, the one that drove her wild, right on her instep, right there. *There.* The spot was a secret pipeline that sent electrical jolts to her sex and contracted her belly with need.

She twisted, but he held tight and it was okay because she couldn't see his eyes and didn't have to face his burning intensity. Her twisting became writhing, and her breath, a moan.

"What's *everything?*"

She could answer because there was no smugness in his tone, only a deep curiosity. And this was only a dream, right? Wasn't she safe here?

"I need to talk to you about Mary. And Allegra. And the inn. And my life. I need my friend back."

"Hmm."

His hands slid over her calves in unbearable, feathery strokes. She stretched out and lay back, letting the sensations wash over her until her hips arched. After tickling behind her knees, he kneaded her calves—one in each hand—with muscle-deep squeezes so satisfying she thought she might die on the spot.

"What else do you need?"

"I need to turn to you. Trust you. I need to know you'll be there if I fall apart or if I need to lean on you. I need to be the only one."

"I see."

She'd known it was coming, but that didn't prepare her for the shock of his fingers heading north, over her thighs, and coming to rest right—ahhh, yesss, right there. They circled the hard nub beneath her panties, driving her higher with a relentless rhythm that had her pumping her hips in a desperate counterpoint.

"Beau."

It was a plea. A down-on-her-knees, intense beg of the worst kind. There was nothing she wouldn't do for that touch, nothing she wouldn't admit or say, no confession too scary.

"What else do you need?"

The words were both on the tip of her tongue and locked behind a thick steel door guarded by armed soldiers and pit bulls. She couldn't get them out and couldn't hold them back. "I need—"

His fingers wandered to the edge of her wet panties. "What?"

I need you to never destroy me again.

But she couldn't say that.

"I need you inside me. Now. Hurry."

He withdrew his fingers, punishing her for her cowardice.

Everything shifted and he was gone, just like that, and she was resting on nothing but a sofa without his sheltering body beneath her.

"No," she said.

"It's all right here—"

His voice faded away—there was some stupid beeping sound drowning him out and she couldn't hear him, but she needed to hear him because this was important. Possibly the most important thing he'd ever told—

"—and all you need to do is ask…"

There was more, but the words were lost to her forever, drowned out by the insistent racket of her godforsaken alarm clock.

Shooting upright, disoriented and infuriated by this lost opportunity, Jillian grabbed the alarm clock on her nightstand, yanked the cord out of the wall and hurled it across the room, where it made a huge clatter and, worse, a streaking scratch in the taupe wall that she'd have to patch sometime today, during her nonexistent free time.

She flopped back onto the pillows, desperation making her crazy. Go back to sleep, dummy. Go back to—

But Beau was gone.

He had, unbelievably, taken some of her anger with him.

Beau had just been buzzed into Dr. Desai's office for his appointment, and was shutting the door behind him, when he turned and ran into a solid wall of muscle coming around the corner.

"Pardon me," he began automatically, making sure he kept his feet under him, but then he looked up and saw who he'd bumped into.

Ah, shit. Just what he needed to get his day off to a winning start. What a nasty coincidence.

It was that prison guy…what was his name? Dawson Reynolds.

Him.

He hadn't gotten any more cheerful, that was for sure. Behind his glasses, his eyes were sullen and challenging, as though he just needed one imagined slight to fly into a rage.

Today he wore knit shorts and a dark T-shirt that revealed the whole neck tattoo thing. It was an African symbol—Andrikan, wasn't it?—that Beau recognized. Something like a tic-tac-toe grid, with curving swirls where the lines ended. It was the sign for, if he wasn't mistaken, peace.

Peace? This guy?

Ha. Funny.

The tense silence grew, so Beau did the polite thing. "How's it going?"

The guy gave him a withering look. "Swell."

Beau could just imagine. If he was smart, he would move aside and let the guy leave. No doubt he had a full day of glaring and seething ahead. But something about Dawson niggled at Beau, and he decided to ask another question or two, at least until the guy killed him.

"You seeing Dr. Desai?"

Dawson's jaw locked and his lips twisted. "Yeah," he said. "Turns out I've got some anger issues."

"Really." Beau tried to keep the sarcasm out of his voice, but he was amused. And a little confused. Desai wasn't cheap, and this guy didn't seem to have any money, so how—

"Not that it's any of your business," Dawson told him, "but this is all part of me getting back on my feet—"

A light went on over Beau's head. "The Innocence Program."

"—but even when you've got people helping you out a little, employers don't want to hire innocent ex-felons in a bad economy—"

"Oh," Beau said, feeling uncomfortable and…guilty.

"—even if you graduated from Duke with honors. Because most people figure that even if you were innocent when you went into prison, you probably learned some bad stuff while you were there. So they don't want you around. But you probably know something about people not wanting you around, don't you, Governor?"

Irritated now, Beau kept quiet; he didn't trust himself to say anything without ripping this guy's head off.

"So, if you'll excuse me," Dawson concluded, "I have an application in to scoop elephant shit at the circus. And if they don't hire me for that, you can find me on the corner, selling drugs to schoolchildren. Have a nice day." With that, he edged around Beau and stalked out the door.

Beau watched him go, barely resisting the urge to plant his foot in the man's ass as he went.

"How was your week?" Dr. Desai asked right out of the box.

How was his week? Ha. Good one.

"Funny you should ask, Doc." Beau settled deeper into the leather chair, crossed his legs and didn't bother to keep the bitterness from his voice. "I think this was the single best week of my life."

Dr. Desai, deadpan as always, played along. "How so?"

"I've had so many successes this week, it's hard to know where to start."

Desai waited.

"I interviewed about a thousand people for my foundation grants. But not that Dawson Reynolds guy who was just here. I don't like him."

Desai absorbed this in silence for a minute. "Did you give him a chance?"

Was that reproach in the good doctor's voice? "I don't have to give him a chance."

"I thought you were all about second chances these days—"

That brought Beau up short.

"But you're not here to talk about Dawson Reynolds. What else happened?"

"What else happened?" Beau pretended to think, and then snapped his fingers. "Oh, yeah. How could I forget? Jillian and I got back together."

"Really?"

"Yeah. We had a long talk, nice and mature, and hashed everything out. She's decided to forgive me and give me another chance. So we're good as new. Better than ever. We'll get remarried by the end of the month."

"Wonderful." Desai's eyes crinkled at the edges, proving that the good doctor may have something approaching a sense of humor. "Sounds like you don't need me today, then. Don't forget to pay the receptionist on your way out."

Beau snorted.

They sat in silence for a minute, with Desai in no particular rush to listen, and Beau in no particular rush to spill. It may have gone on like that forever—that certainly would have been the easy solution—but Beau needed so much fixing they really didn't have any time to waste. Best to get right to the bottom line.

"You want to know something, Doc?"

A pause, and then, "Sure."

"The only souls in Atlanta who don't hate me—whose hate I haven't earned—are my daughter, Allegra, and my dog, Seinfeld. Allegra's too young to know she should hate me, and Seinfeld is too dumb to hate me. That's quite a record, huh?"

"You can add me to the list," Desai said. "I don't hate you."

"Yeah, but I don't care whether you hate me or not."

"Ah. Well…your dog and your daughter. That's a good start, eh?"

"I'll take what I can get."

Desai nodded with what may have been empathy, but that was probably reading way too much into the gesture.

"Allegra's spending the night tonight. First time in my new house. I'm helping her with her Mother's Day gift for Jillian."

"That's great." Desai paused before he got to the heart of the matter, which Beau supposed they'd put off for long enough anyway. "Where should we start? With your foundation?"

"No." Beau's throat clamped down, as though it knew a painful interlude was coming and wanted to get started with the discomfort right away. He tried to swallow back the watermelon-sized lump, but it merely bobbed an inch or so and then settled right back where it'd been. "With Jillian."

"What happened?"

"We had the ugliest scene we've ever had in our entire relationship. And, believe me, that's saying something."

"What happened?" Desai asked again.

What happened? Beau's heart had imploded. Again. He'd felt head-hanging shame for coming up here to the Atlanta area, moving in and upending Jillian's world. He'd wondered, for the billionth time, what kind of sadomasochist he was, or whether he was outright insane. He'd decided that he was, in fact, insane, which was a small comfort because, hey, at least then he wasn't fully in charge of his actions, right?

But Desai was still waiting for his answer.

"I went to her house last week when she was out on a—" the word dried out his mouth and thickened his tongue, even now "—date. The babysitter called because Allegra wouldn't go to sleep without seeing me, so I went over and was still there when Jillian got back. She wasn't real happy to see me. Let's put it like that. She picked a fight. I did the mature thing for about half a second, and then I blew up, too, and escalated the situation."

"I see." Desai tilted back in his chair, looked up at the ceiling and considered God-knew-what. "Did Jillian's reaction surprise you?"

"Yes," Beau said, but that wasn't the real answer, so he amended it. "No."

"How did you escalate the situation?"

"I mentioned…"

Jesus, he was going to fall apart right here and start sobbing like a child getting a vaccination. Man up, Taylor. You can get through this.

"Take your time," Desai said, which didn't help.

He didn't need sympathy right now. He needed someone to call him a punk so he'd get mad rather than let loose with this unbearable sadness again.

Squeezing his eyes between his thumb and forefinger, he ignored the proffered box of tissues in favor of several deep breaths.

There. Better. Just spit it out.

"I mentioned Mary."

Chapter 12

The weight of the ensuing silence told Beau that Desai knew exactly what he was talking about and what this meant.

"Your firstborn," Desai said gently.

"Yeah."

"What happened?"

Oh, come on. Beau jerked his head up as the wave of annoyance hit him. "Since you knew the name and have a copy of my file, I'm assuming you know what happened," he snapped. "So why do we have to go through this exercise? You haven't seen enough of your clients fall apart yet this morning?"

Unruffled—shit; what did it take to get under that guy's skin?—Desai folded his hands in his lap, assuming a posture that clearly said he was prepared to sit there until gravity glued his butt to the seat, but he wouldn't leave or end the session without hearing the story from Beau's lips.

So Beau told him, aiming for a detached and clinical recitation of the bare facts. His voice barely worked.

"We tried to have kids for years. She had three miscarriages. Finally, she got pregnant again and it was the best time in our marriage, which had already been pretty great except for the miscarriages. We knew she was a girl. We named her Mary. I went to all the doctor's appointments. I—"

He broke off, too choked up to continue. So much for detachment.

"—couldn't keep my hands off her. I rubbed cocoa butter on her belly and feet and that sort of thing. We were really… happy."

He wished his voice wouldn't keep giving out on him like this. He felt like the world's biggest idiot. Worse was the uncontrollable fidgeting, which had him shifting in his chair and running his hands through his hair and across the back of his neck. Man, he was a mess. A complete, unadulterated and unmitigated mess. No wonder Jillian wanted nothing to do with him.

"And then?" Desai prompted.

Maybe he needed one of those tissues after all. Jerking one from the box, he swiped it under his dripping nose and crumpled it in his fist.

"And then, in her thirty-seventh week, when the doctor checked her out and said that everything was fine and nothing was happening, I went to Canada for a two-day trade summit. And—"

His mouth was open, his tongue flapping, but the words refused to make an appearance. Just refused to come. It shouldn't be this hard. Not after all this time.

"And?"

"And the baby stopped moving. I flew straight home for the delivery because they, you know, still have the woman go into labor and deliver and all. And I got there just in time to see the birth—only it wasn't a birth, was it?—of a perfect little baby girl with an umbilical cord wrapped around her neck."

Desai bowed his head, looking stricken. "I'm sorry."

Beau shrugged. Sorry. Yeah. Everyone was sorry. And his daughter was still dead and they'd never even seen the color of her eyes.

He felt himself slipping again, wallowing in the darkest depths of despair when, after a short pause, Desai's question pulled him back to the moment.

"Why would mentioning Mary escalate the argument you and Jillian had the other night?"

"Because…"

God, he was tired. So unspeakably tired to the depths of what was left of his soul. If only he could rest. If only getting through every day wasn't such a terrible effort. If only they didn't have to talk about this ordeal.

Beau forced himself to continue.

"Our marriage died the day Mary did. And it was dead for years before I ever had an affair."

* * *

"No, Daddy. Don't take my tiara."

Allegra, the droopy-eyed princess, currently more asleep than awake, snuggled deeper into her fluffy new bed, clutched Archie the lion cub closer with one hand, and grasped the crystal tiara atop her curly head with the other. Across her knees, at the place he probably considered his birthright, sprawled Seinfeld, who watched Beau with drowsy interest.

Allegra was just-showered fresh, with silky purple pajamas and a fresh pink manicure that she'd insisted on applying herself. The thick and mostly smudged result was, as far as Beau could tell, an unmitigated disaster, but Allegra had been thrilled, and that was good enough for him. If she was happy, he was happy.

Staring down at her, Beau felt his heart swell to beach-ball size. His life needed some serious work, yeah, but with this one precious girl, he had the chance to get things right. She was bright and curious, beautiful and kind, funny and everything that was right with his world. The best parts of Jillian and him, mixed together into this precious angel.

With a tiara on her head.

One might think that a full day of princess-izing, followed by a *Beauty and the Beast* movie night with popcorn and Raisinettes, would be enough for a while, but no. This misguided child now thought she was going to sleep with that thing on her head. Maybe it was his fault; he'd certainly fussed and fawned over her tonight, and she had good reason to think he was wrapped around her little finger.

But that didn't mean he was a complete pushover. Sometimes a man had to put his foot down. Beau had said *no* earlier, when she wanted to manicure *his* fingers and toes, and he wasn't afraid to say *no* now. It was all part of the dad gig.

"I told you before," he said, reaching for the tiara, "that you can't sleep in this thing—"

"No-ooo—"

"—because it's hard and it can poke you in the eye during the night. I don't want to make any runs to the emergency room tonight. Do you?"

Allegra wasn't one to concede a point when she didn't have to.

"But, Daddy—"

"Anyway," Beau continued, playing his trump card, "you don't want to bend it. How would you look—a princess with a bent tiara?"

That did it. With a dark, unintelligible mutter, Allegra dropped her hand, allowing Beau to pull the tiara free and untangle it from her hair. Then she fought the sleep for just a few seconds longer.

"Love you, Daddy."

God, she just killed him. "I love you, too, baby."

After Beau pressed a lingering kiss to her forehead, she snuffled and settled, and then, with an abruptness that was exactly like flipping a light switch, fell asleep.

Beau stayed right where he was, on the edge of the bed, watching her and stroking her tissue-soft little cheek. Was it strange for a grown man to be this wildly in love with his little girl? If so, he was the king of strange and would be happy to sit here all night, keeping watch.

But...he still had a foundation to run and applicant files to review.

He was reaching for his cane and getting his feet under him when Seinfeld raised his head and cocked it, listening. Ears perked, he looked to Beau and emitted a low woof. Beau, who had learned to pay attention to woofs, waited.

Another woof, and then a soft knock at the front door.

Ah. Visitor.

Without bothering to be quiet—Allegra slept with the utter, unmoving stillness of a vampire in her coffin during the daylight hours—he went downstairs. His leg protested the steps, as always. As always, he ignored the pain. Tried to, anyway. Seinfeld, who lived for a new adventure or friend, trotted alongside him, tags jangling and tail wagging.

Opening the front door to the sultry Georgia twilight, Beau got the surprise of his life. Jillian stood under the porch light, with a big pink and yellow box in her hands and an unreadable expression in her wide dark eyes.

This was the first time they'd seen each other since the big blowup—Barbara Jean shuttled Allegra back and forth between their houses—and he had no idea what to expect. But she did not, for once, look like she wanted to do him grievous bodily injury with some medieval implement of torture.

She didn't even look angry. She just looked…like Jillian.

"Hi," she said.

Though his chest had seized up at the sight of her, he managed not to stammer. Drawing on all his wits and mental acuity, he managed one syllable:

"Hi."

Wow. They'd each spoken a word to each other, and there'd been no yelling or screaming, no bloodshed or recriminations. Who said miracles didn't happen?

She seemed as stymied by this new civility as he felt, and an uncomfortable beat or two passed during which neither of them risked breaking the peace. Maybe he should just say goodnight and shut the door. His day couldn't end on a better note than this, right?

"Can I, ah…come in?"

In? His spirits rose with unbridled and unreasonable joy, as though world peace had just broken out. Jillian wanted to come in? To *his* house? Was this some sort of cruel hallucination?

"Ah," he said, sure there was a catch of some sort. She probably wasn't here to see him. She probably wanted to kiss Allegra good-night or inspect her new room for suitability. She wouldn't come down here to see him and he was a fool for hoping otherwise. "Sure. But Allegra's asleep already, so—"

Jillian nodded with unmistakable satisfaction, surprising him again. "I don't want to see Allegra. I want to see you."

She wanted to see him? Jesus, God.

He couldn't speak, so he led her into the living room, where they sat on opposite ends of the long leather sofa. She set the box on her lap and stared around the room in a silent assessment of his decorating skills.

He, on the other hand, stared unabashedly at her, afraid to ask what she was doing there or even if she wanted some iced tea. What if his voice jarred her to her senses and she decided to leave? No. Best to sit with his lips together and soak up her presence while he could. That, and pray it took her an hour or two to start talking.

Finally, she delivered her verdict. "The room is really pretty. I like it."

The room. Right. It was a start, he supposed. And a compliment, so that was good. Looking around, he saw what she saw: the leather sofa and love seats, rattan chairs and ottomans, entertainment center and bookshelves, lamps, mirrors and pillows.

"Thanks. I can't take credit, though. It's Pottery Barn 101. I just ordered one of everything."

"Oh," she said, and looked down at her box.

His stupid leg chose that exact moment to tighten up in a spasm, which made him grimace despite all his best efforts not to. Great. Nothing like appearing to be an invalid in front of the woman you most wanted to impress.

When she opened her mouth to ask the obligatory question about how he was doing, he headed her off with an impatient wave and a voice that was sharper than he'd meant it to be. Nothing made him see red quicker than Jillian's pity.

"It's fine," he snapped. "And you didn't come here to check my medical status."

Brilliant, Taylor. Way to encourage her to stay and talk. Why not just kick her out and be done with it? Maybe threaten to call the police?

"No." Reaching for the gold locket around her neck, she gently rubbed it between her fingers the way a pilgrim might handle the Holy Grail, and he had another of those can't-breathe moments of unbearable waiting. "I came to talk about Mary."

Stupefied, he gaped for a good long time, five seconds at least. She…came to talk about Mary? Is that what he just heard?

"What did you say?"

"I thought maybe we could—" she broke off, stroking a hand over the top of the box in a loving caress that was so painful to see it nearly made his eyes bleed "—go through some of her things. I know you don't have any…mementos of her."

No. He didn't. He'd started to ask for something a million

different times, but he'd figured he had a better chance of growing flippers than getting Jillian to give him anything of Mary's.

But now here she was, offering on her own. And he was so ridiculously grateful he'd probably end the evening by dropping to the floor and slobbering wet kisses all over her feet.

"Thank you," he said.

She ducked her head as though she were as overwhelmed by this peaceful moment between them as he was. There might even have been the beginnings of a smile on the corner of her lips, but it was gone before he could get a bead on it.

With a deep breath—yeah, he also felt like he needed an oxygen mask right about now, and that was the truth—she opened the box.

Everything inside had been wrapped with extreme care in pristine white tissue paper, layers and layers of it. Smoothing those back with careful fingers, Jillian revealed a beautiful crocheted blanket of soft baby colors, blue and green, yellow and pink.

God. It was a shock—a jab right to his solar plexus. So much so that he had to blink against that pretty little blanket and give his eyes time to adjust. But…there was no adjusting. No amount of preparation that could make him ready for *this*.

This was the blanket made with love by one of the elderly members of their church, a woman with fingers so knotted with arthritis it was a miracle she could pick up a needle, much less produce anything this intricate and lovely. This was the blanket the woman had made for them to use when they brought their newborn home from the hospital. This was the blanket they'd never used.

Reaching out, he brushed the fluffy softness before he caught himself and stopped. He couldn't…he shouldn't…

"Go ahead," Jillian said.

Their gazes caught across the top of the box, and there were tears shimmering in her warm eyes…tears layered over understanding and empathy. And that was all the permission he needed.

He reached out again, filled to the brim with so much heartbreak and reverence that he couldn't keep it inside. Pulling the blanket to his face—God, it was soft…so soft—he pressed his mouth to it and used it to catch some of his emotion, as if that were possible.

Mary. He missed her. If only he could see her again and hold her, just once. If only he knew what color her eyes had been. If only—

Jillian shifted closer and took the other end of the blanket in her hands and held it. It was almost like she wanted to offer comfort, maybe, or to touch him, but this was as close as she'd allow herself to get.

"Look." Rifling through the box, she produced a tiny pair of pink suede shoes with white flowers on the sides. "She could have worn these when she learned to walk. They're flexible and easier on a baby's toes…"

Man up, Taylor. With a quick swipe of his eyes, he took the shoes and kissed them, grinning. They were so silly. So precious.

"Here's a bathing suit."

A what? "You're kidd—"

No, she wasn't kidding. Jillian passed over a minuscule one-piece with horrifying pink and orange cats on it and a ruffle around the bottom.

He took it, wondering what the world was coming to. "Why on earth—?"

Jillian shot him the exasperated look that was as familiar as his own face in the mirror when he shaved. "You know they start babies swimming early, Beau. They're supposed to get comfortable with the water."

He'd have to take her word for it. Kissing the bathing suit, he waited for the next thing. But when Jillian pulled it out of the box, he had another one of those baseball-bat-to-the-gut moments of shock. So much for manning up.

It was one of those little pajama outfits, with feet. Yellow and white with a bow at the top and snaps on the insides of the legs for changing diapers.

He took it into his lap. Stared. Cried again, with shaking shoulders and the whole embarrassing deal. Jillian kept her head bowed and said nothing, but he could almost swear he felt her edge even closer, to the point that her body heat registered all up and down his side.

After a minute, when he thought he'd collected himself again and braced for the shock of the next thing in the box, whatever it turned out to be, she reached inside and pulled out a silver-framed, black-and-white photograph that nearly knocked him out cold.

It was an extreme close-up of Jillian, with her eyes closed, pressing a tender kiss to Mary's small face. Mary, the most beautiful baby ever, with a full head of dark curls, like Beau's, and Beau's pale toffee skin, and Jillian's arched brows and a thick fringe of eyelashes resting against her cheek as she slept.

Only she wasn't asleep. She was dead.

The hospital had contacted a photographer who specialized in taking pictures of dead babies who didn't look dead, so their parents would have these mementos. This was a larger version of the picture Jillian kept in her locket, which was as close to her heart as she could get it.

And the locket. The locket had been his new-mommy gift, picked out pretty much the second she entered her second trimester, when the baby was supposed to be safe. He'd never thought, on that amazing day so long ago, that the world would crash and burn around them like this.

There was so much he had to tell her, so much explaining still to do. "I shouldn't have gone to Canada, Jill. I should have been with you when you found out. I shouldn't have—"

Turning away, she stared across the room, lost in thoughts that she hid behind a blank face. Finally, she shrugged. "It doesn't matter. You had a—"

"It matters. You needed me and I let you—"

"—trade summit and you were the governor—"

Was he hearing right? That it didn't matter that she had to hear the news that the baby in her belly had died while he was out of the country and she was all alone?

"It matters." Risking what felt like everything, especially the fragile peace they'd established here today, he touched her wrist. "That was the beginning of the end for us—"

"No."

That one word, said with zero inflection, was all she had to say on the subject. With brisk efficiency, she pulled her arm free and began to collect the items again and replace them in the box. Her expression was a mask of serenity that didn't fool him for even half a second.

What the hell should he do now? Press a little harder? Or go along with this fairy tale she was spinning? Watching her raise the blanket high in order to fold it, he just couldn't sit quietly and let it go.

They'd come this far. They couldn't go any further without complete honesty, on this one terrible thing, if nothing else.

"Jillian."

She kept her eyes lowered, refusing to look at him as she repacked the box.

"You're angry with me. You've been angry with me for years—"

"No, I'm not. You were doing your job and you had to go—"

"I wasn't there for you. In the one second of your life when you most needed me, I wasn't there."

"No," she repeated, as if that were the end of it forever.

Stymied and floundering, he took a minute and then decided. To hell with it. He had a lot to say, and he was saying it. He had to say it.

"It was like you were punishing me, Jill."

He hunched down over the box, trying to get into her line of sight so he could force her to really see him, this one time, but she resolutely focused on arranging the tissue paper.

"You wouldn't let me cry with you. You wouldn't cry on my shoulder. You looked right through me. I asked you to talk to me, and you wouldn't. I begged you to go to counseling with me, and you wouldn't."

The emotion rose in his husky voice, all the blocked frustration he'd felt, and he let it come because they needed to get this all out there. It was eating both of them alive, whether they acknowledged it or not, and he was not going to live like this for the rest of his life.

Jillian wouldn't, either, not if he had anything to say about it.

Some days he was sure she'd buried it so deep she didn't even know what was driving her or understand the root of her own anger. She needed his help as much as he needed hers.

Was her spirit still in there? Anywhere inside that body at all?

"You turned your face away from me, just like you're doing now."

"No."

With utter focus, she lifted the lid over the box and slid it into place. There was absolutely no emotion in her voice or expression; they might have been discussing which DVD to watch.

Do you want to watch *War of the Worlds,* Jillian?

No.

A roar of frustration rose up in him and he wrestled it back until his throat burned with the effort. Keep it cool, man. Don't give up.

They weren't going to go down like this. They were going to get past this issue because it was at the heart of everything that was wrong between them, the beginning of their long spiraling descent into ugliness and despair.

He touched her arm again, stilling her hands, and she stiffened to granite.

"You checked out on me, Jillian. I lost my daughter and my wife. Where did you go—?"

Suddenly her head jerked up and she impaled him through the heart with the white-hot flash of her angry eyes, awash in unshed tears, the same as if she'd speared him in the chest at close range.

There was murder in her face, and he shrank away from it.

"Where did *I* go?"

Her voice rang with fury; her body trembled with it, enough so that the wisps of hair around her face fluttered as though a breeze had swept through the room.

"Where did *you* go? That's the real question, isn't it? Where did *you* go? When I woke up that morning and realized it had been a day since I'd felt the baby move, and I put an icy washcloth on my belly and nothing happened, where were *you?* When I called the doctor and she said come in, now, and I got there and she tried to listen for the baby with a stethoscope and then they did an ultrasound, and I had to look at their stricken faces and try to interpret what their silence meant—where the hell were *you,* Beau? In Canada, being a good governor? Well, isn't that nice! Too bad you weren't with me, being a good husband!"

And there it was. The poison that had begun the slow rot of his marriage from the inside out, served up for him on a silver platter.

They stared at each other in the breathless silence. Jillian looked defiant; he felt only grim satisfaction.

Then, without warning, something shifted. It was like a gust of wind swept through a mountain pass, sending a forest fire in yet another direction.

Jillian blinked, and he realized, with sickening dread, what was coming.

Oh, no. Not that.

Yes—that.

Her chin began to quiver. As though she realized she was losing it, she pressed her lips together, but it didn't matter. All at once, her face crumbled and she bent double at the waist, ruined by agonized sobs that seemed to go on forever with no beginning or end.

"Where were *you?*" The words, mangled by her raw emotion, kept coming until he thought the sound would make his eardrums rupture. "Where were *you,* Beau? Where were *you?*"

Jesus, God. He couldn't sit and watch her in this kind of pain without touching her. He'd sooner die. Trying not to startle her, he touched her hair and, damn, it felt right.

This was right.

He leaned closer, ready to take her in his arms, where she belonged, now and always, but she jerked upright and batted him away in a fit of blind hysteria.

"No, no, *no!* Don't touch me!"

Yeah, okay. He let go because *no* meant no and he had to respect her boundaries, even if he hated them, but it felt as unnatural as eating dirt.

He couldn't let her go now. It just wasn't in him.

The best he could do was let her decide, and to hell with what he needed and, come to think of it, his pride. Opening his arms wide, he begged.

"Please, Jill. Just this once. This one time."

She stared at him with her tear-drenched eyes. One tense second passed and then—

And then a miracle happened. Still crying, she crawled into his lap and didn't scream or vomit or call the police when he gathered her close, murmuring to her and rocking her the way he sometimes rocked Allegra to sleep.

Pressing her wet face to his neck, she wept and continued with her one single question, which had been so long coming.

"Where were you, Beau? Where were you?"

Stunned and reacting on pure instinct, he pressed feverish kisses to her hair, that same sweet-smelling hair that had haunted his dreams and waking hours for years, coconut oil or something, the most wonderful smell in the world.

"Shh, baby. It's all right. It's all right."

Thank you, God. Thank you. Thank you. Thank—

"It's all right, baby. It's okay. We'll be okay."

"Beau," she said. *"Beau."*

They went on like that. Three minutes may have passed, or it may have been three hours. He didn't know and it didn't matter. It was enough of a start to get him through three more years, if need be.

She was here. With him. Letting him comfort her in a way she'd never done before, even in the darkest hours right after Mary died. They'd had a moment of complete honesty and made incalculable progress in healing the wounds between them.

Could anything be better?

Jillian. Her arms were around his neck, her hands in his hair, and it was real, not another high-definition, good-enough-to-taste dream that would leave him broken and empty when he woke up. *Real.* He wasn't imagining the need he felt in her grip as she pulled him closer, or the intimacy of this absolute understanding that they could only get from each other.

They needed to be together like this, offering each other

consolation. This wasn't about sex, and he understood that perfectly well. This was about an emotional connection and healing. The purpose of this moment was to get past the pain. That was just fine with him, and it was enough. Hell. Being with Jillian any way he could was more than enough. Sex never even crossed his mind.

Until her fingers at his nape stopped clutching and started stroking.

That was all it took for the tectonic plates of their relationship to shift, until feelings that had been trapped and hidden rose to the surface in a precursor to an eruption more violent than any volcano's.

With that one small thing, the air between them became all about desire. All about the delicious curve of her ass in his lap and the firm pressure of her breasts against his chest. All about her new stillness and tiny gasp of surprise and lust, as though she couldn't quite believe what she'd done, but had zero intention of taking it back.

He shuddered.

She gasped, a whisper of hot air against his neck.

And then she did it again, a curling of fingers in that one spot that wound him up tight.

His breath caught and held because he would do nothing—nothing, God, not even breathe, even if it led to his ultimate suffocation and death—to force her along at this moment.

But…where was this going?

Slowly she pulled back, her face wet with tears and her breasts heaving with uneven panting that sounded, to his confused ears at least, like passion rather than pain. Then she raised her lids to stare at him with wet eyes that glittered with every conceivable shade of brown, from amber to deepest mahogany. And then…

Was he imagining this? Was this a dream after all? A hallucination?

And then she leaned closer…tipped up her chin, just a little…and waited.

Disbelief pinned Beau right where he sat, dazed and frozen,

and he could swear he felt his skin vibrate with leashed tension that strained away from his control.

She had to know that he would swallow her whole right now.

Was that what she wanted?

Could he get this lucky? Was this a test? Did anyone really expect him to let this opportunity pass him by when he'd prayed for it for years?

He wanted to do the right thing, but he'd be damned if he knew what that was. "Jillian?"

There. He'd been honorable and raised the question, dumbass that he was. This was her chance. If she wanted this train to stop so she could hop off and run away, now was the time. Run while you can, Jill.

Only, Jillian didn't run. To his continued and utter astonishment, she eased a hairsbreadth closer, which was just enough for her mouth to brush across his and send him past the point of no return and into the realm of raw desire of the fiercest kind.

"Jillian."

There was no gentleness left in him, no patience. No nothing except for the blinding need to grab back what was his and keep her forever this time, because God knew he wasn't living without her and hadn't lived for years.

A guttural sound raced up his throat and out of his mouth, a surprised cry all wrapped up in a shout of triumph.

Jillian. They belonged together and here was the proof, wild and hot in his arms. He let go of his control because there was only this. Only her. Only now.

Now, God. Now.

Lowering his head, he took her sweet mouth with his and let the need wash over him until it was the only thing left in his universe.

Chapter 13

Was he hurting her? Kissing too hard? Taking too much?

Maybe, but what could he do?

Her mouth was hot and slick, honeyed and urgent. She tasted like the iced tea she served at the inn and something altogether more delicious that was only Jillian. One touch of his tongue was all she needed, one stroking sweep, and she cried out, opening for him and sucking him as deep inside as he could go.

God.

Frantic and unabashedly greedy in a way she'd never been before, she arched against him, thrusting her hips and scratching, licking and biting, ushering him into a world of purest insanity. Lust at its most uncontrollable.

Jillian. Yes. Yes.

But…no.

He couldn't get close enough. Couldn't pour himself into her the way he needed to. Tunneling his fingers through that satin waterfall of hair, he jerked her head back, meaning to thrust his tongue farther into her mouth and take it all, now, but, God, look at her neck. A graceful arch of smoothest brown silk, straining back as he angled her head, it wasn't something he could ignore.

Dipping his head, he licked her. A single long swipe up the perfect column and across her small pointed chin, ending at her lips, which were parted in an earthy moan and waiting for him. The contrast of that cool neck, with its faint tang of salt, and the candied depths of her mouth nearly drove him over the edge into blackest oblivion.

Another kiss. Deeper. Harder.

More.

No…not more. Look at her. Take a minute. Savor this.

He pulled away. She didn't make it easy, raising her head up off the arm of the sofa, where she'd settled, to pursue his mouth with the kind of shameless need he'd only dreamed of. But he took her arms at the elbows and held her back, ignoring her writhing.

"Wait." He tried to smile, but too much emotion was crammed into this moment. "Let me look at you."

She stopped resisting and lay back, stretching out, perfectly still but for the relentless heaving of her breasts. Equally breathless, he rose up over her and settled on his elbows and between her thighs, rubbing his erection against that soft spot there—right there—so she'd know what she did to him.

She knew. The sensual knowledge was there in what he could see of her shining eyes, which were half-closed and partially hidden by her hair in her face. With a shaking hand, he smoothed back that hair and stared, too grateful and overcome to say anything remotely coherent.

Her lips were swollen, her skin flushed. Beneath the soft stretchy cotton of her tank top and the cups of her bra, her nipples jutted out, too stiff with arousal to remain hidden. Her strong legs cradled him on either side, toned and sleek, possessive and determined. When he ran one hand down a thigh, she tightened them around his waist, pulling him closer. She wasn't letting him go. Which was good, because he wasn't going anywhere.

The need shuddered through him as he looked down at her.

He needed to tell her…something…but his vocabulary was too limited to find words big enough for this moment.

"You're beautiful," he said instead, helplessly.

A shadow, just a hint of one, flickered across her bright eyes.

What was this? She didn't doubt him, did she? Did she think anyone in the world was, or ever could be, as beautiful to him as she was?

Yeah, she did. Because he'd been unfaithful and she didn't trust him again. But she would.

Until that glorious day…now was not the time.

Goddamn it.

Rocking her hips, she opened her arms wide and beckoned him.

"Come here. Make love to me."

Make love to her.

This woman was going to kill him.

Opening his mouth, he tried to explain, to tell her they needed to wait, but the words wouldn't come when she was spread beneath him like a glorious banquet.

Tell her, Taylor. Before this goes any further. She'll understand.

Yeaaaaah. In a minute.

Leaning down, he kissed her again because he had to.

And there were a few more quick things on that to-do list.

He had to yank down the front of her top and her bra and let her full breasts bounce free for his gaze. He had to cup one in each hand and squeeze them together. He had to lower his hungry mouth to those plump nipples, which were hard and dark as blackberries, and suck each one into his mouth. Then he had to suck again, and again.

Jillian wrapped her arms around his head, thrusting those breasts up and keeping him close. So he stayed close. Until the rhythm of her surging hips matched that of his circling tongue and her moans echoed off the walls in a thrilling symphony.

Then he had to reach inside her shorts, search for that slick cleft he remembered so well, and see how wet she was.

Ah, God. Honey, hot and thick. So much honey, because she wanted him.

He stroked his fingers through it, lubricating her hard nub.

And then—and he really needed to win a Nobel Prize or some such for an unselfish act like this, especially when his blue balls would probably shrivel up and fall off before the night was through—he pulled his hand away from all that silken heat, without ever tasting it, and sat up, twisting away and letting the treasure in his arms go.

His bewildered body shut down immediately, turning to stone with all his frustrated lust. Clenching his fists, he rested his face on them, barely resisting the urge to pound his temples and hope the pain cleared his head.

His constricted throat wouldn't let him speak, so it took a minute to get his voice to work. When it did, it was hoarse, as though someone had taken a handful of shattered glass and run it over his vocal cords.

"Jillian. Baby. We can't do this now. You're not ready."

God. Was this a punishment for his past sins? Here he was being a noble SOB, doing the right thing, even though the right thing and what he desperately needed were complete opposites, and she wasn't even listening.

She had a glazed look in her eyes and her wet lips curled in a sensual smile that was almost as powerful an aphrodisiac as if she'd used those lips to take him into her mouth and suck.

And then it got worse.

Tightening her thighs around his middle to bring him back, she ran her hands over her bared breasts and then down to her sex, where they did things he couldn't bear to think about.

"You know I'm ready," she said.

He stared, dumbstruck and nearly destroyed by his lust, slowly suffocating with it.

Heh. Nice test, God.

Seeing her spread out this way was like taking the three-day bar exam again, followed by the medical licensing boards and a triathlon just for good measure.

Was he passing? Because it sure felt like he was dying.

Taking a deep breath, he tried again. "We can't. Not yet."

This, finally, seemed to pierce her sensual haze, and her color got even brighter, but with embarrassment this time, not passion. She blinked once, looked around, and landed back on earth with a thud that was almost audible.

"Oh, no." Shrinking in on herself, she yanked her clothes back in place—he almost tipped back his head and howled at the disappearance of those amazing breasts—bolted upright and scrambled as far away from him as she could get, which wasn't far. "I don't know what I was thinking."

She looked like she wanted to die of shame, all ducked head and flushed cheeks, and her lowered gaze didn't come anywhere near his. The sudden distance, when they'd just been all over each other, was way more than he could take.

They would not end their interlude together like this, with misunderstanding and hurt feelings.

"Don't, baby." Grabbing her hand—she tried to pull it away, but screw that—he pressed it to his heart, which was doing a remarkable job of pounding its way out of his chest. A jackhammer couldn't have done any better. "Feel that?"

It was the right thing to do. Some of the fight went out of her, and she flattened her hand beneath his, discovering the truth for herself. Desperate to maintain this connection between them, he scooted closer, until they were practically in each other's laps again, and rested his forehead against her temple.

Man, he was sweaty. Or was that her?

Neither one of them could stop panting. They sat together, trying to get a grip on their runaway lust, for several long seconds, and he couldn't say whose breath was more labored.

His, probably. Yeah—definitely his.

Did she understand? She had to understand.

Peeling her hands away from his chest, he pressed feverish kisses to them and lowered them to his groin, where he was still so hard, so unbelievably, freaking granite hard, that he was no doubt at serious risk of incurring permanent nerve and/or blood vessel damage down there.

"Feel that, Jill?"

Against his face, he felt her faint gasp and convulsive swallow. She cupped him, all on her own, and stroked him right to the edge of what promised to be an embarrassing explosion, not that he gave a damn about that at this moment.

"That's how much I want you." His hips gave an involuntary surge and he wondered how tacky it would be if he unzipped his pants just to give himself a little relief. "I'm dying here. I've never wanted anyone as much as I want you, and I never will. You have to know that."

With a small sound of distress, she tilted her head back and looked to the ceiling, probably praying for any kind of divine guidance she could get right now. After a harsh breath or two, she faced him head-on, and all he could see were her big baby browns, glittering with as much hurt confusion as heat.

"Then why?" she whispered.

Proud, wounded Jillian. He knew what it cost her to ask a question like that.

And he knew what it cost him to give an honest answer.

"Because." Man, he couldn't even look at her right now. Taking their hands, all wrapped together in a tight ball, he lifted them to his lips and struggled to say this right, to get something right, for once. "I've spent too much of my life mixing sex in with things that had nothing to do with sex."

There. That was a fresh piece of his soul, sliced up for her review. Risking a glance, he saw the slight puzzled frown between her eyes.

"I don't understand."

This was so hard. He didn't want to raise the subject of his infidelities, not now, when they'd made this much progress, but it needed to be dealt with.

"Those other women—" she stiffened against him, but he held on for dear life "—that was never about sex. That was about me needing a break from the pain. I needed to look in someone's eyes and see warmth and understanding rather than blame, and I was too stupid and afraid to figure out how to get that back with you."

Try as he might, he couldn't read her expression. But she let him hang on to her hands, so he supposed that was a good sign.

"And what is this about?"

Ah. Finally, an easy question. He was happy to answer this one.

"This is about finally getting it right and not clouding another issue in my life with sex. This is about rebuilding our relationship and making it stronger than it was before. This is about…"

Oh, come on, man. You've made it this far. Don't get choked up now. He cleared his throat to buy himself a little more time and then, when that didn't work, did it again. There. Now he could speak without sounding like a hormonal teenage boy.

"This is about me wanting to see you smile at me again as much as I want you wrapped around me naked. That's all. I want us to be happy, together. And I don't think we're there yet."

Well, he was right about that. Her face twisted and crumpled and she fought, and won, the battle for control. Which was good. But then she untangled her hands from his, which was bad. And she didn't pull any punches, which was worse.

"I'm broken," she said simply. "I'm not sure I can ever smile at you again. I'm not sure I want to."

Jesus, that hurt. He'd earned it, yeah, but it still felt like someone was using a machete to peel his flesh from his bones in long strips.

The fighting instinct was still there, raring to go, but maybe they'd come as far as they could tonight. Maybe he had to let this go. For now. And try to be a man about it.

"I understand." This was partially true. His brain? No problem. His heart? It just wanted her back, wanted her to forget all about the past and start again, right now. "And here's what you need to understand."

Cocking her head, she watched him with keen interest. "What?"

It took him a minute to put it all into words, to summarize what he'd learned about himself and where he wanted to be.

"I'm finished looking back. I'm finished with regret. I'm done beating myself up for stupid things I've done. I'm not going to spend the rest of my life the way the past several years have been. I've had enough misery. I'm done."

Her eyes widened.

"I'm doing everything I can—everything I can think of—to be a better man, Jill. Everything I can to be happy and find a little peace. That's what I want from my life."

He paused, not at all certain he had the balls to stick to this next part, but he was going to say it anyway.

"I'm changing, Jillian. I *have* changed. I'm not perfect and I never will be perfect, but I'm doing a hell of a lot better. Either that's good enough for you, or it's not. Either you want to work on us, or you don't. You want to live in the past, or you don't. You're done hurting, or you aren't. It's up to you. But I'm done wallowing in my guilt. You're the one who needs to decide what to do now."

Chapter 14

What was that *noise?*

Jillian rolled over, struggling to free herself from the tangled sheets.

The shrill chirp of the cell phone sounded again, startling her.

What the hell?

Wide-awake now and yet completely disoriented, she fumbled for the nightstand, where the stupid little thing was flashing red, helping her locate it. Fighting both the blankets and her groggy bewilderment, she sat up and looked at the clock.

Four-seventeen. In the morning. Shit.

"Hello?"

A woman's voice, abnormally chipper for anyone who wasn't a star on a children's program featuring oversized puppets, came on the line after a one-second delay.

"Please hold for the president."

"Oh, for God's sake," Jillian muttered, and hung up.

Idiot.

She'd just flipped her pillow to the cool side and resettled against its delicious fluffiness when the freaking phone rang again. And again. Cursing, the last of her sleepiness gone now, she snatched the phone up again and snarled into it.

"I am not holding for the president or anyone else, and I don't—"

"I really wish," said her older brother, John, the president of the United States, who also sounded revoltingly bright-eyed at this ungodly hour of the day, "that you wouldn't hang up on me every time I call."

"Well, first of all, stop having the stupid operator call me, okay? You're just showing off. You're not so important that you can't pick up your own cell phone and use your precious fingers to dial it yourself."

"I am pretty important now. I'm not sure you appreciate that as much as you should."

The laughter in his voice only irritated her more. It was way too early for him to be having this much fun at her expense.

"The second thing is, it's the crack of dawn, you idiot. Why don't you call at a reasonable hour?"

"It is a reasonable hour. If you're flying back from Tokyo, which I am."

"Well, I've barely gotten any sleep at all, and now I'll get none. Thanks a lot."

"You're welcome. Don't you think it's amazing how we can talk while I'm at thirty thousand feet, thousands of miles away from you? Listen to how clear the connection is."

She rolled her eyes at the ceiling. "You'll have to forgive me if I'm not as amazed as I was the first hundred and two times you called me from Air Force One. My amazement has waned, okay?"

"Fair enough."

"Why are you so cheerful? Are you happy because you're wearing your silly blue plane housecoat with your name embroidered on it?"

He sounded affronted. "It's not a housecoat. It's the commander-in-chief's jacket, which I only get to wear when I'm on the plane. It's very warm and comfortable—"

"How special."

"—but that's not why I'm so cheerful. Liza's having twins. That's why she's so big already."

Twins? This, finally, was worth waking up for.

"That's wonderful, John! I'm so thrilled for you! How's she feeling?"

"She's feeling *great.*"

Whoa. Those three words were filled with so much male satisfaction she could almost smell the smugness leaching through the phone. Man, he was funny, and she knew what this was about.

"Some women find that their sex drives go through the roof when they're pregnant." She clicked on the lamp and sat up. "Something about the raging hormones."

There was a low chuckle and she could visualize his Cheshire cat grin, clear as the lighted numbers on her new alarm clock.

"Really?" he said with forced nonchalance. "You don't say."

"Just let her rest now and then, okay?"

John snorted. "Why aren't you worried about her letting me rest?"

"Okay!" She started to cover her ears and realized she couldn't do that while on the phone. "La-la-la-la-la. I'm no longer listening to you. That's waaaay too much information for me. I'm sorry I even brought it up."

He laughed, a low rumble of delight that cheered her up as nothing had in a while. Maybe there was hope for happiness in the world even if her own life was currently a snarled mess.

"I'm happy for you, John."

"Thanks. What's new with you?"

Should she tell him what was new? Namely that Beau was back in a big way and she'd nearly made love to him a few hours ago? Yeaaah…no. Only if she wanted to kick off her own personal Armageddon. John put Beau in the same category as third-world dictators and terrorists, which meant that he'd be somewhat less than thrilled to hear her ex had made an unexpected reappearance in her life.

Best to just keep her big fat mouth shut.

"Beau's moved down the street and he wants me back," she blurted. "And I…still have feelings for him. I don't want to, but I do."

A ringing silence, louder than a gong's clap inside her ear, filled the line.

It was dumb to tell him, yeah, but she needed help here because she was drowning inside her own thoughts and emotions. Maybe John had some good advice for her.

She waited…and waited…and waited.

Finally she pulled the phone from her ear and checked it, just to make sure they hadn't been disconnected, but no, the tiny little clock display was still ticking the seconds by.

"John?"

More silence, and then, "I'm going to need a minute."

"You've had a minute." Man, he was really pissed; she could hear the anger vibrating in his voice. "Just spit it out."

"I'm trying to be supportive and not fly off the handle, Jillian—"

"I appreciate—"

"—but, that said—*are you out of your freaking mind?* Have you gone insane? Are you off your meds? Is that it? Or have you started taking drugs? That's the only thing that could explain this kind of—"

"This is you being supportive?"

"What the hell's gotten into you?" he roared.

Like she knew the answer to that crucial question. Please.

"I don't know," she said helplessly.

How could she explain Beau's ongoing pull over her and the way, when he touched her, she felt as though she'd finally gotten back that essential piece of herself she'd been missing for years? That she still got lost looking into his hazel eyes and found again when he slid his hands over her? That tonight, when he pushed her away, the frustrated need nearly ripped her in half?

"I'm sure I'm going to regret asking this." John paused long enough to expel an aggrieved sigh. "But is this about sex? If you need to have sex with him, just do that and move on. Exes do that all the time. It's part of the closure process, and it can take a while to tie up all your loose ends."

If only it were that simple.

If only she just wanted Beau's body, sweat-slicked and heavy, buried deep and thrusting inside her, over and over again for, oh, say, the next six months or so.

If only she didn't long to talk to him and share all the daily triumphs and traumas of raising a precocious little girl. If only she didn't wish she could ask him his opinion on the inn and whether she should expand it or update the Web site or change the drapes in the sitting room.

If only she didn't have the strong and growing feeling that

Beau really had changed for the better and was determined to keep changing.

"No," she told John. "It's not about sex. Well, it is, but that's not the main thing. We talked about…about Mary."

It still hurt to say the name, but just a little less this time.

"Oh." John's voice was full of sudden empathy. "Was that… okay?"

Okay? That was a funny word to describe some of the most painful conversations of her life and the surprising and world-altering discovery that what Beau had needed from her back then was shared grief and comfort.

"Yeah," she said. "It was okay."

More silence from John, bewildered this time, if she wasn't mistaken.

The confession refused to stay trapped in her hoarse throat. "I pushed him away when she died. I turned my grief inside."

John snorted. The sound was so derisive that she flinched away from the phone. "Wonderful. As long as no other tragedies strike your family, you and Beau should be good to go. Good luck with that."

"I'm not saying he's perfect now—"

"Well, thank God for that."

"—or even that I'm willing to take a chance on him again."

"Well, what the hell *are* you saying, then?"

Jillian struggled for that answer, her mouth flapping and useless. There was too much inside her, too much she didn't know how to process, and the way ahead was still so dark and scary that she would probably turn back.

But…maybe not.

"I'm saying that I feel hope. For the first time in a thousand years, I feel hope."

John sighed again. She could almost picture him scrubbing his hand over his face. "I'm sure I'm going to regret telling you this, but—"

Her entire body went on alert, desperate for any additional information that might help her figure out what to do with her life.

"—when Beau was campaigning for me early on, I met up with him in California."

Jillian's thudding heart wouldn't let her sit quietly. She got up and paced at the end of the bed. "Go on."

"I went to his hotel suite and he was…a mess. Drinking and… well, I don't need to give you all the gory details. He was a mess."

God, she couldn't breathe. "And?"

"And he asked for my advice. Said he felt like he didn't know you any more and you were drifting away from him. He thought you were angry with him about Mary as much as about the first affair, and I—"

"You what?"

John swallowed audibly. "I told him that was crazy. He wondered if I'd talk to you about going to counseling with him, and I told him that was crazy, too. I thought he was trying to get off the hook for his affair by blaming you. But now—I'm not so sure."

More of that awful hope crept into her heart, leading her down the garden path, no doubt. Along with that she felt anger because her brother had possessed this piece of her puzzle and never even told her.

"Why are you telling me this now?"

"Because. I've always known that Beau loves you as much as he's capable of loving anyone. The question is, how much is that?"

A lot.

Jillian's heart answered without hesitation.

Beau loves me as much as I could hope to be loved by anyone.

This was all so much to think about. Exhausted suddenly, she collapsed on the bed and flopped back onto the pillows. "What should I do?"

"You'll figure it out."

"I'm not sure I will."

"Trust me. In the meantime, I've got to go. I didn't call to offer my sound advice, you know. I called to wake you up and tell you we'll be down in a couple weeks for our weekend off. If you have a room for us."

"I think I can manage something."

"Happy Mother's Day, Jill."

Mother's Day. She'd almost forgotten. Allegra had a big day in store for her, and Jillian couldn't wait. "Thanks."

"Hi, baby!"

Jillian stepped to the edge of the porch and caught Allegra as she flew up the stairs and into her arms. Allegra submitted long enough for Jillian to get a whiff of unfamiliar shampoo and then drew back. With a gleaming smile of brightest sunshine, the girl smoothed her own hair and waited for Jillian's reaction.

"How do I look, Mommy?"

Jillian got a good look at her daughter and felt her jaw drop.

Whoa. Tricky question right off the bat. Allegra's tiara sat, crooked, atop hair that had been clumsily parted down the middle and then twisted into…were those braids? They were supposed to be braids, anyway. The ends were wrapped in plain old red rubber bands, the kind that were made for office use and would have the girl's hair tangled into an unmanageable snarl in another three minutes. Below that, she wore a bright green tutu over her fluttery yellow Easter dress and white patent-leather Mary Janes.

Tinker Bell on steroids pretty much covered the look, but an honest assessment was unthinkable. Jillian settled for a carefully worded half-truth.

"You look amazing."

Allegra laughed with delight, skipping away just as Seinfeld edged in. Taking advantage of Jillian's position down where he could reach her, he nudged her face with his and then, when she didn't move fast enough, gave her a quick lick on the cheek, which was wet, gross and smelled of chicken scraps. On the other hand, she'd had a rough night and would take affection where she could find it.

"You silly dog." Tipping her chin up and into the safe zone well away from his enthusiastic pink tongue, she scratched under his collar. "You're such a silly dog."

"Daddy did my hair," Allegra informed her.

Ah. That cleared up that nonmystery. The child's hair had either been done by a man or a blind, thumbless woman who didn't own a brush.

"That explains it," Jillian said.

Having exhausted all her best stalling tactics, there was nothing left to do but stand up straight and greet Beau, which was easier said than done since her heart was thumping loud enough to violate any local antinoise ordinances.

While she hadn't slept and felt like she'd been forced through a wood chipper, all brittle, antsy and discombobulated, he seemed to be doing…great. Looking well rested and more relaxed than he'd been since he arrived in town, he wore running shoes, shorts, a T-shirt and a Braves baseball cap that gave him the kind of casual appeal that made athletes so irresistible.

And make no mistake about it—he was still an athlete. His scarred leg had seen better days, of course, but as a set his legs were still muscled and powerful, and his toned arms and heavy shoulders, well…she wouldn't go there.

After giving him what she hoped was a discreet once-over but was probably a slack-jawed leer, she tried to focus on his eyes. This was a mistake. He looked virile and intent, as though he'd been infused with the energy and desire to run out and conquer the world and wanted to start right here, with her.

And then he wanted to swallow her. Not whole, but savoring one piece for hours at a time. It was all there in the banked heat, and the way that hazel gaze skated over her body with a deepening of color until it became an earthy forest-green.

She'd worn her sexiest and most cleavage-baring sundress just so she'd see that exact look in his eyes, and it was well worth it. Ice-blue with a scoop in front and crossed straps in back, it highlighted a good fifty percent of her brown skin, much to his subtle pleasure.

"Good morning," he said with an easy smile.

There it was: Greeting 101. Perfectly functional, nothing fancy.

And yet it was infused with so much meaning that her head spun with the possibilities. He didn't look smug. He looked happy, as though the weight of the world was off his shoulders at long last.

As though anything was possible.

Maybe anything was.

"Hi."

He stared at her, his smile fading away to a deepening of his dimples that was somehow an even more devastating test of her nerves and strength.

Her own face, meanwhile, was doing strange things. Her cheeks burned, and she realized, with a jolt, that she wanted to smile back but was fighting the urge.

It felt unnatural, denying him. Or maybe she was only denying herself.

Flustered, she turned back to Allegra, who was twirling on her tiptoes, dancing to a tuneless song that she hummed under her breath.

"How long did it take you to manage that hairstyle?" Jillian asked.

He laughed. God, he had a beautiful laugh. And she'd missed it with the phantom ache she imagined she'd feel if she lost her right hand.

"With Allegra rolling around on the floor with Seinfeld? About two hours."

There was that urge again, to laugh with him and commiserate.

As though he knew she was all tied up in knots, he rescued her by calling to Allegra. "Are you going to give Mommy her present?"

Present?

It'd barely registered because she'd been so focused on Beau.

"Yes." Allegra bounced over in a remarkable imitation of Bambi frolicking in the woods, and grabbed at the box Beau held—a round hatbox in a beautiful blue floral pattern wrapped with satin ribbons. "Let me have it, Daddy. I can do it."

"No, you can't." Beau gave the girl an indulgent grin as he lowered the box to the porch swing and waved for Jillian to sit down. "This box is bigger than you are."

Allegra shot him a glaring pout and scrambled onto the swing next to Jillian with a flash of her pink My Little Pony panties.

"Open it, Mommy. Open it!"

The one-second wait proved to be too much for the girl, who reached for the ribbon and tugged it. Jillian started to push her little hands away—whose present was this, anyway?—but then she noticed that Beau was leaving with Seinfeld.

Jillian's heart lurched. "Where are you going?"

Stupid, Jill. Stupid, stupid, stupid. Way to wear your heart on your sleeve.

But Beau didn't seem to make anything of it and shrugged as he gathered the dog's leash in his free hand. "I'll let you ladies enjoy your Mother's Day in peace. We're going for a long walk and then I'm going to work in the backyard a little."

"Oh." Jillian, who'd had vague and half-formulated plans of inviting Beau to stay for the Mother's Day brunch extravaganza, which was, even now, in full swing on the back porch, tried to keep her expression indifferent. "Well...don't strain your leg too much."

"I won't. I took some Tylenol and it's feeling pretty good."

What? He took some meds? Was that why he looked so good today?

What did this all *mean?*

She watched while he smiled up at the sky for no apparent reason, breathing deep. Then he gave her a look that was as pointed as his next sentence.

"I think it's going to be a beautiful day, Jill. Don't you?"

It already was a beautiful day, not that she could bring herself to agree with him on this point. They both knew they weren't talking about the day at all, but the birth of a new era between them. An era that was here whether she admitted it or not.

He left without waiting for an answer. She watched him go, the dog ambling at his side, and fought against the *Come back, Beau!* that was right on the tip of her tongue.

And then it hit her.

God, she was sick of herself. She was up, she was down, she was back, she was forth, and she couldn't decide where she wanted to be and muster the courage to get herself there. She gave new meaning to the word *pathetic*.

"Open it, Mommy! Open it!"

Allegra had worked off all the ribbons and had the hatbox lid more than halfway up already. Trying to get back in the game, Jillian took over the box-opening duties and got the surprise of her life.

A kitten with a blingy blue rhinestone bell collar poked her head out and looked around.

Oh my God.

It was a beautiful Siamese, just like Ramona, her childhood pet, all white fluffiness with enormous blue eyes, pointy gray ears and a blackish muzzle that looked like she'd smudged her face in some fireplace ash.

They blinked at each other for one arrested moment, and then the kitten meowed, a long, whiny sound that spoke of much suffering inside the box, the desire to bounce and play in the grass and, probably, the need for a fish treat of some sort.

If there was anything more adorable on the planet, Jillian doubted that she'd ever live long enough to discover it.

"Hi, kitty." The creature, who couldn't have been more than three months old at the outside, was a squirmy fit for Jillian's hands as she raised her up for a better look. Gorgeous. She had bright eyes the color of the glowing gas flame on her stovetop, and Jillian fell utterly and completely in love with her.

Before Jillian could press a kiss to her fuzzy little forehead, however, Miss Attitude meowed again and swiped Jillian across the nose with one black-tipped paw.

And Jillian laughed with a belly-deep delight she hadn't known she could still feel. Leaning her head back and pointing her toes to get the swing going, Jillian held the kitten high over her head and nuzzled her soft fuzziness despite the kitten's obvious and growing displeasure. The little thing made a sound that was much more squealing disgust than meow, and Jillian laughed again. She couldn't stop the laughter even if she wanted to, which she didn't. It came and came and came, an endless bubbling wellspring from inside her chest that would no longer be denied.

Next to her, Allegra was bouncing and clapping, thrilled that her present had gone over so well. "Do you like her, Mommy? Isn't she cute? What's her name, Mommy? What should we call her?"

Jillian didn't know and she couldn't think about it now because she only had eyes for Beau, who'd obviously remembered her Ramona stories from a thousand years ago.

Halfway to the street now, he stopped and turned, drawn, she knew, by the commotion and the rusty sound of her laughter, which was rarer than a Diana Ross and the Supremes reunion concert. As though in suspended animation, he watched her over his shoulder, his lips parted in surprise.

For the first time in years, she didn't look away. She didn't punish him with the killing, aloof glare that she'd perfected, nor did she deny him what he said he wanted most. To her astonishment, she no longer felt the need. This was, after all, a beautiful day, and she could smile about it.

She could smile at him. She *wanted* to smile at him.

"Thank you." It was a blanket acknowledgment for the kitten, the cathartic lifting of that terrible burden between them and this thrilling feeling of hope, of the possibility of happiness. "Thank you."

He took a moment to come back to life, and when he did, it was with a devastated twist of his face, quickly hidden. He looked away and looked back just as quickly, with a swift, heaving breath in between, and she saw the jerky bob of his Adam's apple as he swallowed back his emotion.

They stared at each other, words unnecessary.

At last his eyes lit up and a corner of his mouth curled, but this time he was the one who couldn't manage a full smile.

It was okay, though. She understood.

"You're welcome." He swallowed again, trying without much success to clear his voice. "It was my pleasure."

Chapter 15

When Beau didn't answer the front door, Jillian figured he was around back.

She also figured maybe she should turn herself around and return to the B & B, where she belonged, and where Barbara Jean was currently putting Allegra to bed, but she couldn't force her body to walk in that direction.

Instead, she kept to the stone path skirting the front of the spotlit house and took a moment to enjoy Beau's handiwork, a springtime wonderland of glorious flowers and shrubs. Everything beautiful was here, planted by his hands this very day, and she should know because she'd peeked out her window to watch him about, oh, seven or eight thousand times.

Forsythia in the same fierce yellow as the edges of today's sunset, potted impatiens in hot-pink and white, peach and red. Coleus and elephant ears, hostas, black-eyed Susans and fragrant lavender and Russian sage. The path, which had footlights to guide her, wound around, past the right wing of the U-shaped house, and slipped through the open door of the decorative wrought-iron gate that protected the courtyard.

"Oh," she breathed, the sound lost to the gentle splash of water.

It was fabulous, the kind of hidden paradise that reminded her of her occasional visits to the old homes of Savannah. In the middle stood a large fountain with a beautifully sculpted figure. It was, Jillian realized, stunned, a smiling mother. She wore a draped gown that clung to her curves and balanced a pigtailed daughter on one hip. With her free hand, she poured water from a jug, nourishing the profusion of marble flowers at her bare feet.

Though the figures looked nothing like Jillian or Allegra, the symbolism was unmistakable and breathtaking.

The perimeter of the courtyard held more potted flowers and ferns, palms and shrubs she didn't recognize, all fragrant on the warm night breeze. There were wrought-iron benches and tables, chairs and footstools, and the French doors leading into the living room were open, letting out the strains of Frank Sinatra crooning about doing things his way.

And there was Beau. Stretched out on a lounge chair facing the fountain, with a drowsing Seinfeld draped over his calves.

Jillian's heart kicked into overdrive, and the pulse at the base of her throat pounded with nerves and excitement. She crept closer, her hands tightening reflexively on the handles of the heavy picnic basket she'd brought with her, and wondered what she would say.

Another visit to Beau's house, another basket, more food.

She prayed this visit would be significantly less disastrous than the first.

Her sandal scuffed on an uneven stone. The tiny sound made Seinfeld raise his head, look around, ears perked, and meet her gaze with a low woof. Beau turned his head, following the dog's line of sight, and saw her.

They both stilled, except that Beau's eyes widened with surprise and his lips parted with an *oh* she couldn't hear.

The arrested moment between them lengthened, lasting well past the time that Seinfeld yawned, stretched and ambled over to nuzzle Jillian's elbow.

She didn't have eyes for the dog. Only Beau.

With a slow unfurling of his big body, he got to his feet and kept one hand on the back of the lounge chair for balance. He'd apparently showered and changed after his long day of yard work, and he now wore a pristine white T-shirt and dark shorts, the perfect clothing to highlight a god's perfection—if he had to wear clothes at all, that was.

His shoulders were wide, his defined torso rippling and sleek through the thin cotton, his endless legs powerful despite the jagged scar that ran from thigh to calf on one side. His skin gleamed and his eyes glittered in an unrelenting stare that held her right where she was, suspended in this hidden world of incredible beauty and possibility.

She waited, but Beau wasn't ready to speak yet. Neither was she.

The breeze brought her a knee-weakening whiff of his subtle deodorant, which was something fresh and sporty, and her body remembered that scent and tightened accordingly.

She wished, in a secret, shameful part of her brain, that he would do something to take all decision making out of her hands, but she knew he wouldn't. Then she wished she'd drunk a frozen margarita or six and had an excuse, something to point to later that would relieve her of all culpability for anything that might happen between them, but she was dry as a Prohibition-era tavern.

This was all up to her and there could be no excuses tomorrow, no backtracking.

"Hi," she said.

"Hi."

God, his voice. It was deep and quiet, nothing that could be heard from more than ten feet away, and yet it surrounded and echoed through her, affecting her as strongly as fingers trailing down her spine or the gentle press of lips in the bend of her elbow.

"I brought you some dinner."

"I see that."

No, he didn't. Those intent eyes saw her bare shoulders and the plump valley between her breasts. They saw her hips and her fluttering skirt, which revealed hints of her thighs as the breeze swirled around her. They saw her hair trailing across her face and the subtle heave of her chest as she tried to get air.

Beau didn't care about any basket, or any food.

"I figured you hadn't eaten much, and after all that work in the yard..."

She trailed off, well aware both that she was in danger of babbling and that Beau would soon run out of patience with her. Still, he played along, and they glanced at the small side table, where Seinfeld was now sniffing hopefully at a bowl sitting next to a half-full glass of what looked like iced tea.

"Chicken noodle?" she wondered.

"Chicken noodle."

She wanted to laugh but couldn't manage a smile. "Some things don't change."

"Some things don't change at all."

Were they still talking about food preferences? Did it matter? Nothing was sure in her world anymore, and that didn't matter right now, either.

Beau took a step closer and held out a hand for the basket. She took a step closer and extended the handle to him. He took it and pulled. Gently…gently…exerting just enough force to reel her in until they were face-to-face and she had to tilt her chin up to maintain eye contact.

Then he tugged the basket out of her hand and stooped to put it on the table. It took him a long time to straighten up again, long, slow seconds during which she could almost imagine that his nose skimmed the folds of her skirt, absorbing her scent. When finally he stretched to his full height, he was a scant inch away and his body flamed with a heat she could feel through her clothes.

Heavy lidded, she stared at him, not daring to breathe.

Taking his time about it, he settled his fingers at her temple and then slid them through her hair like a rower's oars gliding through water. She sighed, a tiny whisper of emotion that turned into a gasp as his fingers emerged from her hair only to trace down the side of her neck, across her collarbones and lower.

"You came to bring me dinner?"

His breath was honey-sweet from the tea, as delectable as a box of milk chocolates chased down with champagne.

"Yes."

"I think," he said, his hands now skating over her breasts, his thumbs unerringly centering on her nipples and circling with an increased pressure that was as unbearably sweet as it was electrifying, "that you came to tell me what you told me when I was in the hospital and you thought I couldn't hear you." He paused, letting her heart skitter with fear because she'd known it would come to this and she'd marched over here anyway, helpless to choose another fate. "Didn't you?"

"No." She tried to sound strong, but her voice was a scratchy mess of nerves.

"No?"

"No."

"Hmm."

A slight frown made his brows flatten, but it didn't slow his hands down any. Still on their relentless circuit of her body, they settled low, one each on the globes of her butt, and pulled her up against a full and heart-stopping erection that was so hard she didn't know how he had enough blood remaining in his head to talk.

Oh, God. The pleasure was so unspeakably sweet and he hit the ache between her thighs just right with his circling hips. Just right.

Helpless to do otherwise, she held tight to his heavy forearms so she wouldn't collapse, let her head drift back and moaned, low and earthy. When he licked across her lower lip and into her mouth, she opened for him and moaned again, from her chest this time, and her soul.

Ah, God. He tasted so good…so unbelievably good, like tea and Beau and, better than that, like home. She had to get closer and pour herself into him any way she could, any possible way. But when she arched closer, brushing her swollen breasts against the solid wall of his chest and her sensitized lips over the thrilling stubble of his cheeks, he pulled back.

Just a little, but way too much.

His hands went to work on the back of her skirt, bunching it up, inch by slow inch, exposing her to the night air until only her black tap pants stood between her and the paradise she needed him to give her.

His lips rubbed their way across her face to her ear, but she was much more concerned about his fingers edging under her panties, to the throbbing wet folds that desperately needed his attention. And then he spoke, bringing her back to the reality she couldn't escape.

"I think you're still scared," he whispered.

She didn't know how he did it, but those words went directly to her damaged heart, making one more place in her body ache for him.

"No."

"Don't be scared." He nipped her lobe, just sharp enough to make her cry out, and then sucked the tender flesh into his mouth to soothe it. "Don't be scared."

"I'm not."

Man. The lies that came out of her mouth were really unbelievable.

There'd be hell to pay in a minute, no doubt, but right now he had better things to do than punish her. Freeing up one hand while keeping the other at work between her legs, sending her higher and higher, he planted it on the top of her head, tilted it back, and kissed her again, long and deep until she began making uncontrollable sounds of animalistic pleasure that were like nothing she'd ever heard before. She writhed against his fingers, and when he slipped them inside her overheated body she rode him without embarrassment, too overwrought to work up any shame.

He broke the kiss off to look at her. There was so much love in his eyes, so much tenderness, that it nearly blinded her to see it.

"Beau."

What she thought she was trying to say to him in that moment, she had no idea.

Nothing. Everything.

If only she knew where to begin.

"Don't be afraid, Jillian. Okay?"

She wavered, teetering between hugging her doubts closer and absolute surrender to this moment, and he drifted forward to take advantage. Nuzzling her lips and alternating between licks and nipping bites that sharpened the pleasure a million times over, he kept stroking between her legs until they were both wet with honey and she felt it on her thighs, slick and hot.

A wicked smile gleamed in his eyes. Naturally, he knew what he was doing to her. "You remember this between us, don't you?"

Remember? As if she could forget in a million lifetimes.

"I remember."

"Good." His lids lowered into such a look of sultry promise that her breath stopped dead. "This is going to be better. We're better."

She managed the beginnings of a smile and a shaky nod. Ninety-five percent of her believed him, and wasn't that enough? "We are better."

"I want to make love."

"God, so do I. I'm shaking with it."

That was putting it mildly. A quivering tremble had begun in the depths of her belly and quickly spread to her heavy limbs. She felt languid and agitated, petrified and ecstatic, the same and yet fresh and clean as a newborn blinking up at the world for the first time.

Beau felt exactly the same beneath her hands—the silky-coarse hair, the sleek skin, the restrained power in his tense body—and yet he felt…more. More intense, more determined and more of a man than he'd ever been before. And she wanted this new Beau in a way she'd never wanted anything.

"Now," she whispered against his mouth, panting, kissing and biting, melting down in his arms with the sheer effort of holding back her climax because she wanted him inside her when she came. *"Now."*

"Not yet." Maintaining a rigid control that tightened his muscles until he felt like marble vibrating against her, he shifted his one hand. Now it assaulted her from behind with a slow stroking torture that crept between the halves of her butt and through her wet cleft and up…up…up…just grazing her engorged clitoris before retreating to assault her again. "Tell me what you said at the hospital."

Another feathering touch had her knees buckling.

"Ahhh," she cried, her head falling back. "Beau, please—"

"You love me?"

That murmuring voice, raspy, low and hot against her lips, was as much a torment to her overwhelmed body as anything else. She wasn't ready to admit anything, not yet, but the clenching muscles inside her tightened another notch.

In that one second, the swirling sensations surrounding

her receded enough for one crucial truth to become perfectly clear:

If she didn't come right now, she would die—and he wouldn't let her come until she confessed what they both already knew.

"Do you love me?"

Those fingers hovered a fraction of an inch from where she needed them to be.

"Yes."

His chest heaved with a startled gasp of surprise, and he kissed her, long and hard until she tasted all his gratitude and his overwhelming relief.

"Tell me, Jillian. Tell me."

With his strong body loving and protecting her and his adoring eyes watching her, she couldn't be afraid. Not here. Not now. Not anymore.

"I love you. I never stopped loving you. I couldn't even when I wanted to."

There was another great contraction of his torso and he made a choked sound. Whether it was a laugh or a sob, she didn't know. And then he tilted his head back for a quick glance up at the starless sky.

"Thank you, Jesus."

He took her mouth again with a greedy sucking kiss, ran his fingers over her hard nub and then thrust them inside her, catching her by surprise.

She came with a violent jackknifing of her body and astonished cries that echoed off the courtyard's stones. Seinfeld, who was somewhere nearby, emitted a *What the hell's going on?* kind of whine that she barely heard.

The piercing pleasure washed over her in pulsing waves that crested and rose again, on and on for what seemed like forever.

Something happened then. She may have crumpled, or maybe he picked her up. She never knew. But suddenly he was carrying her in his arms, her face pressed to his neck, and then swinging her around and settling her onto the nearest chaise.

His face dark with purpose, he went to work on her clothes.

Chapter 16

Melting into the cushions, she had a dazed awareness of him sliding his hands under her skirt to relieve her of her panties, and she lifted her hips to help him. He tossed the panties aside and yanked his own T-shirt off. Then he sat on the edge of the chaise and stared down at her.

She was bared to the waist, the vibrant night air cool against her legs and excruciatingly intimate against her sex. He studied her with utter absorption, his gaze focused on the nest of curls and the still-quivering flesh. Unsatisfied, he reached up to pull the bodice of her dress lower until her aching breasts bounced free. A breeze swept through just then, puckering her dark nipples down to jutting points.

Over the water's gentle splash came the sound of his harsh sigh, which was awed and utterly masculine. "Look at you, Jill."

When his naked torso gleamed, rippling and golden, in the moonlight? And his erection strained for her, tenting the front of his shorts with an insistence that made need curl deep in her belly all over again? She didn't think so.

"I'd rather look at you."

He grinned and their gazes met.

"I'm sorry," she said.

"For what? Making me the happiest man on the face of the earth?"

Flushing and feeling more feminine than she had in her life, she shifted so she could prop her chin on one hand and stroke his heavy length with the other.

"No, silly. For coming too soon."

He groaned and thrust his hips, developing a rhythm that

had him growing longer, harder. She tightened her grip and he groaned again.

"There's no such thing."

"I wanted all this inside me," she murmured, pouting.

"Don't worry."

Breaking free as though he'd slammed headfirst into his limit, he got to his feet and turned toward the open French doors with a last glance at her. His gaze lingered, savoring her breasts and bare body south of her bunched-up skirt.

"Don't move," he said.

"Don't worry."

Raising her hands overhead to rest them on the back of the chaise, she sprawled, feeling deliciously like Cleopatra. He cursed and disappeared. In less than ten seconds, he was back, his limp almost undetectable and a red package in his hand.

That flash of red troubled her, and he seemed to know it because he worked it on while watching her with turbulent eyes. As a married couple, they'd rarely used condoms, and she'd had no other lovers. But he…

"Don't think about that, Jill," he said, crawling over her to wedge her thighs farther apart and settle between her legs. Balancing on his elbows, he spoke with the kind of ferocity and conviction she'd never seen before. "None of that was ever important. You're important." Taking his penis, he rubbed it across her thick flesh, lubricating himself, and she cocked her hips to take him in. "You're everything. You're everything."

He penetrated her just a little, which was all she could take because it had been so long, and he held himself in such rigid check that a light sheen of sweat broke out across his forehead.

"God," he said.

"I know."

Killing her by degrees, he worked another inch inside, and then drew out just as slowly. Another inch…another withdrawal… and another…until her muscles eased, her eyes rolled closed and her body moved on its own and rose up to meet him.

Testing them both, he withdrew to his engorged tip, swiveled his hips just a little and then thrust. She cried out, her voice surprised and raw, and her eyes flew open to discover that her dream had finally come to life.

Beau rising over her, muscles bunched and neck straining, sweat glistening on his chest as it rubbed against her breasts, his eyes wild and fierce with determination. Everything she'd dreamed, and more.

Digging her short nails into his heavy shoulders, she scratched down his back and grabbed his butt as he flexed and released. Those perfect globes pumped beneath her hands, and he settled into a hard, driving rhythm that had the pleasure building again, darker and more primitive this time, and stars sparking across her vision.

She drew her legs into her chest, taking him deeper, and he faltered, losing his tempo as he gave himself over to pure sensation.

"Jillian," he said as his head dropped.

Before the oblivion took her, she felt a moment's savage satisfaction and a ruthless determination to make this a night he would never forget. Beau needed to know who she was and what she could do to him.

"Jillian," he said again, a whimper. *"Jillian."*

Tightening her thighs around his torso, she worked him harder, demanding more and then more again. "Harder."

"Jill—"

"Harder," she urged. "Now. Hurry."

He knew what she was doing. She could see it in his face. Staring down at her, his features a dark kaleidoscope of emotions, he gave her what she needed, physically and emotionally.

Driving into her with all he was worth, he matched the beat of his words with the thrust of his hips. "You're everything, Jill. Everything. *Everything.*"

She almost believed him.

His chanted *everythings* went on until the darkness claimed them both, and her cries, joyous and triumphant, drowned out the sound of his voice.

The night was so balmy and beautiful, the splash of water so peaceful and relaxing, that they saw no need to go inside, to bed.

Maybe later. Right now, they spooned together on the chaise, her back to his front, while he enjoyed the silky slide of her dress and the silkier glide of her bare skin against his, and tried to convince himself that this was real. That it wasn't impossible or, hell, illegal, for him to be this happy with life.

Having never felt this way before, he feared the imminent arrival of a speeding bus or a lightning bolt with his name on it. If that was his fate, he almost didn't care. At least he'd die having made love to this amazing woman one more time.

He couldn't seem to stop rubbing, stroking, caressing, squeezing and otherwise touching her every way he could. Every inch of Jillian was endlessly fascinating to him, from her sweet-smelling hair, which tickled his chin, to her exposed breasts, which weighed heavy in his hands, as plump and ripe as he'd remembered them, to her thighs, which were strong, lean and perfect for anchoring him inside her.

Yeah.

Life was good.

Loud smacking pierced his sensual haze, and he looked around, raising his head just high enough to see Jillian slip Seinfeld some cheese from the picnic basket. They'd cracked it open and enjoyed the best cheeses and crusty bread, meat-loaf sandwiches, pasta salad and fat fudgy brownies that he'd ever tasted, all washed down with sparkling cider since he no longer drank.

Now Jillian was sneaking remnants to the dumb dog, who looked every bit as thoroughly sated and pleased with her as Beau was. He pretended he didn't know what was going on for a few seconds, but then his pet-ownership gene kicked in.

"You know," he said, smoothing her hair back and kissing her temple, "you're not supposed to feed table food to dogs."

"Really?" Amusement oozed from her voice. "What if it's low fat?"

"Nope. It's not healthy and it spoils them."

"Ah, but he's not my dog. I can spoil him and then go home and leave you to explain why he's getting Alpo for his next meal."

"Don't even try it."

Wondering if a few more things had stayed the same over the years, he bit her on the shoulder and then, holding her tighter, tickled her ribs.

Bull's-eye.

Her whole body spasmed, and she laughed a belly-deep laugh that was the earthiest music he'd ever heard. When she squirmed to get away, he slid his hands onto her breasts, flattened his palms against those tight nipples and circled. Just for good measure, he latched his lips onto the sensitive tendon between her neck and shoulder and bit.

Another bull's-eye. Like magic, she loosened in his arms, as fluid and hot as molten lava trailing down the side of a Hawaiian volcano.

And then she made a move herself, grinding her butt against his erection and twisting her neck to kiss him. God. She undid him, this woman did.

Always had, always would.

Needing more, again, needing everything, he reached for the throbbing heat between her legs just for the thrill of hearing her gasp. She broke the kiss and arched, her face twisted with agonized pleasure.

Before they got sidetracked, though, and, make no mistake, there would be some serious sidetracking before the night was over, it was a good time to mention some things she needed to know.

Returning his hands to her breasts, he spoke against her ear. "Seinfeld is your dog, Jill. This is your home. Everything I have is yours."

She stilled, her unspoken uncertainty as clear as the moon overhead. Then she turned to face him and, with a sly smile that did nothing to hide the wariness in her eyes, reached for his rock-hard length, which he'd foolishly encased back in his shorts.

"This?"

Don't do that, Jill. Don't make something so serious and absolute into a moment for teasing. He stared with all the bottled intensity he was feeling and watched her eyes widen.

"Yeah, actually." As her smile faded, he guided her hand and pressed it to his heart. It was, predictably, pounding like a rap concert, so there was little chance of her not getting the message. "And this. Understand?"

After a slight hesitation, she blinked and risked the beginnings of a smile. And that was enough, for now.

Baby steps, Taylor, he reminded himself. Just take baby steps.

They twined their legs and settled together with his erection cradled in her sweet spot. God, she was soft. Unsatisfied, he slid a hand down to her thigh and brought it up, higher, until it was snug against his hip and there were no parts of them that weren't fitted together like the dovetails of a finely made antique cabinet.

"I'm worried about your leg," she said, even as she tightened her grip on him. "I don't want to hurt you."

He raised an eyebrow. "Do I look hurt?"

A sudden burst of laughter had her head tipping back and his lungs struggling for air. She was so freaking amazing he just couldn't get over it.

"I was scared," he told her, cupping her face and running his thumb over the happy apples of her cheek, "that you'd never smile at me again."

"You were wrong, weren't you?"

He snorted. "I'm good at being wrong. It's a cottage industry with me."

"Ah, well. It gives you something to work on, doesn't it?"

A second or two passed while he stared at her, considering. Maybe now wasn't the time, but they needed to get some of these things out from between them. Forever.

She sensed his new seriousness, and her features clouded over. "What?"

"Can I tell you something?"

It took her a while to answer. "Do you need to?"

"Yes."

There it was, that subtle bracing of her shoulders and darkening of her features. He knew those gestures so well because he'd taught them to her. He'd taught her to be afraid, and to fear the worst, and, God, he was sorry to the depths of his soul for it.

"The women—" he began.

She flinched, resisting him, and he tightened his hold and ran his hand over her thigh, soothing her.

"The women—during the marriage and after—they all looked like you. They all reminded me of you. I got drunk when I was with them and usually wished I were drunker. I tried not to look at them too hard because then I would see—"

The emotion rose up to strangle him, and he had to clear his voice.

"—then I would see that they weren't you." He paused, wondering how much to confess, but what the hell. He'd come this far. "The night of the accident, I was with this woman in the limo. I barely knew her. I didn't want to know her. And I was so disgusted with myself that I could almost vomit. And that's how I felt all the time. But I didn't know how to get out of the nightmare."

The shadows had taken over her expression now. "Did you ever think about…hurting yourself?"

He paused, hating to tell her.

"I'm not going to lie, Jill. I was relieved when I saw that semi coming, and I was sick when I woke up in the hospital, alone, and realized I was still alive. What you said to me when I was out of it—that you still loved me—that was the only thing that kept me going. Because I decided that if I had a second chance—with life, and with you—I wanted to do the work. I wanted to deserve it."

"You do deserve it."

The sudden ferocity in her voice stopped him cold, and that was before she grabbed his face and pressed kisses all over it. Both eyes first, forehead and cheeks and then, finally, his mouth. She poured herself into him, and he thought that maybe everything they'd endured to get to this point was worth it.

"Don't you hurt yourself, Beau. Ever. Do you understand me?"

He understood the hard glitter in her eyes, all right. "Yeah."

They needed each other now. Nothing else. Pausing only long enough to reach over the side of the chaise and pick up another condom, he struggled out of his shorts and worked it on.

They were still facing each other. Widening her thighs with

much eager help from her, he took his engorged length—God, he was going to explode in another second here—and slid inside all that tight heat with her breathless gasps to spur him on. She was looser this time, but not much, and the delicious friction nearly blinded him.

Once he was seated to the base, he drew her closer until they formed one seamless whole from chest to toes. And then he nuzzled her mouth with shallow kisses and the kinds of feather-light licks of his tongue that had always driven her wild.

Still did, apparently.

As he set the slow pace, her cries rose up to the night sky.

Chapter 17

"What's this room?" Jillian asked.

It'd gotten too cool for sleeping outside on the chaise, not that they were likely to get much sleeping done anyway under the circumstances, so Jillian had asked him to show her the house, which she'd been dying to see.

Thought it was still a work in progress, with stepladders, drop cloths and sawhorses every few feet, the place was well on its way back to being a gorgeous home after years of neglect.

"Remains to be seen." Beau hesitated, shoving his hands into his shorts pockets and staring at his bare feet. "I was thinking—"

Looking up, he shrugged and worked at a nonchalant smile that never gained strength. And was he blushing? Not that she could tell in this light, of course, but still. After the night they'd had together?

"Tell me," she said.

"I was thinking…maybe it could be a nursery, if we have more children."

That was the last thing she'd expected—she'd been thinking game room—and the room swayed accordingly.

Whoa.

Breathe, Jill. Don't freak out now.

That was easier said than done, considering that the ch-word was a hard slap of reality in what had otherwise been a fantasy night. She stared into his intent eyes, trying to think, but…no. She couldn't think. She could only feel, and the thought of trying to have more children with Beau felt like the panicked slamming of a speeding Porsche into the Great Wall of China.

No. God, no. And also…yes. *"Children?"*

Already his brows were lowering, and he looked as though he wanted to take it back. "Children. Little humans with continence issues."

"I'm old," she reminded him.

"Not that old."

"I've had several miscarriages—"

"And a healthy child."

"—and a stillborn child. Have you forgotten?"

"Jill," he said.

God. She hated that reproach in his voice. How dare he make her feel guilty for pointing out a few details that should be obvious to anyone with even half a functioning brain?

She turned away, wishing the walls would back up a little and stop closing in on her.

"Don't you want any more children?" He seemed genuinely bewildered. "Is that it?"

Not want any more high-maintenance divas like Allegra, sweet angels like Mary or—she hardly dared to think of it—hazel-eyed, curly haired boys like Beau? The possibility made her insides clench with the worst kind of need.

"That's not the point. The point is that it took a lot of tragedy for me to produce one healthy child. And besides that—we're not even married. I'd never have a child out of wedlock. I'm surprised you'd even suggest—"

He raised one eyebrow and settled into the kind of terrible stillness that made her squirm every time. "Is that what you think I'm suggesting?"

Marriage? He wanted to talk marriage *tonight?*

The walls continued their relentless advance, blocking off the room's air and leaving her with none. That familiar feeling of naked vulnerability swept her up, and she tugged the bodice of her now-crumpled dress up a little higher, even though it felt like she was about to suffocate.

When that provided no protection, she folded her arms and tried to use sarcasm to get this night back on track. "Having sex doesn't cure everything between us, Beau."

The darkness didn't disguise the wounded look in his eyes, or the subtle slump to his shoulders, as though he'd absorbed a blow.

"No, but making love and admitting that we still love each other is a pretty big push in the right direction, don't you think?"

Yeah.

She just hadn't figured it'd still be so scary.

The rising fear made her go on the offensive. "What? Did you think we'd head off to the justice of the peace in the morning?"

"No." He smiled ruefully. "Things with us would never be that easy."

She stared, absorbing the implication that he'd fire up the car right now if she only gave the word. "How can you be so sure?"

Another smile, this one so sad and beautiful it was almost blinding. "If there's one thing I've ever been sure about, it's spending my life with you. It's everything else that causes problems."

Why was this so hard to hear? It wasn't as if he'd kept his intentions a secret; he'd told her the day he arrived that he wanted them to remarry.

And—she had to admit it to herself, if not to him—she wanted it, too.

In her entire life, she'd never loved a man the way she loved Beau, and she never would. When she'd said *I do,* she'd meant it—forever. If she had a magic wand to wave or a bottled genie, remarriage and rebuilding their family was what she'd wish for, no question.

But this was no fairy tale, and she and Beau were two seriously flawed human beings.

And, God, she still couldn't breathe.

She circled her throat with her hand, trying to massage her heart into slowing down and her airway into opening. Now was not the time for a panic attack.

"We've been apart for years, Beau."

"I know."

"We've changed."

"I know that, too."

"We can't…we can't just—"

Thinking and talking were getting pretty hard what with the

severe lack of air and all, and her hand slipped to her now-heaving ribs. Brilliant, Jill. That wasn't obvious at all.

"We can't just pick up where we left off and—"

"I know we—" He materialized at her side with a sudden burst of movement that didn't help her spinning head. "What's wrong?"

"Nothing," she tried.

"Don't tell me *nothing.*" Wrapping her in his arms, he steered her to the window seat, where they sat and he looked her over with a gaze made all the more penetrating by the moonlight. "Are you in pain, or—"

"No."

What she was, was gasping for air like a swordfish on a line, and she had no intention of ending the night curled in the fetal position inside his nearest closet.

"Should we get you to the ER—"

"Shh." Leaning her head against the glass, she closed her eyes. "I just need…a minute…or two. Okay?"

Instead of answering, he pressed his lips to her temple and tightened his hold on her rib cage, his hands atop hers. A quick surge of anger at her ongoing weakness helped her pull herself together and, after a few harsh breaths that made her sound like a near-drowning victim, she was more embarrassed than anything.

"I'm fine."

She tried to pull free and act like the strong woman she wanted to be, but Beau held her close, his expression closed and unreadable.

"You mentioned having panic attacks."

Why couldn't she have had a simple heart attack? It'd be so much easier to explain. "Occasionally, yes."

"Since when?"

"Do you really want to know?"

Cursing, Beau looked to the ceiling, and his body thrummed tight with tension. For a minute she thought he might jump up and punch a wall or something, but he swallowed all that emotion back and got control of himself much faster than she had. When he looked at her again, all that intensity was banked to a manageable level that didn't scare the wits out of her.

"Maybe I should let you go," he said. "We both know it would be better for you."

"Taking the easy way out again, are you?"

His gaze wavered, but he didn't answer, and that wasn't good enough.

"Should I expect you to turn up with a new girlfriend next week?" She didn't bother to keep the taunt out of her voice. "That's what you do, isn't it? When there's trouble between us? Turn to someone else?"

Just like that, he was all focus again, all fighting determination. His jaw squared and she knew that this man, this better Beau, was worth all the trouble and pain.

"Not this time," he told her. "Not ever again."

"But you want to let me go."

"Don't twist my words. I want to marry you, and you damn well know it."

"I'm not ready for that."

His expression softened. Leaning in, he nuzzled the curve of her neck and, oh, man, she could feel all their joint need heating up again and the uncertainty in his trembling lips.

"I know. And I can wait. But whatever happens, I don't want to make things harder for you—"

Giving him a sly smile that she sincerely hoped would drive him out of his mind, she slipped her fingers under the waistband of his shorts, to where his growing length was already straining and hot.

"Some things are better when they're hard, Beau."

He gasped and let his head fall back while she stroked him. But then, suddenly, he'd had enough, and grabbed her wrist to stop her. Fixing her dead in his sights, he waited until he had her full attention.

"Jill," he said.

Fear tried to break free inside her again, but she willed it back with several deep breaths before she spoke. One near-panic attack per night was more than enough for her, thanks.

"Yes?"

"Can we work on recommitting to this family? Can we think about it?"

Whatever he wanted, she was pretty much there. A new commitment? Her body, heart and soul? Her right kidney? It was all good if Beau needed it and asked nicely.

"Yeah," she said. "We can do that."

"We're getting there, aren't we, Jill?"

She laughed, the sound every bit as shaky and vulnerable as she felt. "I sure hope so."

They lapsed into a delicious silence, staring at each other without much need for anything else. He was doing it to her again, that trick he had of filling his hazel eyes with so much raw love and adoration he seemed to glow with it. Being scared when they were connected like this was as remote a possibility as swimming to the bottom of the Atlantic to live with mermaids.

Finally his half smile widened into the rueful, self-deprecating grin that always made her skin flush and her heart skitter. He shook his head and reached around to massage her nape with those strong fingers. She almost passed out with the unbearable pleasure.

"Can I tell you something?" she asked.

His gaze, which gleamed bright and hot in the moonlight, drifted to her mouth as she spoke. Shifting closer, he ran his thumb over her sensitized bottom lip, tugging it gently to one side and bringing her to life in ways she'd never known were possible. She felt wicked and decadent. Surprising him, she sucked his thumb into her mouth, where she pulled on it, hard and deep.

He shuddered and then went still, except that his entire body tensed and seemed to hum with restraint. "As long as you don't tell me we're done making love for the night, you can tell me anything."

Laughing, she freed his thumb, which he seemed reluctant to take back. "I'm so glad I don't have to hate you anymore. It was exhausting."

"Yeah." His fingers dipped to the curve of her breast, tracing circles across her skin until she felt the gooseflesh rise. "That wasn't working for me, either."

"Tonight seems to be going okay, though."

That got her the full smile, dimples and all.

"Tonight's shaping up pretty well."

With that, his mood shifted into hot and dangerous territory. Using just a bit of his phenomenal upper-body strength, he shifted her around until they were face-to-face and she was on her knees, straddling his lap. He tipped his chin up and stared at her above him, his gleaming gaze wicked as his fingers inched under her skirt and up.

"What'll we tell Allegra?"

A moment of cool sanity penetrated her sensual fog. "Do we have to make an official statement just now? Can't we just take things slow?"

The line of his jaw hardened because she'd given the wrong answer, one that hurt him. One that, judging by the harsh set of his lush lips, he meant to punish her for.

"We can take that slow, yeah."

Without warning, he grabbed her arms and twisted her until, in one breathless heartbeat, she was flat on her back in the window seat, and he was wedged between her legs, a couple of hundred pounds of relentless determination.

A tug and a rip, and then her panties were flying off in the darkness, ruined and gone. Shoving her thighs apart, he shifted down her body, pausing only to shoot her a warning glance and settle one of her legs on his shoulder.

Jillian waited, panting, the cries collecting in her throat.

"But we're not taking this slow," he told her, and lowered his head.

Chapter 18

Jillian, Blanche, Barbara Jean and Allegra stood on the front porch and watched the caravan of big black SUVs crawl down the street toward the inn. Behind them stood the rest of the staff here at the B & B, their white polo shirts blinding, their black pants pressed to a razor's edge.

Omnipresent Secret Service agents, complete with dark suits and those intimidating sunglasses, swarmed the house and lawn; the advance team had been there for several days already. They all looked dour, and Jillian couldn't blame them. If she'd been in charge of security on this, the sitting president's surprise weekend getaway trip for the first lady's birthday and all the corresponding headaches, she'd look dour, too.

In preparation for this important visit, the place had been closed to the public and all the employees at the inn had cooked and cleaned to the point of exhaustion.

All for her brother, John.

The fathead.

The SUVs stopped at the curb and the agents swarmed like caffeine-drunk bees as John climbed out and reached behind to help Liza. Jillian had to laugh. They were doing the whole *Don't mind us, we're just tourists* thing, which was as inconspicuous as a flying saucer trying to blend in with rush-hour traffic.

They'd also told the press that they had no public events scheduled for the weekend, which meant, naturally, that the press was right on their tails. Already, satellite trucks were lining up at the ends of the street, on the other sides of the barricades to block traffic. The neighbors would love her for this.

Liza came up the path first, looking glamorous and beautiful, as always. She'd cut her hair in a sleek pixie style that highlighted her come-hither dark eyes and cheekbones. Pregnancy had done something to her, some intensification of her looks that made her a walking sex kitten, all lush cleavage, hips and glowing skin. She wore a black sundress that hugged her basketball of a belly, and judging from the wide grin on her face, she'd stopped scowling completely these days.

"Wow, Mom." Stepping forward, Jillian caught Liza in a big hug. "You look great. No wonder John can't keep his hands off you. I almost want to do you myself."

Liza laughed and shot her husband a glance over her shoulder. "John's got a big mouth. I'll have to cut him off tonight."

"No, you won't," John murmured behind Liza's back, waiting for his turn with Jillian.

"Hi, babies," Jillian sang. She rubbed Liza's belly and stooped closer, just to be obnoxious, half expecting Liza to snarl at her. Liza didn't suffer fools, displays of affection or most people lightly. But to her surprise, Liza just laughed again and submitted to the handling with good grace. "Hi, babies. This is your Aunt Jillian. Start memorizing my voice, okay?"

Finally, she let Liza go and turned to John, who gave her a stern look. "I didn't see a marching band when we drove up. Who's going to play 'Hail to the Chief' for me?"

"No one. And I didn't have commander-in-chief—" she made quotation marks with her fingers "—embroidered on the bathrobe in your suite, either. Welcome back to the real world, John."

"I told you to call me *Mr. President.*"

Jillian worked hard to keep her lips pursed. "I still remember when you used to stand in the mirror for hours, grooming your invisible mustache. You're lucky I don't call you Mr. Fuzzy."

John opened his arms to her. "But you'll still put a plaque on the door to our suite, right? *The president slept here?*"

She smiled sweetly. "There's already a plaque on the door. President Nixon stayed here in 1970. You'll be sleeping in his bed."

John froze, midhug, and staggered back a step with a hand clapped over his heart. "You really know how to hurt a guy."

They erupted with laughter. Jillian was about to swoop in for her bear hug, when John abruptly stopped laughing—it was like a needle being yanked off a record halfway through a song—and stared at her as though she'd just kicked a puppy down a flight of stairs.

"Don't tell me," he said with open horror.

Uh-oh. Jillian pulled her most bewildered face, but she knew where this was going. "Tell you what?"

John narrowed his eyes, nailing her right where she was, on her own damn porch. "You haven't laughed like that in years. *Years.* You're back together with him, aren't you?"

Oh, man. This was sooo not good.

Jillian fidgeted, uncomfortably aware of their avid audience and of Liza, bless her heart, hurrying to greet everyone else and steer them into the house so they could have a moment of semiprivacy.

John, meanwhile, clamped a hand on Jillian's elbow and frog-marched her a few steps away, around the corner of the porch, where no one but the milling agents could see them.

Irritated, she yanked her arm free and glowered up at him, wishing he didn't know her so well. Why couldn't he pretend he didn't see whatever he thought he saw in her face? Why did he have to confront her on this within ten seconds of his arrival?

"Answer my question." He puffed up and gave her the speechmaking voice that was supposed to strike awe and respect in hearts everywhere. "Are you back with Beau again?"

"Will you get over yourself? Do I look like one of your flunkies in the West Wing? You're not going to boss me around in my own inn. I don't care who you are. You can stay at the Motel 6 down the road, for all I care."

This diversionary tactic, naturally, didn't work.

"Are you seeing him?"

Jillian thought about the fourteen glorious nights since their reconciliation, nights when Beau climbed the back steps to the veranda outside her bedroom and let himself into her bed. She thought of the mornings when he snuck home to change and then reappeared half an hour later for breakfast with her and Allegra. She thought of the phone calls and texts during the day, and all the catching up they'd done. She remembered the furniture she'd ordered for his home office, the miscellaneous fix-it projects he'd done around the inn and the massages she'd given his leg when she caught him frowning with the ache. She thought of their walks together, which strengthened both his leg and their relationship, and how, with her encouragement, he was taking medications to manage the discomfort. She thought of how they'd both agreed that this was the best time of their lives, and they'd never been happier together.

Was she seeing Beau?

"Sort of," she told John.

There was no point lying; John wouldn't believe her. And why should she lie, anyway? She was a grown woman who didn't need her brother's approval. Even though she wished she had it.

John cursed. Then cursed again, worse. Stalking away, he went to the edge of the porch and stared up the street, squaring his shoulders inside his black polo shirt.

"That his house?"

"Yep."

"Hmm." His jaw tightened, making his moody profile even harsher. "I should arrange to have some Air Force training mission go awry and bomb it. The base at Moody isn't that far from here."

"You'd never do that."

"Wanna bet?"

The light in his eyes was distinctly murderous, so she decided she might want to take this conversation in a different direction.

"Look, John, this is America—the country you're in charge of. In America we're free to make our own decisions. Maybe you've heard something about that…?"

"Forgive me, Jill, but your decisions suck."

What? Oh, no, he didn't.

She pointed a finger in his face, half an inch from his nose, and resisted the urge to poke him with it. "The only reason I'm not taking your head off for that is because I'm giving you credit for loving me so much that you're being overprotective."

"I don't want him to break your heart. Again."

"You think I do?"

"I think you're not a good judge as far as he's concerned."

"I think that A, this is really none of your business, and B, I really wish you'd give Beau *and me* a little credit for changing and doing the work we need to do to make this thing a success this time around."

"I want to, Jill," he said helplessly. "I'm sorry, but I'm just not sure that Beau is capable of permanent change."

Neither was she. Not entirely sure, even now—not that she'd admit it. Still, she shrugged and put on her game face. "That's your problem. Not mine."

They glared for a minute and then John opened his arms and pulled her into a fierce bear hug that said everything between them. Then he spoke against her hair.

"He makes you happy?"

"Yes."

He let out a sigh so dejected that she felt his ribs contract against her arms.

"I was afraid of that." He paused. "You might as well invite the bastard to dinner."

Jillian smiled up at him. "Wow. Thanks for that ringing endorsement."

"Best I can do."

They laughed and were just linking hands to head back and catch up with the others, when Allegra poked her head around the corner. The kitten, who was still clutched in her hands and tucked under her chin, emitted a long-suffering and generally disgusted mewl that seemed to go on forever.

"Uncle President," Allegra said, "do you want to meet our new cat?"

Much as she hoped for it, the floor refused to open up and swallow Jillian whole. Which meant that she had to play the gracious hostess and endure a meal so fraught with peril that it made a joint Hatfield-McCoy reunion barbecue seem like a good idea.

Good thing the Secret Service was hanging around, ensuring everyone's safety. The best she could hope for was that everyone emerged from dessert…alive.

Liza, seated to Jillian's right, kept up a determined and

cheerful conversation, thank goodness. "Do you always serve dinner family-style, Jill?" She spooned another helping of collard greens on her plate and added a splash of vinegar. "And how many sides do you cook normally?"

"Family-style is easier, and it encourages the guests to sit together and talk. We always have four or five sides—we send the leftovers to the homeless shelter every night—but I made a couple extra tonight because I know they're John's favorites."

She and Liza risked cautious glances down the other end of the table, past the mashed sweet potatoes, black-eyed peas, creamed spinach, lima beans, rolls, biscuits, roast chicken, meat loaf and mashed potatoes, to where John sat, glowering at Beau, his overloaded plate untouched.

Beau glared back.

He'd arrived a little while ago, exchanged restrained greetings with John and Liza, then slipped upstairs to tuck Allegra in bed before the adults had their dinner. Now here he was, sitting quietly and politely but with a fire in his eyes to rival the flames in the flickering candles.

Yeah. The countdown to World War III had begun.

Was it hot in here? Taking the napkin out of her lap, Jillian used it to dab her forehead, which felt sweaty. Then she exchanged nervous glances with Liza and reached for the wine. Once her glass of zinfandel was refilled way past the traditional four-ounce mark, she felt equipped to resume the conversation.

"Do they ever let you cook at the White House, Liza?"

"Every now and then, the colonel and I sneak down and bake some cookies. We try not to make too big a mess and get ourselves in trouble."

"How's he doing?"

Liza's smile was wistful. "He's okay. Good days and bad. But I'm so grateful that he's able to live with us, and he's got his nurse—"

"Pass the sweet potatoes." John, who was still flashing death rays at Beau and hadn't eaten the sweet potatoes he already had on his plate, seemed to realize his barking was rude. "Please," he added grudgingly.

Beau's jaw tightened.

"John," Liza began, but Jillian was all over this one.

"Listen, *Mr. President,*" she began, lifting the heavy china bowl of sweet potatoes and thinking how lovely it would be to flick a heaping spoonful into her brother's face, "you can take these sweet potatoes and stick them where the sun—"

"It's okay, Jill." Beau's voice was quiet, but his honeyed skin was pale and his scar looked stark and red, a sure sign of turmoil. "It's not your job to defend me. And I think the president and I need to have a conversation. It's overdue."

John sneered, baring his teeth in a way that made Jillian want to snatch the butter knife away from his fisted hands. "Don't call me 'the president,' you son-of-a-"

"John," Liza cried.

"I don't mind, Liza," Beau said. "I've been called worse. And your husband and I have some air to clear."

"Gee. You think?" John said. Reaching for his goblet, he drained it, then signaled to Jillian.

Without a word, she passed the nearly empty wine bottle down to him. It probably wasn't a good idea to get him drunk, but things weren't going so hot with him sober, either. At this rate, they'd need another three or four bottles before dessert, and Liza and Beau weren't even drinking.

Thus fortified, John faced off with Beau while the women fidgeted in their seats and tried to become invisible.

"I'll start," John said. "My sister is a grown woman. She's strong and smart and gets to run her own life and make her own decisions. If she wants you back, I support that a hundred percent."

Though these were all the right words, Jillian knew better than to relax.

"Great." Beau's jaw tightened with grim satisfaction.

"That said," John continued, "I still want to rip your balls out through your throat for what you did to her, and I retain the right to do that in the future if you break her heart again. Just so we're clear."

"Great," Beau said again. "I'm all for clarity, so here goes. I don't blame you. I'd've kicked my ass at the front door if I were you. I have it coming. That and more."

John gaped at him, utter disbelief etched in every line of his face. "You always know how to say the right thing, don't you, Beau? Always know how to play the game—"

"Do I look like I'm playing?" Beau roared.

More glaring ensued. John's mouth hung open and he seemed startled into silence, but maybe he was only storing up energy for a final climactic assault.

Right. Time for distraction.

"Do you two, ah, have any idea yet about the twins' sex?"

"One of each," Liza said.

What a fantastic blessing. "Oh, that's won—"

But Beau and John weren't finished with their conversation.

"See that you don't hurt her again," John said, his powers of speech returned at last.

Beau glanced at Jillian and gave her one of those private, unsmiling looks so full of meaning that the intensity of it sizzled up and down her spine. She dimpled with encouragement, and he turned back to John.

"I know I'll never change your mind about me," Beau told him with utter sadness but no self-pity. "I wish I could, but I know I can't."

Staring down at his plate, Beau picked up his fork and started to take a bite of something. "This looks great, Jill—"

Without warning, John lashed out, snatched the plate away and plunked it down on the other side of the table, well out of Beau's reach. A sound dangerously like a warning growl vibrated from Beau as he dropped his fork and faced John again, shoulders bunched with tension.

John planted his elbows on the table and jabbed two fingers in Beau's face. "The thing you don't understand, *Beau,* is that you didn't just betray Jillian. I loved you, man. You were my *brother.* Are you feeling me? For years, you were my *brother,* and if anyone had warned me that you were going to do what you did, I'd've laughed in their face and called them a liar. But you made a liar out of me, didn't you? You couldn't keep your shit in your pants and you blew all that to kingdom come, didn't you?"

This conversation was killing Jillian—just ripping her open

down the middle and pulling her guts out. She could hardly stand to look at either man and see all that harsh animosity, which was compounded to the nth degree by the raw hoarseness in their voices. Ducking her head, she used her napkin to swipe at her unexpected tears, but Beau sat tall, ready to take all this and more, if need be.

"How many times can I tell you I'm sorry?" he asked.

"No idea." There was no mercy in John's flashing eyes, and no signs of it coming anytime soon. "Why don't you keep saying it, and I'll let you know."

Wincing, Beau tossed his napkin on the table and turned his head away, staring out the window at nothing. Jillian and Liza exchanged silent glances of commiseration, but no one said anything. Jillian wasn't sure what, if anything, to say. Beau had made himself this bed with John; maybe he needed to lie in it for a while. That was between him and John, wasn't it?

The stalemate might have continued forever, but a quiet new voice entered the fray. "I'm wondering," Liza said to her husband, "if you should be throwing these particular stones."

Whoa. If anyone had thought the tension at the table couldn't get any thicker, they'd been wrong. Absolutely wrong. Dead wrong.

John's nostrils flared; Liza, looking placid, folded her hands in her lap and stared him down; Jillian wished she had two fingers of scotch, neat.

"What the hell," John asked, his voice low and gravelly, as though someone had fed his vocal cords through a paper shredder, "is that supposed to mean?"

Liza shrugged, displaying the calm levelheadedness that had served her so well as a news correspondent. "This was all before my time, Mr. President, so you'll have to correct me if I've got my history wrong. But it seems to me that, number one, you cheated on your first wife during a rough patch in your marriage." She held up one finger, and then another. "Number two, you changed and asked for forgiveness, number three, she forgave you, and, number four, you were a wonderful and loving husband after that."

Now holding up four fingers, Liza waggled them at John,

whose face was a vivid red bordering on purple. "Did I get that wrong? I want to make sure the record is straight."

Wow. The air had effectively been sucked out of the room.

Jillian was going to have to award this round to Liza.

Several seconds passed before John was able to pick up the battered remnants of his ego off the floor and formulate a rebuttal.

He cleared his throat. They waited. He turned to Beau, whose lips seemed to be twitching with the repressed beginnings of a smile.

"Since my wife is pregnant with my twins, and in a fragile and delicate condition—" John began.

Liza snorted with outrage. "You are so going to pay for that later."

John pretended he hadn't heard her.

"—and since I don't want to upset her because she probably doesn't realize what she's saying, what with the hormones and all, and, more important, since I want to get laid later—"

Laughing now, Liza balled her napkin up and threw it across the table at him.

"—I will allow for the slight and outside possibility that you *might* have changed and *might* be ready to be a good husband to Jillian."

"Wow." One of Beau's heavy brows crept toward his hairline. "I feel reborn."

The sarcasm seemed like a bad idea, especially since the tension was still pretty thick in here, and Jillian wished she could thump Beau on the head. She started to reach for her wine again, but John scooted his chair back, stood and extended a hand to Beau.

Beau hesitated, blinked and then looked to Jillian as though he needed an explanation about what a hand was and what the hell he should do with it.

She gave him a tiny encouraging smile. He stood.

The men studied each other, exchanging all kinds of subliminal manly signals that Jillian couldn't begin to decipher. There was one second where they seemed to shake, but the next thing she knew, they were hugging each other, slapping backs and clearing throats. Neither smiled. Then they broke apart, both determinedly looking in opposite directions, and resumed eating.

Jillian looked to Liza, eyebrows raised.

"You playing any soccer these days, Beau?" John asked around a mouthful of baked beans. "We can play in the morning. I feel like whupping up on your ass."

This, finally, did the trick. They all laughed, and it was relieved and joyful and the greatest gift Jillian could have imagined, because she'd been sure she'd never get Beau and her brother in the same room again without bloodshed, if not homicide.

And Beau… God, he was looking at her with one of those half-smile, quietly intense looks that shouted out things like love, desire and the fierce determination to get her naked and flat on her back at the earliest possible opportunity.

A hot blush collected over her breasts and traveled up her neck to her cheeks, a dead giveaway that she was thinking the same thing and was happy to indulge him in whatever his heart desired for the rest of the night.

Beau's smile faded, leaving a desperate desire that had nothing to do with sex. He burned with it; she felt him ache with it. He held her gaze, dinner and guests forgotten, and Jillian tried to breathe, but she couldn't remember how.

Marry me, he mouthed.

The *yes* was right there, on the tip of her tongue and in her heart. She felt her flush deepen and the beginnings of a smile curl her lips, but it hardly mattered because he could surely see the answer written all over her.

And then someone's cell phone rang with a muffled chirp.

The unwelcome sound came again, piercing the wonderful candlelit intimacy of the moment, and Jillian blinked, dragged back to the real world even if she didn't want to go.

"It's not me," John said as the cell rang again.

"I don't have my phone on me," Liza said.

"It's me. Sorry, Jill. I thought I turned it off."

Shooting an embarrassed and apologetic look at everyone in turn, Beau unhooked the cell from his belt, turned it off midring and took a quick glance at the display just as he was putting it on the table next to his plate.

And froze with shock while the color leached from his face, as though he'd drunk a gallon of extra-strength bleach.

Oh, no. Jillian felt the ripple of concern sweep around the table even as her stomach dropped. "What's happened?"

Beau, who seemed too stricken to speak, just shook his head.

Now he was really scaring her. Someone must have died.

"Beau, who was it?"

He met her gaze and she read the answer in his eyes even before he spoke. "Adena Brown," he told her.

Chapter 19

Dinner went south after that, and all the guests and personnel scattered to other parts of the inn, which was fine with Beau. Screw dinner.

He had more important things to worry about, namely bridging the divide—*again*—with Jillian. He wasn't about to lose all the precious ground he'd gained with her over an unwanted phone call.

Shit. Why hadn't he blocked that woman's number from his cell? How unspeakably stupid was he? Very, apparently.

"What did she want?" Jillian asked.

Beau had known terror a time or two in his life. The screaming seconds before his accident came to mind. That was number one. What he was feeling now was definitely in the top five.

It was the look in her wide eyes that had his heart stuttering now.

No—that wasn't it.

It was the vacancy in her eyes that scared him, the absolute lack of emotion. Those empty eyes were a painful reminder of the dark days after Mary's death, when Jillian's body stayed with him, but her soul left the building and wouldn't come back. Right now, there were no signs of the happy, confident, glorious Jillian he'd rediscovered over the past few weeks, and he prayed she wasn't gone forever.

She sat on the sofa in her private upstairs living room, catty-corner to where he sat on a chair. Her chest heaved a little more than it needed to, like she was on the verge of another one of those excruciating panic attacks.

Yeah. He'd sworn he'd never hurt her again, hadn't he?

And look where they were now, right back at square one,

if not lower. His promises were still as valuable as Monopoly money, and that seemed to be his bottom line, no matter how he struggled against it. Hell, maybe it was his destiny.

He braced his elbows on his knees, gripped his hands together and rested his forehead against his interlocked fingers.

Help me, God. Help us.

Dropping his hands, he took a deep breath and faced Jillian head-on. "She's starting a political think tank back in Miami. She wants me on board."

Jillian unscrambled this code in no time. "She wants you back now that she's divorced."

Beau hesitated. Adena hadn't said as much, but he was pretty good at reading between the lines, especially when it came to women. "Probably."

"She was in love with you."

He wouldn't lie, no matter how much easier it would make things right now. "She said she was."

Jillian was no fool. "She was."

Be a man and 'fess up, Taylor. "Yes."

"Were you—" Jillian began.

"No."

Try though he did, he couldn't quite keep all the frustration out of his voice. Jesus. They'd been over this. He'd told her he'd never loved another woman. Told her how meaningless that faceless sex had been—both during his extramarital affairs and since the divorce.

He loved Jillian. Only Jillian. Hadn't he lived that these past few weeks? When would she believe him? What more would it take? Why should he be on the hot seat just because that woman called him out of the blue? He hadn't gone looking for trouble, nor would he ever.

How many more hoops would he have to jump through?

But then the wave passed and all that dark emotion faded away. It was his fault Jillian was insecure. He was the one who'd cracked the foundation of their relationship. Apparently he needed to shore it up a little bit more.

"Jill," he said, reaching for her hand.

She jerked away. "Don't," she said, but it was in that dead, emotionless tone, the way she might have told a server in a restaurant, "Don't overcook my steak." Just *don't.*

It drove him wild, losing her like this when she was right here, not three feet away. They wouldn't go through this again. Not again.

Without thought, he swung around to the sofa and grabbed her arms, pulling her resistant body as close as he possibly could.

She went rigid and strained to get away. "I said, *don't—*"

"Don't you tell me that." He tightened his grip. "I *will* touch you. I'm not going to let you go again, Jill. I'm not going to let you pull away like you did before."

"Get your hands off me!"

"No. And if you're pissed off, you need to tell me. Don't pretend you're not. Let it out."

That did it.

Her face twisted, snarled beyond recognition. With a terrible sound like a roar, she unleashed all her fury, which was enough to make a grown man scurry to the nearest closet and hide.

"How could you do this? How could you let that woman back in our lives?"

"I didn't ask for this, Jill. I didn't call her. She called me. I don't want this."

"She wants you back!"

Sliding his hands down to the hard balls of her fists—he was surprised she didn't take a swing at him—he kissed one hand, and then the other. When she jerked free, he clamped his hands on either side of her hot face and turned her head so that she had nowhere to look but at him.

Believe in me, Jill. Believe in us.

"It doesn't matter what *she* wants," he told her quietly. "It only matters what *I* want. And you know what that is."

Jillian went absolutely still.

Her breath hitched and he feared he'd made a terrible mistake and shoved her over the edge into a full-blown panic attack. Just when he started to let her go, she surprised him by scrambling to her knees and straddling his hips.

Wha—?

For a minute she stared down at him, something feverish

burning bright in her eyes, and then she kissed him. She was a hot, aggressive little demon, taking his mouth with her soft, sweet lips, silky tongue and nipping teeth. When she pulled back at last, he was breathless, fully aroused and dazed.

Ferocious and mind-blowingly sexy with her damp and swollen lips and wide eyes, she held his face and drew her line in the sand.

"She doesn't get to show up out of the blue and do this to us, Beau. I won't let her."

Much as he wanted to hold that thought, lower Jillian to the floor, strip and ride her until she was sweaty, shaking and limp with satisfaction, here was yet another crack in the foundation of their relationship, and the damage had been done. They had to address it.

"What can I do?" Gripping her butt, he anchored her to him so they could be as close as possible while they had this awful conversation. "I've already told her never to call me again. I blocked her number, so she can't get through, but I don't want you to go through this again—"

Jillian shook her head, seeming to deflate beneath the weight of her bewilderment. "I don't know. I thought I was past this. I thought I was ready for reminders to pop up, but I—"

"I can't control when something like this will happen, Jill. I wish I could, but I can't."

"I know."

"How can we get past this?"

"I don't know."

Wow. Stalemated just like that. And here he'd thought they'd come so far.

He let her go when she slipped off his lap, and they sat side by side, dejected and a million miles apart.

After a minute, she took a deep breath that had dread collecting like cement in his gut even before she spoke.

"I think you should go."

"Go…where?" he asked, but he knew.

"Go to Miami. Talk to Adena. See if you want the job."

He waited for the punch line, but there didn't seem to be one. So he replayed that last bit in his mind and tried without success to process it. He'd've had more luck processing a dinner of dried corn kernels mixed with poison mushrooms.

It took him a good ten seconds to respond. "Is this a joke?"

"No."

No? "You're…sending me away?"

"I'm setting you free to make a choice."

Suddenly he couldn't sit still for this, couldn't let her touch him with her soft skin while she calmly lobbed a grenade into the middle of their relationship and blew it straight to hell.

Standing and trying to get his freaking weak leg under him, he pivoted to face her, his frustration quickly turning to anger.

"Setting me free?" He held his arms wide, wobbled and had to grab the back of the chair for support. "Do I look like a damn butterfly?

"Beau," she began, getting to her feet.

"I've already made a choice."

She flinched and that was just too damn bad. It was her fault he was shouting; her fault that he was coming unglued while she stood there, cool and aloof, and watched; her fault he was teetering on the edge of sanity.

"I chose *you.* I chose this life with our child. Don't you know that?"

For a minute, she wavered. Closed her eyes, rested her hand against her forehead and seemed to struggle with her emotions, which bunched up in her face and gave her a vivid flush. But when she opened them again, her light brown eyes were as clear and placid as a mountain lake at dawn.

"You want me not to withdraw and to be honest, right?"

No. Not when being honest meant she was about to lay some dark confession on him that would surely rip his heart out. Not when it would rock their little boat, which had been sailing along so smoothly with nary a wave on the horizon.

"Yes."

"It's hard for me to say this because I want to be a strong woman. I want to have confidence. I want to believe that you think I'm the greatest woman in the world—"

"I *do.*"

She held up a hand, silencing him. "But there's a part of me that still wonders whether you won't get bored here in the country with me. Whether you don't miss a faster life in a big city. Maybe you want to be a mover and a shaker again—"

"Cut to the chase, Jill," he snapped. "You wonder if I'll cheat on you as soon as I get a chance."

She hesitated, looking like she wanted to deny it, but then she smiled a rueful smile that was exactly the kind of knife to his belly that he'd feared.

"Yes. I'm sorry, but I do." Blinking back glittering tears, she swiped at her eyes and took a moment to collect herself. "I wonder if you're only hiding here with me because your leg bothers you and you have nowhere else to go while you lick your wounds. But now you have the chance to do the kind of thing you've always enjoyed doing in a city you love. And I wonder if this is the opportunity you've been waiting for."

God.

He tightened his hold on the chair, trying hard not to collapse under the weight of all her doubts, when he'd foolishly thought doubts between them were a thing of the past.

Fear made him lash out. "You know what I wonder, Jill? I wonder if anything I do will ever be good enough for you, or whether you've made up your mind to punish me forever."

He must have hit the nail on the head, because she spluttered with words that didn't seem to want to come. "That's not—" she finally managed.

"Oh, I think it is."

A hard moment passed, full of so much bitter pain on both sides he was surprised he didn't smell fumes. He stared, loving her mostly, but hating her just a little, too. Because there was a tiny dark corner of his soul that wondered if she wasn't right—not about the other women, but about tucking his tail and running from the glittering and successful life he'd had before.

And he wondered if he wasn't the same old Beau underneath, a leopard who'd put on a lion suit rather than truly changed his spots.

Most of all, he hated her for doubting him when he had absolute faith in her.

"You want me to take this little test for you and go to Miami?

Fine. You want a break from me? Fine. Whatever you want. It's your world."

Anguish lined her face, making him feel better and worse. Better because this wasn't as easy for her as she was pretending. Worse because they'd had enough pain between them to last three lifetimes, and he didn't want to leave with anger between them, not even for a single night.

"Beau, please—"

He reached for her hand, which was smooth and soft and still a perfect fit after all these years. She came eagerly, settling against him, where she belonged, and sighed when he rested his lips against her forehead.

"Here's what I want, Jill." Pulling back just enough, he cupped her face and tilted it back so he could see her eyes and she could see his. "When I get back here—and I *am* coming back—I want your decision. You're either in, or you're out. You either trust me, or you don't. We either build a new life together, or we let each other go."

She stiffened, probably because he'd pushed her much further than she wanted to go, and her brows snapped together in the beginnings of a frown. "You can't just—"

Turning her loose, he stepped back and found his cane.

"Yeah, I can. One of us needs to decide what we want, and it's not me."

Silence. There was nothing she could say to that, and she knew better than to try.

Wheeling around, he headed for the door. "I'll see you in a few days."

"Why are you so angry, Beau?" Dr. Desai asked right off the bat at the next session.

Beau snorted. "How much time do we have?"

Desai bowed his head, doing his waiting patiently thing, and that was all the encouragement Beau needed.

"I'm not mad. I'm pissed."

"Why?"

Beau could barely get the words out, maxed out as he was on bitterness. "Because why the hell does this woman get to call me out of the blue and ruin all the progress I've made with Jillian?"

"Why else?"

"Why should I have to go to Miami for this test of Jillian's?"

"Why else?"

"Because I'm…a little, ah…scared."

"Of what?"

"Of discovering that I miss the city or the excitement or something."

"Not the women?"

Beau thought of the nights in Jillian's arms, of the unspeakable pleasure and the addictive need for more pleasure from that one source only. "No," he said, the top edge of his anger leaking away. "The one thing I'm not worried about is the women."

"Why else are you angry?"

"Because when the hell is she going to trust me?" Beau didn't mean to roar like a snared lion, but he was beyond self-control, and this had been bottled up inside him for too long. "Why does my entire life have to be defined by my infidelities? When is she going to stop judging me?"

Dr. Desai considered his fingers, which were folded in his lap, for a long time before he spoke. "This is interesting. You're very critical of Jillian's inability to get past this one thing, but I'm wondering, how good are you at forgiveness?"

"Me? What the hell are you—"

"You haven't forgiven Jillian for her doubts, have you?"

Beau nearly gagged on his surprise.

"You run a foundation that gives people second chances and yet there's a young man who's a lot like you—"

What? That Dawson Reynolds guy? "He is not like—"

"—and you have the unique opportunity to mentor him and change his life. Are you being a model of forgiveness to him?"

"This is your best advice, Doc? That situation has absolutely nothing to do—"

"Isn't the principle the same?" Dr. Desai asked. "When we're talking about second chances and redemption?"

Beau struggled, unable to answer.

And then Dr. Desai dropped the nuclear bomb on him.

"Or maybe your biggest issue is that you haven't forgiven yourself for not being the perfect man you hoped you were."

Beau ran his Range Rover through the car wash on his way to the airport. It didn't take him long to find who he was looking for.

Dawson Reynolds stood at the far end, drying the cars as they emerged from the automated wash. The dude looked truly sad on this sweltering morning, hot, wet and miserable, his T-shirt and khakis damp with what was probably an unholy combination of sweat and soapy water. His back pockets were jammed with towels, and he worked on a shiny BMW, putting some elbow grease into it and taking care to buff a couple of hard-to-reach spots.

Then the car's owner strode up, climbed into the driver's seat and drove off, paying Dawson as much attention as he'd've paid a passing ant on the sidewalk. No tip, no thanks, no nothing.

Dawson glared after the man, swiped his wet face with his forearm and turned to the next vehicle. Which happened to be Beau's.

The poor guy cringed, probably thinking that an unfortunate coincidence had brought Beau here to see him at his lowliest. Beau felt a twinge of discomfort. Maybe he should've called ahead, but then he wouldn't have the pleasure of seeing the brother's face when he told him the news.

Dawson wheeled around, nostrils flaring, and went to work on the Rover, looking so furious he probably wanted to take a swing at Beau.

Beau took his time about walking over, drawing out the moment. "How's it going?"

Dawson grunted, now drying the rims.

"That gig at the circus didn't work out?"

Dawson straightened, narrowed his eyes at Beau and stretched out over the hood, drying it.

"You're not very angry today." Beau slid on his sunglasses and turned his sarcasm up a notch. "Did those sessions with Dr. Desai finally do you some good?"

That did it. Dawson straightened and squared his shoulders, his skin vibrating with rage and threatening to split his clothes down the seams, like the Hulk. "What the hell do you want, Governor?"

Beau shrugged and flashed his most innocent look. "Can't a brother get his car washed? And anyway, I thought you wanted an interview."

Dawson gaped. "An inter—"

"This is it," Beau told him. "But you're not doing too hot so far. I'm not real impressed."

Dumbstruck, Dawson stared off at the next car emerging from the wash, then looked back to Beau, his lips twitching in what might have been the beginnings of an uncertain smile. "How did you find me?"

"Well, I checked all the playgrounds in the area and didn't see you dealing to children, so I thought you might be here."

Dawson snorted a quick laugh.

"Desai told me," Beau said.

"Desai. I'll have to talk to him about client confidentiality."

But Dawson didn't look upset with Desai, and Beau wasn't upset with the good doctor, either. The man had asked him some hard questions and made him think enough to cause his brain to bleed.

The bottom line was that Beau was finished with anger—at Adena Brown, Jillian and especially himself. He wasn't perfect. Big freaking news flash. He was doing the best he could, which was a day-to-day thing, but looking pretty good right now. He had something to offer Jillian, Allegra and the world.

That was enough.

And this guy here, Dawson Reynolds. Buried underneath all his anger was a dude who had some promise, if he didn't let his self-destructive big mouth get in the way.

Self-destructive. Yeah, Desai had been right about that. Dawson reminded Beau of himself when he was young and stupid. Which wasn't that long ago, come to think of it.

"I read your file and application again," Beau told him. "You're pretty smart."

"Hell, yeah, I'm smart—"

Beau held up a hand, silencing him. "Let's work on you shutting up a little bit more. How about that?"

Dawson snapped his jaws closed.

"You put together a good proposal," Beau continued, "and I think you'd be great at flipping houses. You might have a Donald Trump in there, waiting to come out, and I'm willing to give you a chance."

Dawson's eyes widened, but he kept quiet.

"So I want you to quit your job here, unless you think you have a future in drying cars—"

He paused, and Dawson shook his head hard enough to jar something loose.

"—and show up at my office on Monday. I'm going to train you up, see if I can't do something with you. Got it?"

Dawson nodded.

"You might want to think about it," Beau warned him. "If you accept the grant, you'll have an obligation to pay it forward and mentor someone else coming up after you. If you think you can stop flapping your jaws long enough to teach someone else, I'd be glad to have you. Okay?"

"Oh," Dawson said. "Am I allowed to speak now?"

Beau had to laugh as he extended his hand. "Smart-ass punk."

Dawson laughed, too, but it flashed by, as though he'd only given himself permission to loosen up for half a second every three days or so. Then he sobered and gripped Beau's hand, serious and earnest. "You won't regret it."

"See that you don't make me regret it. By the way, you missed a spot."

He pointed to the side panel and Dawson jerked around to see what he was talking about, but Beau laughed again.

"Just kidding," he said.

He climbed in, slammed the door and adjusted the mirrors. This was a good thing he was doing here with Dawson, and it felt right. It also felt right to feel proud of himself about something, and wasn't that a switch?

Pulling away, he kept his muttering voice loud enough for

Dawson to hear him. "A man with a degree from Duke shouldn't have to work in a car wash."

Dawson's joyous laughter followed him as he turned into the street and headed for the airport.

Chapter 20

Beau wished he could hate Miami, but Miami didn't cooperate.

When the car picked him up outside the airport, the sky was the unreasonable, blazing blue that only the tropics could manage, with fat gray storm clouds on the horizon that promised the usual afternoon rain.

He breathed deep, realizing that he'd missed this sultry air, fragrant with unknowable flowers, the damp earth and the bay, missed the bustling excitement that came with a big city full of millions of people.

Yeah, he felt a twinge. Slight, but there.

"This is it, Governor," the driver said, pointing to a Mercedes idling at the curb.

Beau winced. His former title, which was such a vivid reminder of the past, was always like the amplified scrape of a thousand nails across a blackboard, and enough to make his ears rupture.

"Just call me Beau."

Smiling, the driver relieved Beau of his carry-on and swung it around to the trunk, and Beau took a minute to redistribute his weight on his cane. The last thing he needed was to fall on his butt and—

Oh, shit.

There she was, inside the car, waiting for him with the kind of glowing-eyed excitement that confirmed his suspicion that she wanted to resume their affair.

Adena Brown, the woman he'd turned to for comfort when he should've been turning to his wife.

His stomach pitched, but he kept his expression politely neutral.

She hadn't gotten any uglier in the years since he'd seen her. She looked good, in fact, with her skirt hiked up to thigh level to reveal bare legs that were sun-kissed and shapely, shoulders bare and breasts straining against the bodice of her strapless dress.

He wasn't quite sure how this sexy little outfit jelled with her go-for-the-jugular business demeanor, but it really didn't matter. She'd dressed to impress, and he was impressed.

Shoring up his manners, he got in and shut the door before some lurking airport paparazzo—they were never far away, always waiting for Jennifer Lopez or some other celebrity of the day—snapped a picture of them together.

"Hi," she said, her smile widening with obvious delight.

"Hi."

"You look great."

He hesitated, but what the hell. He was all about honesty now, and she'd gone to a lot of trouble for his benefit. "So do you."

Unfortunately, she seemed to take this statement of the obvious as encouragement, and caught him by surprise as he was resting his cane against the seat.

Leaning across the leather seat and bringing with her the faint scent of some sophisticated musk that probably cost about a thousand dollars an ounce, she cupped his face in her soft manicured hand and kissed him. Too close to his cheek to be a lover's greeting, but too close to the corner of his lips to be platonic, the kiss registered with the purely male side of him and made his nerves prickle with awareness.

He remembered that scent. He remembered that hand and those lips.

They'd had some fun together, he and Adena. She was an athlete in bed, as enthusiastic and memorable a lover as he'd ever had, and he'd had plenty.

The kiss lingered for a startled moment, and then she turned him loose, her voice husky now. "It's good to see you."

Yeah. He could see that in her brown eyes, so like Jillian's and yet not like hers at all because they had sexual heat without any human warmth.

Since he couldn't say the same, he decided just to be pleasant. "Thanks for bringing me in."

Holding his gaze, she uncrossed and recrossed her legs, to great effect. Old Adena kept herself in great shape; he had to give her that. The driver got in and they pulled away from the curb and merged with the traffic exiting the airport.

"I didn't think you'd come."

"Well...as you know, I almost didn't," he told her.

"What changed your mind?"

I'd do anything to earn Jillian's trust once and for all, that's what.

"I thought I'd see what you had to say."

Adena twisted around in her seat, coming in as close as she could without climbing into his lap, and displaying a pair of breasts that were still spectacular, as she no doubt knew. Why didn't she just take the dress off and rest her girls on a silver platter for his perusal? Or, better yet, she could have them photographed and run off on business cards to hand out to prospective lovers. That could simplify things for her, right?

She touched his arm. "I've missed you."

He didn't doubt it. She was just that delusional and self-destructive.

"That's funny," he told her, "since our affair ruined both our marriages and our lives. Why would you miss me? If you were smart, you'd have yourself hypnotized to have all memory of me wiped from your mind."

Blinking, she gave him the puppy-dog eyes, all wide bewilderment and open adoration. "Don't say that. You know how I felt about you."

"I know how you felt about my penis, yeah. I'm not sure we ever knew each other, though."

His cool bluntness didn't make so much as a chink in her thick ego, nor did it cause her to stop this line of conversation, which disgusted him and would leave them both embarrassed. He hadn't expected it to.

"Don't say that, Beau. I've always loved you. You know that."

Love. Huh. Yeah.

Funny.

Turning away, he stared out the window and absorbed the bitter disgust rising up over the back of his tongue. Took a minute to absorb it, to wallow in it. To imprint this moment—this feeling—on his brain so he'd never forget, even if he lived another sixty years.

Adena seemed to sense that things were going south on her; he heard the rising desperation in her voice. "Did you ever care for me?"

That would be a big negative.

She was beautiful, she reminded him a little of his wife and she'd been able and oh-so-willing to give him some comfort during one of the darkest periods of his life.

Their affair had amounted to some heated looks, a few frantic screwings that had never made him feel any better and a lot of guilt and scrambling to cover up his infidelity.

He hadn't wanted to build anything with her, hadn't missed her when she was gone and would never have thought about her again in his life if she hadn't called him.

She was, in short, utterly forgettable, and he only wished she'd disappear so he could carry on with the forgetting.

"I'm in love with my wife. She's the only woman I've ever loved."

"The tabloids have been saying you're back together." Adena's eyes darkened to black. "But she's your ex-wife, isn't she?"

"I'm working on that."

For a minute she didn't say anything, and he knew she was retooling her strategy, rethinking and refining her approach. Then she eased closer and let her hand drift up his thigh.

He tensed, but that didn't seem to bother her.

"Beau." She nuzzled his ear. "Please. I know you remember how it was."

Yeah, he remembered. It'd been fun, for about thirty seconds. And it'd been the stupidest thing he'd ever done in his life or ever could have done.

It was so obvious to him *now,* but why hadn't he seen it *then?*

Still, he took a minute to really consider what he was ejecting from his life forever, to really decide.

It would be as easy as falling off a horse. The car had a divider, and he could have Adena flat on her back, legs spread, screwed and happy by the time they reached the office.

Or, if he wanted, he could get out of this car, head to the nearest hotel bar on the beach, and find a beautiful and willing woman there. Miami was full of beautiful women. The only things more plentiful here were palm trees.

He could have one-night stands every evening for the rest of his life. He could have ménages or orgies. Whatever he wanted, the sky was the limit because he was handsome, notorious and had a little money. Endless fun and games were his for the taking. All he had to do was take.

Except that if he went down that road again, he'd lose the one thing he really wanted and needed—his soul. Jillian was his everything, and he was finished trying to eke out a bearable existence without her. More than that, he was finished with this sordid scene and Adena. There wasn't anything remotely tempting about any of it.

His girls were back home at the B & B, waiting for him, and he had no idea what the hell he was doing here when he belonged with them.

Clamping his fingers on Adena's wrist to stop her upward progress, he removed her hand from his body and shoved it back in her lap.

"Pull over," he told the driver.

Adena's jaw dropped as the car edged to the nearest curb. They hadn't even made it out of the airport yet, and their little reunion visit had lasted five minutes at the most.

"What're you doing?"

Beau picked up his cane and opened the door, desperate to be anywhere but *here,* with *her.* "I'm going back home where I belong."

"What?"

Ah, shit. She looked weepy and shaky all of a sudden, as if she might really cry. It was probably all an act, but even so, he'd hurt enough women in his life and didn't want to hurt this one any more than he had to.

"I'm sorry I wasted your time, Adena. I wish you all the best." He paused and glanced over his shoulder so she could see he meant it. "And I don't ever want to hear from you again."

Her face turned a flaming red, somewhere between hurt, anger and abject humiliation, and she opened her mouth to let him have it, but he didn't have time for any nonsense.

Climbing out, he shut the door without looking back. The driver, meanwhile, rushed around and met him at the trunk to hand him his rolling overnight bag, stammering about driving him back to the terminal.

"No, thanks." Beau settled his cane in one hand and the bag's handle in the other. "I think I'll walk."

Why shouldn't he? His leg wasn't bothering him too much today, and the weather was nice. The terminal wasn't that far, and he could use the exercise and the time to clear his head, although his goals had never been in sharper focus.

If he hurried, he could probably catch the next shuttle back to Atlanta and be home by midafternoon, with his girls and his dog and their new kitten.

His life was waiting for him.

"The princess and I are off to go swimming," Barbara Jean announced.

Jillian and Blanche, who'd been sitting on the bench at the weathered kitchen table, reviewing the dinner menu for the rest of the week while taking a quick breather after the lunchtime rush, looked around for Allegra's grand entrance and exit.

The girl, sure enough, wore her white terry-cloth cover-up, which presumably hid one of her pink bathing suits. The tiara du jour, a towering cardboard number with silver loops and shedding sparkles, sat atop her sandy-brown head. In her small hands, she carried a purple lace fan and her leopard-printed purse. Inside the purse, with only her head sticking out, her expression disgruntled, sat the kitten.

"Bye, Mommy."

Allegra trotted over for a quick kiss, and Jillian eyed all the accessories, including the feline.

"Hannah needs to stay here," she told her daughter.

"Hannah Montana."

Jillian rolled her eyes. "Hannah *Montana* needs to stay here. And take your tiara off before you get into the pool, pumpkin. You don't want to ruin it."

Allegra submitted to the removal of her headwear, which was strange, and then lingered for an extra hug from Jillian, which was stranger. Jillian gave her a critical once-over, but she didn't seem flushed or anything.

"What's wrong, pumpkin?"

"When's Daddy coming home?" Allegra asked for the millionth time that day.

"Not until tomorrow."

The girl wilted with the utter despair that only a child could manage, looking orphaned, homeless and friendless all at once, and her eyes filled with fat tears. "I miss him."

Not as much as I do, honey.

Much as Jillian wanted to whine and cry like her daughter, her pride wouldn't allow it. She was the genius who'd insisted that Beau meet with Adena, and she couldn't very well backtrack now. This little test separation was a good thing that they both needed. In the end, their relationship would be the stronger and better for it.

She hoped.

Either that, or Beau and Adena had rekindled their little spark and were now in bed together.

"I know." Focusing on Allegra, she pushed that devastating image far from her mind's eye. "But I'll bet he'll bring you a souvenir when he comes back."

The girl's tears vanished, burned off by the sudden flare of hot interest in her greedy little eyes. She hopped up and down in her tiny flip-flops.

Hannah Montana, who didn't appreciate this kind of commotion, meowed a protest, jumped out of the bag and slunk into the shadows down the hall.

Jillian and Blanche watched Allegra bounce out the door after

Barbara Jean, and were exchanging an amused glance, when Jillian's cell buzzed from the pocket of her flowered sundress. She fished it out.

"Hello?"

"I'm back," said Beau.

Oh, God. Beau? Back already?

The silky drawl kicked her heart rate into turbo-overdrive because she recognized that tone. There was only one thing on his mind when he spoke to her like that, and it wasn't airports or Miami business trips with former lovers.

"That, ah…" Excruciatingly aware of Blanche's keen and interested gaze on her now red-hot face, Jillian smoothed her hair and tried not to stammer. "That was, ah, pretty quick."

"I did everything you wanted me to do, Jill, so now it's my turn. I want you to do something for me."

"What, ah…what's that?" she asked.

She met Blanche's gaze—jeez, the woman didn't even pretend she wasn't listening to every single word—and managed a lame smile as she got up from the bench and hurried to the window for some modicum of privacy.

"I want you to meet me at my house in one minute. Okay?"

"Su-Sure." Jillian cleared her wobbly voice and tried not to sound like a creaky door hinge. But there was nothing she could do about the absolute lack of oxygen getting to her straining lungs. "I can do that."

"Are you wearing one of your sexy little summer dresses?"

Jillian had to glance down to make certain. Even then, she was such a hopped-up mess of nerves and anxiety that she wasn't sure what was what. Halter bodice that tied at the neck? Check. Full skirt? Check. Strappy sandals? Check.

"Yes."

"Good," he said. "Take your panties off before you come."

Chapter 21

Jillian was halfway up his drive when the sound of a powerful engine caught up with her. Nearly shaking by now with a wicked combination of nerves and anticipation, she turned to see Beau pull up in his Range Rover and park.

He got out, his eyes dark and fathomless.

Jillian froze.

Without speaking, he headed straight for her, one hand on his cane and his free hand outstretched. She took it and almost had to drop it again because the hot flash of electricity between them was that strong.

He must've felt it, too, because his eyes widened and he squeezed her palm as though to make sure she didn't get away from him. She would have laughed and reassured him if she wasn't too choked up with lust and emotion to speak.

Fingers intertwined and gazes locked, they walked up the path to the house. His leg didn't slow him down one bit and, if anything, she wasn't moving fast enough for him.

It was strange now to remember how he'd nearly died after his accident, how his poor body had been such a crumpled mess. There wasn't an ounce of weakness in this man, not one part of his body or, probably, his spirit that wasn't more powerful than it had ever been before.

He let her go long enough to unlock the front door, and then they were inside the foyer, where the afternoon shadows fell across his face, highlighting the absolute determination in his glittering eyes.

And then his cane clattered to the marble floor and he was all over her, driving her backward to the nearest wall with his hands gripping her face and his mouth claiming hers with the kind of aggressive, biting kisses that would leave her lips swollen and her heart singing. He tasted minty and desperate, and she couldn't wait for his passion to swallow her whole.

He pulled back to stare down at her, and it was all there in his face: the intense need and raw vulnerability, and the overwhelming love.

"You're home early," she gasped.

Flashing a look of purest annoyance, he focused on sliding his big hands up under her skirts to see if she'd followed his instructions, and crooned with approval when he discovered that she had.

He went to work kneading her butt. When she was weak-kneed and wobbly, with only the wall at her back and his muscled thigh between her legs to hold her up, he eased back just enough to assault her from the front. His fingers zeroed in on her slick cleft, which was swollen and open, aching for him.

"I have a tough time staying away from you."

"Good," she said flatly, and then cried out as his fingers circled her hard nub, lubricating her and winding her tighter… tighter… "What happened in Miami?"

He licked his way deep into her mouth, his tongue surging and retreating in time to what his wonderful fingers were doing down south. She tried to keep quiet, lest she miss what he was about to say, but that was as impossible as keeping birds from singing in the morning.

"What happened is that a beautiful and sexy woman met me in the car and tried to seduce me."

"And?"

"And all I could think about was getting back here, to you, so we could be doing this and I could tuck Allegra in bed tonight. So I passed your little test. Satisfied?"

God, she was.

So much so that she couldn't stop her laugh of triumph, which was quickly swallowed up by another cry as he stroked her again.

"Not yet," she told him. "But I'm getting there."

With only a quick grin at her innuendo, he leaned in to kiss her, and then pulled back to hit her with a stern warning. "Don't try to send me away again. I'm not leaving."

"I'm counting on that."

"Marry me," he said.

Man, she'd been hoping he'd bring that up again, but that didn't mean she had to appear needy. "Is that a question?"

"No. It's a command."

"Oh, too bad." She pretended to pout. "I was going to say yes."

He almost smiled, but was too busy to give it much effort. Working quickly, he unzipped his pants, freed himself and took his length, which was ruddy and engorged, in hand.

Oh, thank God. If he took any longer, she was going to collapse and then die from her lust. She eyed the rug at the center of the room, but he grabbed her behind one knee, hitching up her leg and spreading her wide.

A distant corner of her brain spluttered a weak protest even as she eased him closer, anchoring them together with her leg around his waist.

"Your leg—"

"Screw that." He paused, the plump head of his penis poised for entry. "We have a baby to make. Don't we?"

She stared into his face because they'd waited too long and worked too hard for this moment, and she didn't want to ever forget anything about it.

"Yes," she said. "We've got another beautiful baby to make."

Bending his knees, Beau angled himself just right, and then he was inside, stretching her until the delicious friction swallowed her up inside the pleasure. He shifted his weight, getting his balance, and she wrapped her legs tight around his waist, ready for the ride.

Kissing her again, he pumped his hips and found a punishing rhythm that drove her right out of her mind. She made a sound that was so raw and animalistic that he hesitated, his brows knit with worry.

"Am I hurting you?"

"Oh, yeah." She nipped his lip and enjoyed his corresponding shudder. "And I want you to hurt me harder this time."

"You got it," he murmured, and then, laughing with pure male satisfaction, Beau picked up the pace, as good as his word.

Epilogue

One year later

"Ease up, Jillian," the doctor said. "Let your body do the work. You don't want to shoot this baby across the room."

"The hell I don't," Jillian snarled. "Get this thing out of me NOOOOOOW!"

Beau, who was sitting on a stool up by Jillian's head, helping her hold her thighs to her chest while the baby crowned, didn't know when to leave well enough alone. This unfortunate deficiency kept him from keeping his big mouth shut.

They could see the growing patch of thick and curly black hair in the overhead mirror—it and the steady thump of the baby's heartbeat on the monitor were about the most thrilling things Beau had ever experienced—and he should have been happy with that, but no.

This was Jillian's third birth but his first, they'd chosen not to find out the baby's sex, and he was pumped up on adrenaline and the fervor that came from weeks of classes to prepare for this moment. Plus, Jillian's labor had progressed too quickly for anything civilized, like an epidural, so he felt that he should say or do something to ease her through this process before his dwindling time ran out.

So he looked down into her twisted and sweaty face and said, like an idiot, "We're almost there, baby. Take a deep breath and ease up. We can do it."

Jillian, panting and wild-eyed, looked around at him with intent so murderous he wished the doctor would roll his tray of scalpels, scissors and other sharp instruments a little farther out of her reach.

"Uh-oh," the nurse murmured, looking amused.

Beau shrank back and wished he'd been born with a modicum of common sense.

"*We* can do it?" Jillian rose up on her elbows and nailed him with a glare that made him want to sprint to the nearest nurses' station and schedule an emergency vasectomy. "Did you say *we,* jackass, when *I* am the one up here trying to birth this eight-pound baby with a watermelon for a head? Are you that stupid?"

There was no denying it. "Apparently, I am—yes."

The doctor and nurse kept their heads low, but they made quiet sounds that were suspiciously like snickering.

"Well, unless you've ever passed a bowling ball through your penis and have some sort of experience with this kind of thing," Jillian continued, gaining steam and outrage, as though she planned to put this whole labor thing on hold until she'd finished reading him the riot act, "then I suggest you shut the—*Oh, God.*"

That was it. Jillian grabbed her thighs again, twisted up her face and emitted an earthy sound that was somewhere between a groan and a roar of triumph.

Up in the mirror, a full head appeared, paused long enough to turn and have its little nose suctioned by the doctor, and then was followed by the easy slide of the rest of the slimy and squirming body.

"It's a big, strong boy."

"Oh, thank God," Jillian said.

The wonder swelled up from Beau's soul, filling him to bursting. "A boy," he echoed as the doctor put the baby on top of the green sheets covering Jillian's belly. "Did you hear that, Jill? It's a boy."

Jillian, who'd slumped back, closed her eyes and taken several relieved breaths, said wearily, "I don't care if it's a three-eyed toad. As long as it's out."

Beau laughed.

And then he cried.

It wasn't manly or pretty, and he'd be mortified about it later, but for now there was nothing he could do. All through the cutting of the cord, the cleaning and weighing of his son, the nurse's snapshots and Jillian's cleanup, he hovered, laughing and crying and useless. Finally, the nurse got sick of him and pressed him back into his stool, where he leaned in to kiss his wife on her cheeks and forehead, anywhere he could reach, and thank God for this moment.

"I love you," Jillian told him.

He could hardly get the words out around his sobs. "God, I love you, Jill. I love you. I can't believe you did this. I'm so proud of you."

"*We* did this."

Yeah. They had.

"Here's your boy."

The doctor passed the blanket-wrapped and squalling bundle to Beau, and Beau lost another little piece of his heart forever. Resting the baby on the bed between them, they stared at the newest member of their family.

Red-faced and angry, the baby waved his fists and shrieked like a stuck pig until Jillian nuzzled his fat cheek with a kiss.

"You stop that right now," she chided in her mother's singsong, massaging his little arm. "There's nothing wrong with you."

And the baby, to Beau's astonishment, took one last, snuffling breath, stopped crying, blinked and looked up into Jillian's face with keen, whiskey-colored eyes just like hers.

"That's better," Jillian cooed.

Beau examined his son through his tears, unable to believe he'd had any part in the creation of something this amazing. The boy had a curly head full of black hair, so much that they'd need to run him by Great Clips on the way home from the hospital for a trim. He also had sleek black brows and Jillian's pouty lips.

He looked plump and healthy, alert and absolutely perfect.

Beau cupped the baby's head. "Allegra's going to love you, Kenyon."

The boy was smart. Blinking again and clearly trying to get his bearings, he turned his head just enough to see Beau leaning over him. Their gazes connected, father and son. This, naturally, kicked off more tears, which fell fast and heavy, threatening to drown the poor child even before he'd had his first diaper change.

How pitiful was it that he was doing more crying than his newborn son?

Laughing at his own silliness and overflowing with joy, Beau swiped his eyes, determined to collect himself sometime today, while they were all still young.

He looked across Kenyon to Jillian.

Apparently, she'd forgiven him for his earlier cheerleading stupidity, because her eyes were wide and blazing, bright with love and what looked like gratitude.

"Thank you," she said.

"For what?"

"For putting this family back together."

God. So much for no more crying.

Beau sat on the bed next to her and gathered them both close, his wife and his son, two of the three most important people in the world to him, his family, his life.

He'd walked through fire to make it to this moment, and he'd happily do it again if he needed to. The joy he felt now had absolutely been worth it.

"My pleasure," he told his wife, taking her left hand and kissing the band of sparkling diamonds that he'd placed there, where it belonged. "My pleasure."

* * * * *